Collision Control

Book Four

Crossing Forces

COLLISION CONTROL

CROSSING FORCES BOOK FOUR

USA TODAY BESTSELLING AUTHOR

C. A. SZAREK

Paper Dragon
Publishing

Other Books by C.A. Szarek

Crossing Forces — Romantic Suspense

Collision Force (Book One)
Cole in Her Stocking (A Crossing Forces Christmas) — *FREE read!*
Chance Collision (Book Two)
Calculated Collision (Book Three)
Collision Control (Book Four)
Superior Collision (Book Five)
Incendiary Collision (Book Six) — *Coming soon!*

The King's Riders — Epic Fantasy Romance

Sword's Call (Book One) — *Also in Audio!*
Love's Call (Book Two) — *Also in Audio!*
Rogue's Call (Book Three) — *Also in Audio!*
Fate's Call (A Novella from the World of the King's Riders) — *Also in Audio!*

Highland Secrets — Historical Fantasy/Time Travel

The Tartan MP3 Player (Book One)

The Fae Ring (Book Two)
The Parchment Scroll (Book Three)
Highlander's Portrait (A Highland Secrets Story) — *Coming soon to Audio!*
Highland Valentine (A Highland Secrets Story) — *only .99*
The Princess and The Laird (A Highland Secrets Prequel)

Highland Treasures — Historical Fantasy/Time Travel

Highland Oath (Book One) — *Coming January 2018!*
Highland Essence (Book Two) — *Coming soon!*

Anthologies

Deep in the Hearts of Texas — *FREE read!*
  Story: Promise (A Crossing Forces Companion)

Crossing Forces

Small Town Texas doesn't always mean small time crime.

Welcome to Antioch, population fifty thousand.

With a police department full of detectives and officers who are good at what they do, throw in the occasional FBI agent, and the bad guy doesn't have a shot, no matter how big the crime.

They work together and fight together. Relationships will be forged and changed along the twists and turns.

When fate intervenes, love and happiness can be found in unlikely places.

Dedication

Book *four*. Really?

I love this series and these characters so much I guess
it went faster than I realized.
I need to thank my husband, Shane, for input and
continuing interest in my 'cop' stories. I'll just have to
keep working on you for the rest of the stuff I write.

Thanks, once again, to my former FBI friend, Holly.
Your expertise and having ready answers to all my
questions never ceases to amaze me. I really think you
do know *everything*.

Thanks to my friend Christine for always keeping me
going when I wanted to stop. Also, Amee, for always
having encouraging words. I know you love Jared
almost as much as Cole, but don't worry, I won't tell if
you don't.

Alanna, you always have two pom poms for me, and
for that I will be eternally grateful.

To my two Jo's: Y'all rock. End of. Thanks for always
being there for me, no questions asked.

Toni, you're made of awesome. Don't worry about Joe
so much. You'll see.

Alison, thanks for the race to the word count contest.
Looks like you were right. *Again.*

Thanks to everyone who follows me on Facebook and
Twitter, checks out my blog and website. Without you
guys getting the word out about my books, constantly
cheerleading, and awesome support, I couldn't do
this!

Chapter One

Her laugh got his attention first.

Jared looked over his shoulder. Four women at a table. A blonde, a brunette, redhead, and the last had long wavy hair somewhere between blonde and brown.

Which had the laugh that intrigued him?

She laughed again and his eyes shot to the one in the corner, facing the bar.

They were all pretty, but he couldn't tear his gaze away from her long, almost-curly locks.

He watched them talk, wearing a smile.

Jared needed to see more of her body. Her purple shirt was tight and displayed large breasts. She was curvy. He could see it even from his distance at the bar. Not heavy by any means, but not his normal type.

Gorgeous.

Nowhere in sight was his usual wannabe supermodel. Maybe in the others — but not her. He didn't care, he was drawn to *her*.

Too bad he couldn't tell what color her eyes were.

"All right, dude, I need to hit the road." His buddy's voice made him jump. Amusement flashed across Pete's green eyes. "You okay?"

He bit back a curse. "Yup."

His fellow detective probably needed to get home to his wife, Nikki.

Jared's partner, Cole, had left to head home to his

wife and two kids, too. Cole was married to Pete's partner, Andi.

Both the detectives had someone to go home to.

Envy made his gut heavy.

Since when do you give a shit about that?

He swallowed a groan. He needed to get laid or something.

Pete glanced at his watch. "See you in the a.m., then. Chief wants us all in for morning patrol briefing. Did Lucas tell you?"

"Yeah, but he didn't say why."

"Neither did the boss. We'll find out in the morning."

"Guess so."

"Hope it's not a long day. Hell, make that a long week." The guy sighed.

"Everything okay?"

Pete made a dismissive gesture. "Yeah. My brother and Lee are coming in Wednesday, with the baby for Thanksgiving. They're staying through the end of next week. First time meeting my niece, and all that. She's two months old now, so I'd like to actually spend time with my family, ya know?"

"Ah." Jared nodded. Yeah, he got it. His adoptive parents were in Antioch, and his little sister away at school in Corpus, but they were all important to him.

Although, he had no clue where his older brother was. He had Joe's cell number, but he hadn't talked to him in almost a year.

"So, I hope it's not a big deal, is my point," the detective said.

"We'll deal, no matter what. It's always tough before we get into the holidays. Hell, maybe he wants to talk the on-call schedule or some shit."

Pete arched and eyebrow and smirked. "At seven in the morning? Doubtful. Gut says it's a case. Hopefully Andi and I get to say *'not it'*."

Jared laughed. "Me and Cole got your back. We can always make Sully and Jamison take it."

"Not likely. They're immersed in that crap they're helping the Sheriff's Office with."

"Damn. That's right. No worries. Me and Cole can take it." He thumbed his chest.

"Good deal. Really gotta run. Pregnant wives get sorta grumpy when you're late." The guy's expression belied his statements. Pete was on cloud nine about becoming a father. Everyone knew he adored his wife, too.

Word was it'd taken them longer than expected to conceive—not that Jared paid attention to the girl-talk at the office. Of course, he was happy for them and all that.

"Tell Nikki I said hello." He offered one last wave and watched his friend jog out of the bar.

Love?

Kids?

No thank you.

Jared liked kids all right—his partner's boys were a blast to play with. He'd gotten stuck with babysitting duty once or twice, but he'd enjoyed hanging out with five-year-old Ethan, and sixteen-month-old Micah. However, he was grateful he got to return them to their parents afterward. He only remembered their ages from Cole beating it into his head.

That kind of responsibility wasn't for him.

And diapers?

Eww.

He blew out a breath and surveyed the local cop hangout. *McAuley's* had been in Antioch before he was born. The boys in blue of the small Texas city had adopted it when a retired detective, Mike McAuley, had opened the doors back in the sixties. It was an Antioch Police Department institution.

Jared swept his gaze along the walls full of police paraphernalia, from antique to modern day. There were pictures of cops everywhere, too. A framed one of McAuley himself was mounted over the bar. He'd passed away when he was a kid. The man's three sons ran the place nowadays.

The girl laughed yet again.

His eyes rested on the four women, but none of them were looking his way.

He grabbed his shot glass and gulped the Scotch, even though he didn't need a fortifying drink to approach a woman. Never had problems with that.

Perhaps that *was* the problem.

Oh shut up and do your thing.

"Ladies."

Silence reigned as four sets of eyes looked up at him.

The blonde flashed a smile. Yeah, she was the hottest one at the table. Slender. Tight clothes. Pouty lips with bright red painted on. Supermodel material he usually went for.

Red winked. She was cute, too.

The brunette obviously checked him out, roving his jeans and blue button-down before she smiled, too.

The last woman—the one Jared *wanted* to stare at him—looked away, breaking quick eye contact.

He begged for her to look his way again.

She finally did after he cleared his throat.

Blue.

Her eyes were like blue ice.

Jared flashed his signature smile. The one old girlfriends had told him had melted them on the inside and made their legs fall open.

Even in the dim light of the bar, her pink cheeks were obvious.

His stomach fluttered.

Her beauty stunned him as much as the color on her cheeks pleased him. Her hair was more brown than blonde. Full of waves he wanted to run his fingers through. High cheekbones, creamy skin and plump lips. If she was wearing makeup, it was minimal, and she didn't need it.

"Can I buy you a drink?"

She didn't look away, but she grabbed the full bottle of beer in front of her. Didn't tell him no, but her eyes did. At least she'd recognized he was addressing *her.*

He swallowed a groan and shifted in his combat boots.

Since when am I uncomfortable in front of a woman?

Deeper crimson stained her cheeks. Endearing, but

his gut told him she was uncomfortable, too.

For some reason, he wanted to make her feel better.

She looked around, as if doubting Jared had been talking to her.

Odd, considering the eye contact, and earlier non-verbal answer. "I'm Jared." He shoved his hand out.

Show her you're talking to her.

Her blue eyes widened.

He'd expected a smile. Not the look of abject horror she was wearing now.

The redhead to her right not-so-subtly jabbed her side and his intended jumped.

"Umm…hi." She sounded as enticing as her laugh.

Jared wanted to drag a chair over and sit next to her. His voice took a hike and he chided himself not to stare.

"Well, it's getting late," someone said.

His gaze shot to the blonde, just as she exchanged a look with the brunette.

The other woman nodded.

Blondie pushed her chair back and swung a *Coach* bag the size of Texas over her shoulder.

Brunette and Red also stood.

"Yeah, I think I need to get home, too," the redhead said.

The brunette agreed, grabbing her jacket. The shuffling of belongings and chairs combined with the clopping of high heels happened fast.

Jared blinked and they were headed to the door without saying anything to their abandoned friend.

But now we're alone.

He looked down at her, but his smile stalled.

Betrayal dominated her expression. She glared when the blonde paused at the door. The woman flashed a smile and wave that was obviously lost on the woman before him.

Jared cleared his throat. "Can I sit next to you?"

Her head whipped back around. "Why?"

He rocked back on the heels of his shitkickers.

Why? Charm. Focus on being charming.

"I like to keep the company of a beautiful woman." He smiled.

She frowned.

He stared. Couldn't help it.

She frowned at a compliment?

Jared quirked an eyebrow and slid onto the chair next to hers, because she was never going to invite him to sit. That made him want to join her even more. Intrigued the hell out of him. "What's your name?"

Cocking her head to one side, she studied him. "Uh...Ren."

"'Wren' like the bird? Cool name."

"No." Her cheeks reddened again and she looked away. "Umm...it's...short for Renee." She fidgeted before she'd meet his gaze again.

His stomach churned at the thought of her being uneasy with him. He forced words out. "Can I call you Renee?"

Those eyes met his and he swallowed. Hard. Crystal blue, like a morning summer sky. Jared had never seen anything so beautiful in his life.

"O-o-o-kay. I mean, sure." More shifting, so he reached for her hand.

Touching her resulted in a zing of energy up his arm.

Their gazes locked.

Her lips parted and his mouth went dry.

He wanted to kiss her.

No.

Jared *needed* to kiss her.

Before he could even lean in, Renee gasped and moved away.

"Which one of them put you up to this?" she demanded.

Her obvious suspicion made him rear back.

He blinked.

Wanting to kiss a woman two seconds after meeting her was fast...even for him.

Get it together, seriously.

"Excuse me?" he croaked.

She looked away. "Never mind."

Jared studied her. She was nervous. No...*uncomfortable.*

Why?

"Renee."

When she met his eyes, his heart skipped.

"I want to have a nice evening. A drink. A dance. With you."

She cleared her throat and he wanted to kiss it.

"With. Me." It wasn't a question.

He nodded. "With you. Is that a problem?"

Renee's pale gaze raked his face. "No. I guess not.

My friends are always telling me I need to loosen up."

"Are they now?" Jared flashed his best charming grin. "Just so happens I'm pretty good at helping that along."

"I don't doubt *that*." She looked him up and down and something made him want to squirm. "Okay, rules."

"Rules? How can you relax if there're rules?" He reclined in the chair, fighting a smile.

"No small talk."

"Really?"

"Really. None of that *'Where do you work?' 'Do you like your job?' 'What's your family like?' 'What do you do for fun?'* Blah blah blah."

He laughed. "So, no politeness?" Jared had some ideas if she didn't need him to be polite.

"I didn't say don't be polite. Just…let's keep this in the here and now." Renee averted her eyes again, something flashing there, but it was gone by the time she turned back to him. A slight smile curved her luscious mouth.

He didn't buy it. Grabbed her hand. "You okay?"

"Nope. Not going there. That breaks the rules."

"Already? Well then, I'm sorry, ma'am." Jared grinned until she smiled back and he inclined his head. "I think the jukebox needs a coin or two, and I need a dance."

"But no one's dancing." She gestured to the small area that passed for a dance floor.

"Not a problem for me. Let's help you loosen up." He stood, extending his hand.

"Why the heck not?" Renee chugged the beer and slammed the empty on the table. When she looked up at him, she flashed a lopsided grin that made his insides wobble.

He arched an eyebrow and chuckled.

It's gonna be one hell of a night.

Her drink melted into two, then three…four…or five?

Shit, he'd lost count, but he'd only had one more shot of Scotch himself. Jared had to drive home, not to mention be at work earlier than normal.

They danced until it was almost eleven and the place was pretty cleaned out, given it was a week night.

The youngest McAuley, Brian, kept throwing Jared knowing looks from the bar. The guy was paying more attention to them than the counter he was supposedly cleaning.

Yeah, I know, I'm thinking what you are, dude.

He wanted Renee. Wanted to take her back to his place, throw her down on his bed and give her the time of her life. She'd have no problem *relaxing.*

Jared pulled her closer and swayed to some random country song about long lost love. It could've been any one of the greats crooning as they danced, but it didn't register. He couldn't keep his mind off the gorgeous woman in his arms.

Soft, curvy. *Perfect.*

He wanted to taste her. *All* of her. His cock twitched as her pelvis brushed his. Tried to tell it now wasn't the time, but *'let's get out of here'* was on the tip of his tongue.

"Hard," Renee whispered, lifting her head from his shoulder.

Jared stilled and their eyes met. God, he'd die if she realized he was half-aroused.

Then again, it's a good way to see if she's on the same page.

"What?" he croaked.

"Your chest. It's so hard." She poked his right pec. Her cheeks went rosy for the hundredth time, but she was adorable.

Most of the flush was alcohol related. He needed to remember that. Pin it to his brain.

He got the feeling she didn't drink much, but he hadn't lost track of all the beer she'd downed. His conscience chided, *'put her in a cab. Send her home'.*

Jared couldn't. He wanted her.

If she was willing, he'd have Renee.

You are such a sleaze.

She peered up at him as if she was waiting on him to say something.

Right. Hard.

Heat crept up his neck. "Uh. Yeah. I work out."

She blinked, then giggled. "Guys who look like you don't notice girls who look like me." Renee backed out of his embrace, gesturing to her curvy form. The movement of her arms made her skirt play at her knees.

A tease.

His dick jumped and he almost groaned. Wanted to see more. But what she'd said sank in and he cupped her face. "*You* are absolutely gorgeous."

She scoffed, rolling her eyes. "Right. Me."

Jared dipped down and took her mouth, swallowing her surprised squeak. Beer and sweet, *sweet* woman greeted his tongue when he forced her to open for him.

God, she tastes good.

Like a sugary treat mixed with the stout lager she'd consumed, her kiss was a drug he had to have more of.

Renee stepped into him, wrapping her arms around his neck. She moved her mouth under his, kissing him back, giving when he took. Her hips against his made him granite, and when she rocked into him, his body took over and pressed right back.

He kissed her long and hard, until his cock threatened to blow in his jeans. Considering the three shots of Scotch, he was pretty damn impressed.

Jared needed to get her to his place.

Now.

Panting, he made himself end their lip-lock before he wrapped her legs around his waist and pushed her skirt up right there on the dance floor just to get inside her faster. "Wanna get out of here?"

Large, perfect breasts rose and fell against his chest. Purple fabric shifted as she struggled to breathe evenly, giving more than a mere hint at cleavage. Her eyes were hazy, but she nodded.

"Yeah?" His heart kicked into overdrive and he chided himself to calm down.

They were both inebriated, but '*this isn't a good idea*' went unheeded. He wasn't exactly thinking with his big brain.

"Yes."

The word was breathless and made him groan.

"My place or yours?"

Her hesitation made him cringe.

Please don't change your mind.

"Yours." Renee nodded, as if she was trying to convince herself so he kissed her again, cupping her ass and pushing his erection into her pelvis.

"I want you," he breathed.

No way was he sleeping alone tonight.

Chapter Two

They fell against the apartment door as soon as it was closed — but at least they were on the right side of it.

The short drive in his big black truck was a blur.

Jared's kisses were burning a trail down her neck and Mel's legs wobbled.

She clutched him to say upright. The heat of his skin warmed her hands and her whole body, even through the cotton of his shirt.

What is he doing to me?

Alcohol muddled her brain but she was right with him.

Wanted more…wanted *him*.

Is this a dream?

The guy was *hot*.

No one that looked like him had *ever* given her a second glance.

"Bedroom," he ordered in a warm blast below her ear.

Mel froze. This was real.

She was about to go to bed with a guy she'd met *tonight*.

Sex with a stranger.

"Renee? You still with me?"

Renee.

Right. She'd told him her middle name.

Why?

Because one of the girls had put him up to this. Was sex a part of the deal?

Was he…an escort or something?

Who cares?

"Yes." She forced the answer out.

He was holding her, kissing her.

Val always said she needed to loosen up. So, by God, she would.

Jared straightened and cupped her face.

God, he's tall.

Warmth enveloped her and Mel closed her eyes. When she opened them again, she fell into his, pools of midnight that melted her half-hearted resistance.

If he kept looking at her like that—with heat and desire—she'd give him anything he wanted. Although, she didn't like being naked alone in front of a mirror. How was she supposed to manage it with the male model/linebacker in front of her?

She gulped as everything sank into her hazy brain.

Naked. Sex.

With this guy. Jared.

A tremor shot down her spine and her thighs quivered. Mel was already hot, achy. Her body wanted him.

So shut off the rest.

"I want you," she blurted.

A slow, sexy smile spread across his kiss-swollen lips. Then his expression sobered and he stroked her cheeks with both thumbs. "Do you really want to be with me tonight?"

She nodded. The concern in his dark gaze made

her heart patter. Drunk off her ass or sober as a nun, she'd be stupid to walk away—or stumble, in her current state. "I know what I'm doing."

"Good. 'Cause I want to *do* you."

Mel giggled. "Nice romance there, Casanova."

He flashed a lopsided grin. "Do I really need to worry about having game? You're already at my place."

She kissed him in answer.

Jared spun her away from the door, kissing her until her toes curled and her sex pulsed. They staggered around in the dark apartment.

Mel let him lead the way; their mouths remained fused as they moved across what had to be his living room. One of her borrowed purple stilettos slipped and she yelped into his mouth, clutching at his broad shoulders.

He broke their kiss and laughed as he steadied them.

Their eyes met and she couldn't look away.

This man was beautiful. And he wanted her.

Her stomach fluttered, and she reached to undo the top two buttons of his shirt.

Jared took her mouth again her as her fingers worked, and he moved them both forward. He groaned against her lips as she slipped her hands inside his button-down. Thick muscles greeted her seeking touch.

Hard. Hot.

She wanted to see what she was touching. Mel ended the kiss, walking backwards to his forward step, her eyes glued to the expanse of gorgeous male in front of her. "You look…like a model."

He laughed and her cheeks burned.

Geesh…give you a little alcohol and it's like truth serum. Shut. Up. Melody Nash.

"So do you." Jared pressed a tender kiss to her mouth to stop her protest.

Her? A model?

Right.

The dream of every size-fourteen kindergarten teacher.

I couldn't even pull off plus-sized model.

Desire made her belly quiver as she commanded her brain to turn off. Kissing him harder, she twined her tongue around his, forcing deeper into his mouth, rocking her hips into his.

His erection pressed right back, long and hard, making her even hotter for him.

Jared swallowed her moan and slid his big hands down her back, over her bottom. Something brushed her hip and a loud crash made them both freeze.

"What the—?"

"I never liked that lamp." They spoke at the same time.

Mel tried to laugh, but it came out as a nervous titter. She bit back a cringe.

He shoved the debris out of the way with a combat boot, then released her and put out his hand. "C'mon. Maybe we should watch were we're going. My bedroom's not far."

Heat suffused her again when she touched him. She shivered and bit her bottom lip.

His dark eyes were molten.

How could he look at her like *that*?

God, don't let it just be the alcohol.

Jared kicked off his boots and shoved his shirt off his shoulders as soon as they made it into his room.

Mel couldn't stop watching the play of his muscles as he moved.

He had a smattering of dark hair across his defined chest. Dark curls narrowed into a strip that disappeared into his jeans. Powerful thighs, though she couldn't see them just yet. He was sculpted — everywhere.

She gulped.

I'm really doing this.

Goody-two-shoes was going to have sex with a stranger.

"Renee?" He froze with fingers on his zipper.

"Yeah?"

"Lose the clothes. I wouldn't want to damage such a nice outfit." He smirked.

It was sexy and made the butterflies in her stomach swarm.

Her head spun and she backed up to the bed, sitting down hard. A soft comforter cushioned her butt. She looked at the bedding. Deep red sheets peeked out from the black sea of thick blanket she sat on. So masculine.

A very naked Jared was at her side in seconds.

Darn, she'd missed the rest of the show.

He cupped her cheeks and tilted her face up, but she wanted to take in all that bare skin. His erection in particular. It jutted proudly.

Mel's fingers itched to touch him there.

Where's that ounce of bravery coming from?

"Are you okay?"

"Y-y-yes." Stuttering?

She wanted to melt.

Great way to move right to 'idiot'.

He flashed a smile and tugged on her shirt.

Mel lifted her arms and let him take it off, fighting the urge to cover her black lacy bra—the only non-practical one in her wardrobe.

Jared groaned and took a step back. "Gorgeous."

She stood, digging deep for courage she didn't know she had.

Thanks be to alcohol, after all.

"I need to touch you."

She ignored his whisper and lowered her skirt's zipper. With a shimmy of her rounded hips, it fell to the carpet, a heap of royal purple. She made herself meet his gaze.

His Adam's apple bobbed, and it made her feel like she was on the red carpet—wait, was there a naked red carpet?

"You make me feel pretty." The sentence fell from her lips and heated her cheeks.

Truth serum strikes again.

"You're not pretty, baby. You're *gorgeous*."

Baby.

Mel sucked in a breath and pushed her black bikinis off the most flawed part of her body.

Don't look at my hips —

Jared gasped and urged her to him before she

could even step out of her heels and kick her panties away. His mouth descended on hers hard, while his fingers worked the clasp of her bra.

His erection pressed into her pelvis and stole her concentration as she returned his kiss. She wrapped her arms around him, caressing the muscles of his back.

She yelped when he lifted her, and she scrambled for a grab at his shoulders, but the bed took their collective weight, Jared following her down. Without breaking the seal of their mouths, he divested her of the bra and threw it.

Then he grabbed her shoes and panties, tossing them across his bedroom. He returned to her quickly, dragging his mouth down her neck.

She melted under the movements of his lips.

He cupped her breasts, kneading them and kept his kisses moving south, until Mel was squirming.

Jared's stubble teased her inner thighs and she froze, a hand on his thick shoulder.

Squeezed her legs together.

"Baby, let me in. I need to taste you."

Taste her? As in…

No one had ever —

She stopped that truth before it could tumble out and made herself relax into his bed. Mel loosened the rest of her body, inch by inch.

Jared didn't waste any time. He dove between her legs and licked the sensitive bundle of nerves at the top of her sex.

She cried out and arched.

"Did that feel good?" He gripped her hips and

held her firmly, but didn't hurt her. "We're just getting started."

She didn't answer him, but wouldn't have had time anyway.

He parted her slick folds with his tongue.

Mel whimpered.

"Good? Hmmm, you taste good and you're so wet for me."

Writhing beneath his touch, she couldn't have said a thing if she'd tried. So she let go and just *felt.*

Jared added his fingers to his kisses, gently probing before thrusting into her. At the same time, he sucked her clit.

She screamed his name and her thighs trembled as inner muscles gripped him. The slow pumping of his fingers made her hips lift of their own accord.

He was relentless, stroking into her until she wiggled and moaned.

"You're so tight. Squeezing me. Hmmm…you're close. Let go for me, baby. Come hard, Renee."

His words were a trigger.

She couldn't take any more.

Mel arched her back and cried out, orgasm roaring over her. She panted and gasped, collapsing into the bed.

He shot up her body and held her close, caressing her forehead and kissing her there, despite the dampness of her heated skin. "Did that feel good?"

His warm breath whispered over her face and made her whimper.

She burned for him, burned for more, despite the

soul-rocking climax.

Mel had never felt like this before.

Their eyes met and he smiled. Slow and sexy with a touch of tender. How could a stranger look at her like that?

How could Jared make her *feel* so much?

She trembled and reached for him. Cupped his stubbled cheeks and dragged him down for a kiss.

He took it from there, deepening their lip-lock. Her essence swirled around with their tongues. It made her body warm all over again.

Her core ached. She wanted him inside her.

Jared pulled away from their kiss as if he'd read her mind, his muscled chest heaving against her breasts. "You're killing me, baby. I need you."

Mel closed her eyes as his declarations washed over her, as strong as his touch. Her whole body was a live wire for him. "I need you, too."

"Thank God." He rolled away, leaving her cold, but wrenched open the drawer of his nightstand.

She sucked in a breath when he flashed a smile and ripped the foil packet open with his teeth.

Condoms at-the-ready. How often does he do this?
Should I…do this?

She ignored the sudden dose of conscience and watched with rapt attention as he rolled the latex on his impressive erection.

Need took over her brain, and that was just fine.

"Jared," she whispered, as he came back to her, pulling her into his arms.

"Hmmm, baby?" His mouth hovered millimeters

over hers.

Mel lifted her face, brushing her lips against his.

He kissed her back and parted her thighs with a knee.

She wrapped her arms around his neck and held him close as Jared settled on top of her.

Her sex bloomed again, throbbing as the tip of his erection brushed her sensitive clit. Then he was there, pushing inside her, filling her.

Pleasure was instant and hot, rolling over her. She gasped and tilted her hips to take him deeper.

He groaned into her mouth. "Damn, you're tight." Jared panted, his powerful chest heaving.

She kissed him harder, lifting her bottom to meet his first thrust.

Now was not the time to think about the *one* lover she'd had in her life, nor that he'd left her at the altar.

She hadn't had sex since… No.

Mel wasn't even going to say his name in her head.

Jared was with her, *inside* her, scrambling her brains with every movement of his hips.

She pushed away insecurities about her body and inexperience and let physical demands take over.

He trailed his mouth down her neck as he propelled forward.

She buried her hands in his hair, leaning her head back to allow him better access.

He nipped her chin and licked the spot, making her pant.

Her body was on fire.

They were both covered in sweat, but she didn't

care. Mel followed the curve of his shoulder as Jared found her mouth again, moving his tongue in rhythm with his hips.

She caressed his damp skin, reveling in the hard muscles of his back, then slid her hand lower, grabbing his rear end with both hands, kneading and squeezing.

He groaned and her body responded, muscles tightening, as if his pleasure was a trigger to her orgasm.

Climax hit her like a ton of bricks.

Mel panted his name as he stiffened in her arms.

He threw his head back and whispered her middle name.

Biting back a correction, she locked eyes with him.

No use having him call her '*Mel*' now.

His dark gaze was hazy, sated, and it sent a shiver down her spine.

She had made this gorgeous man have that particular expression on his face.

Jared buried his face against her, rolling to his side and taking her with him. He pulled her into his chest as his softening arousal slipped from her body.

Her sex trembled with a small aftershock of pleasure and she shivered.

"Sorry," he whispered.

Mel pulled back and met his beautiful dark orbs. "Why?"

"You felt so good. It was too quick."

Too quick?

What to say to that?

He'd made her feel better...feel *more*...than she

ever had before. Two orgasms was a first for her, too. She'd never admit that out loud. "It was…fantastic." Truth serum struck again, and her cheeks warmed.

The lopsided grin he flashed made her heart stutter.

"*You're* fantastic, baby."

She fidgeted against his chest and he pressed his mouth to hers.

"Be right back." Jared left the bed and disappeared into the attached bathroom.

Mel looked around the room. Even the dimness lent to the fact that the place was masculine. There was a framed picture of some sort of badge on the wall, but it was too dark to make it out.

There was a rack with a few rifles and a shotgun on it. That gave her pause, but it was no different than the one on the wall in her dad's den.

Texas. Guns everywhere.

Her head was clearer now. She glanced down at her naked body and flushed. She'd been naked…been with him.

Somehow, she didn't feel so imperfect anymore.

Mel smoothed her hand over the curve of her too-round hip, touched her inner thigh. Her core ached pleasantly. She'd remember this night, always.

But she should leave.

"Are you all right?"

Jared's voice made her jump and her eyes flew to his bare form at the end of the giant bed. Her mouth went dry.

Muscles galore.

Just watching him move was enough to make her hot for him all over again. He was beautiful.

"I'm fine. Really good, actually." Her head swirled as he climbed back into the bed and caressed her cheek.

Maybe the alcohol buzz wasn't gone.

Or maybe it was just him.

"Me too." He pulled her closer, pressing a kiss to her mouth. It was tender, gentle. Was that normal for a one-night stand lover?

Mel told herself to pull away, but his warmth enveloped her, and she didn't fight him when he wrapped his arms around her and lay them both down. She snuggled into his chest and sighed when he pulled the covers over them. "I should go," she whispered.

Jared didn't answer, and when she lifted her head, his eyes were closed, his expression relaxed.

He caressed her back and she settled down. She'd leave after he'd fallen asleep.

"I want you to stay," he murmured.

How do I answer that?

She glanced up at his handsome face and smiled. Couldn't help it.

He sighed, the sure strokes of her skin falling off as his breathing evened out. Jared was drifting off and Mel wanted to snuggle into his side.

So she did, cushioning her cheek on his defined pec.

Chapter Three

Something was pinning her down.

Mel wiggled and opened one eye. She was too hot. Her arm was cramped against something large and warm.

She straightened and stretched it. Coarse hair greeted her seeking fingertips and she lifted her cheek.

Mel jolted all the way up, both eyes flew open. "It wasn't a dream," she gasped.

He made a noise in his sleep and she glanced at his face.

Please don't wake up.

What did I do?

Visions of them entwined, his mouth on hers—not to mention other *un*mentionable places—his hands all over her body. Them moving together.

It all slammed into her head at the same time.

Denial wasn't going to work.

She hadn't been *that* drunk.

"Nice, Mel. Good job."

The way he'd made her feel was a part of her memories, too. Warmth suffused her limbs, settling low in her belly.

Forget about it. One-time thing.

Get the heck out of here.

His arm was flung across her hips like he owned her, and their legs were tangled.

Why doesn't that bother me as much as it should?

This man was a stranger.

Mel gently disengaged herself. She stilled, praying Jared remained asleep. A glance at the clock on his nightstand told her it was just after five.

Crap.

Tuesday. Last day of school before Thanksgiving, and the short break. She had work—school—in less than three hours.

Thank God for early release. The school day would be over at noon.

Her head spun.

That was the *last* time she'd let her friends take her out to feel better.

Yeah, you feel better now?

Sex—fantastic or not—wasn't going to help her forget.

She sucked in a breath and slipped out of Jared's bed. Forced her gaze away from his naked body so she wouldn't be tempted to stare.

The man was *beautiful.*

Mel frantically searched for her clothing, trying to silently gather her things. It was still dark out, plus the curtains on the two windows in his room were black to match his bedding. Light couldn't have leaked in if it'd wanted to.

She bent to grab her skirt off the carpet just as he groaned and rolled over.

Great, 'cause I need him to catch me doing the naked dance.

Gritting her teeth, she snatched her underwear, blouse and skirt, but couldn't find the other one of Val's purple stilettos.

Move, move, move.

She sprinted into his living room, cringing when she noticed the broken lamp.

Their conversation flitted into her brain, because of course, she needed to feel even more stupid. Gasped when she remembered poking his chest before they'd left *McAuley's*.

She'd told him how hard it was.

Mel smacked her forehead and crushed her eyes shut. God, how had he been able to stand sleeping with her?

Unless he was normally attracted to *idiots*.

She yanked skirt on, donned her bra and shoved her panties into her small purse. Looking at them made her scowl, but she dug her cell out of her purse.

Please don't be dead. Please don't be dead.

When she pressed the center button and the screen lit up, she crept to Jared's front door.

Thank God.

After sneaking out like a pro, she closed it as quietly as she could.

She tucked the shoe under her arm and released a breath. Then Mel hurried down the stairs and out the front of the brick apartment building, ignoring the sting when a small pebble bit into her bare heel.

Slipping around the side of the building, she searched the parking lot.

Crap!

Mel had ridden with Jared. Her car wasn't there.

Her stomach twisted.

Son of a gun!

She needed a rescue — *McAuley's* was on the other side of town.

Mel groaned and scrolled through her contacts.

Val was going to be ticked about the shoes. They were Louboutins.

The phone only rang once, but her best friend was an early riser.

"Hello?"

"Can you come pick me up?"

"Where are you?"

"I'll find the address." She looked around in the dark to try to spot *something* on the building. "Um…I'm at those apartments…*The Enclave*."

Dead silence on the other end for a good twenty seconds.

Mel cringed. "Just come get me. Please."

"Where's your car?"

"*McAuley's*." She closed her eyes.

More silence. Then a muffled giggle. "You didn't."

"Val, I swear to God I will *never* speak to you again if you don't come get me. Right. Now."

"Awful demandin', doncha think, Needy-Frieda."

"Forget it! I'll walk back to the bar."

Her best friend and fellow teacher laughed long and hard. "I'll come get you, but you have to tell me about every *second*."

"Yeah yeah." She wanted to knock her head into the building.

How could she have had sex with a stranger?

At least Jared had been gentle. Had made her feel

good.

More than good.

Fantastic.

Then why did you sneak out?

He sure as heck had made her forget about David.

She snorted. Making love with David—her high school sweetheart, college boyfriend and later, loser fiancé—couldn't hold a candle to *sex* with Jared. A guy she didn't even know.

Well, she *knew* him in the biblical sense.

Mel shivered and a tremor shot down her spine as a visual of the night flashed into her mind. She closed her eyes against the memories, because she didn't want to admit that she didn't regret being with Jared. Would do it again.

Maybe she should've stayed.

Had breakfast with him?

"Yeah right. For what?"

Like she'd told him last night, guys that looked like him *never* noticed girls that looked like her. He'd been horny, she'd been there.

The nearby condom supply said it all. No reason he'd even want a repeat.

What if one of her friends had put him up to picking her up?

Mel's heart stuttered. Something that felt suspiciously like hurt made her frown. She swallowed back a gulp.

A quick double tap on a horn made her jump.

Val pushed the passenger door open from the driver's side, flashing a grin. "Slut puppy taxi at your beck and call. No charge for the first ride. Congrats on the end of a looooooooong drought! Step on up."

She glared and stalked to the car, ignoring her bare feet.

"Oh. My. God. You look like you're having a walk of shame. Wasn't it good? That guy is smokin'."

"Shut. Up." Mel climbed into the Jeep. Slammed the door and snapped her seat belt on.

"Hey, now. Don't take your bad sex life out on my baby. Least you got some."

She reclined in the bucket seat and closed her eyes.

Can't believe I'm gonna say this.

"It wasn't bad. It was…awesome."

"Then what's with the 'tude? And where the *hell* is my other shoe?"

"I couldn't find it." She flashed her friend a sheepish smile.

Val frowned and tapped on the overhead light. "Dude, those are Louies!"

"Val, seriously. I don't think I can take you without caffeine."

"Mel, seriously. They were expensive."

"I'll buy you another pair."

"What is *wrong* with you?" She frowned. "You should be relaxed if your new friend is good in bed."

"I'm fine, but thanks."

"I have a better idea than buying me new shoes."

"What's that?" Mel arched an eyebrow.

"Go back upstairs, get his number and tell him you want to see him again. After all, if you got laid on the first date, the second one's gotta be awesome. Oh, and you can get my damn shoe."

"No."

Her bestie's blue eyes narrowed. "I will totally kick your ass if you're going to let that piece of shit, David ruin a perfectly good romp with the hottest guy that's ever given either of us the time of day."

She bit her bottom lip.

Right.

Like beautiful Val—natural blonde, big blue eyes, five-foot-seven, *real* double Ds and one-hundred-twenty-five pounds soakin' wet—couldn't get a guy like Jared to give her a second glance.

Mel didn't know what to say, so she looked out the window.

"That's it, isn't it?" Val demanded, finally pulling out of the parking lot of the apartment complex.

Her best friend's tirade against her ex continued down Main Street.

"No. It's not David," she said. It was only *half* David, but she wouldn't admit it aloud.

Val snapped her mouth shut and stopped at a red light. "Then what is it? I know seeing him at school was more than a shocker, but I'm sure Jared helped. There's something wrong in your head if he *didn't*."

"First of all, finding out that the guy I *thought* was the love of my life, not only left me at the altar but also had been *cheating* on me the last *six* years of our relationship, and had a child with someone else and didn't bother to tell me, is *more* than a small 'shocker'. David Junior better not end up in my class. I might kill a kid."

She giggled.

"You're laughing?"

"I like you riled up. I didn't say you couldn't be upset. That's why I took you out last night. Emily and Kara both agreed you needed *out*. And 'lo and behold', Mel got herself a new man!"

"I did not."

"Why not? Damn, he's hot."

"Yeah. I have eyes."

"Hmmm. Lucky ones. And lucky hands...and lucky everythings. You got to do a hell of a lot more than *look* at him."

Mel sighed and shook her head.

She loved Val to death, but her friend would never get it. Val looked like someone Jared should be with. *Mel* didn't.

"I was going to ask you how much you paid him."

Her friend's head shot around, and their eyes locked. "What're you talking about?"

"He walked up to me."

"Right."

"When I was at a table with you, Em the-hot-redhead, and Kara the bad-boy-magnet."

"Correction, *I* am the bad boy magnet."

She glared and Val smirked. "You know what I mean."

"No, actually I don't."

"You guys are hot...and I'm...me."

It was her bestie's turn to glare. "Melody Renee Nash. I'm going to stop this car and kick your ass. You're so stupid sometimes, I wonder if you have mirrors in your house. You're flippin' gorgeous."

Mel rolled her eyes. "I do have mirrors in my house. Which is my point."

Val pulled the Jeep into *McAuley's* parking lot and shut it off. She grabbed both her hands and squeezed, her blue eyes serious. "I love you. We've been through a lot of shit together, but I hate what that son of a bitch did to you. You put up with it for *way* too long. I thanked God the day he didn't show to your wedding. I'm *glad* you didn't marry him."

"What're you talking about?"

"Because of David, you have this horrible image of yourself, and you're one of the most beautiful women I've ever met. Inside *and* out."

Scoffing, Mel tried to pull away, but the grip tightened.

"This guy, Jared. He saw what *I* see, or he wouldn't have taken you home."

"Right. So neither of us was drunk and horny."

Val flashed a smartass smile. "Well, the horny I believe, it's been a while for you…"

She yanked away and shoved her shoulder. "I have just enough time to shower and get dressed for *work*. I have twenty-two five and six year olds to entertain for the day."

Her friend laughed. "I believe the word is '*teach*'."

She smiled and nodded. School would help her feel normal. Mel loved her job. Thrived when teaching the little ones. "I'll see you at school."

Just as she opened the driver side door of her blue Sportage, Val called her name.

"You'd be stupid to leave things at a one-night stand. Especially if he was awesome in bed." She waggled her eyebrows.

Mel laughed and shook her head, not answering as she climbed into her SUV.

Then I guess you get to call me stupid.

She had no intention of looking Jared up again.

Chapter Four

"**S**on of a bitch!"

Why hadn't his alarm gone off?

Jared shot out of bed, his eyes zoning in on his digital alarm clock. *6:53* taunted him in bright blue. Briefing was in seven minutes.

Fuck.

Chief *hated* tardiness.

It wasn't often he ordered the detectives to morning shift briefing, so it had to be something big.

"Double fuck."

Like he needed his boss pissed at him all day.

He snatched his cell out of his discarded jeans from the night before. Shit, he hadn't charged it, either. It'd be dead by nine a.m., if that.

Gonna be late.

Jared texted his partner, not waiting for a response.

The phone dinged from where he'd thrown it on the bed, but he ignored it. Grabbed a fresh pair of jeans from the closet and shoved his legs into them.

He took a moment to snatch his blue shirt off the floor, draping it on the back of the overstuffed chair in the corner. Caught a whiff of Renee's sweet scent and paused.

She's gone.

Not like he could've forgotten their night, but his urgent need to get to the police department was leading.

Too bad, too, because he *wanted* to think about her.

He glanced over his shoulder at his rumpled bed.

She'd been…fantastic. Sweet and hot, with a touch of innocence. He'd never had such a responsive lover.

Jared tugged on a short-sleeved, black button-down, his mind consumed by Renee as he hastily tucked it in.

Why'd she leave?

No time to look for a note.

He slid his holster onto his belt and rushed from his room. Jumped over the broken lamp fragments.

No time to clean that up, either.

He groaned when he spotted his coffeemaker on the kitchen counter. He hadn't taken the time to set it up the night before like usual, so no java for him.

Yeah…you were a little busy.

Jared smirked and rushed out of his apartment. He'd take an armful of beautiful woman to hot coffee in the morning anytime.

Renee's perfume was in his truck, too.

He shook his head, trying to convince his cock now wasn't the time.

She'd been…perfect. He *needed* to see her again.

"Shit. Don't even know her last name."

Why'd she left without a word?

She should've woken him up. He would've taken her again, if she'd been willing.

Renee had been gorgeous in passion, her long

wavy hair spread across his pillow, her head tilted back. Rosy full cheeks, gorgeous lips parted. Full breasts rising and falling. Every gasp and whimper had made him burn for her more.

Jared's stomach fluttered and he gunned the accelerator out of the complex parking lot, ignoring the three beeps in a row from his phone. He'd be at work in a few minutes.

He ran down the hall, almost mowing down his boss's assistant when he rounded the corner toward the briefing room.

Nikki scooted out of his way, a hand on her rounded tummy, big brown eyes wide.

"Sorrrrrrrry, late!" he called. That was all he needed, to accidently hurt Pete's pregnant wife. He hurried on his way, not giving her a chance to answer.

He sucked in a breath and skidded to a halt at the closed door. Needed to slip into the room silently.

Of course, his boot caught the metal doorframe with a loud clang.

Jared winced as all heads turned his way.

Chief glared. "Nice of you to join us, Detective Manning."

He wanted to close his eyes, but forced a nod for his boss. Chief Paul Martin's temper wasn't to be trifled with.

Gonna hear it later, for sure.

His partner smirked when their eyes met, but at least Cole had saved him a seat.

"Nice of you to join us, Detective Manning." The guy kept his voice low, but it was a fair impression of their boss's bark.

"Thanks for the seat, Detective Lucas. Considering I woke up at exactly six-fifty-three, I wouldn't say seven-twenty-one is all that bad."

"Yeah, guess you have something to be proud of." One corner of his partner's mouth shot up.

"I need coffee, though."

"You two shut up," Andi, Cole's wife and fellow detective whispered, but her tone was amused.

"What kept you?" Cole asked, throwing a wink at his wife. "Everything okay?"

"I'm cool. Alarm didn't go off." If Renee had still been there, it would've been a different story.

"Right." His partner's gray eyes were skeptical.

"You two *might* wanna pay attention, since you're supposed lead this." Pete scooted to the edge of his seat beside Andi in the row behind them.

"Lead on what?" Jared looked toward the projector screen at the head of the room.

Chief was in lecture mode, pointing to pictures as he talked.

"Auto theft ring. Dallas FBI office called, Special Investigations Unit. I'm sure the agent—Carrigan or something—on the bigger case will pop up sooner or later. From what Chief said, she's wrapping up something else right now. But this is a big deal," Cole said. "The oversized tatted dude is their leader. The pic that's front and center. On the last job, he killed an undercover FBI agent, John Murray. Murray's the dark haired guy on the left. He was undercover as a member of their team. A lot of the info is just best guesses."

"Shit."

His partner nodded. "They were spotted near Antioch, and we're supposed to run point. We do have a lot of expensive rides around here and the feds want this guy bad."

Jared's heart dove to his stomach when he took in the photo on the screen.

His brother's dark brown eyes stared right back.

The morning would definitely require extra coffee.

Mel closed her eyes and swallowed a yawn. She'd made it to her classroom about ten minutes before and was fighting the urge to plant her cheek on the cool oak of her desk while her kids all filed in.

She'd pretty much fled the teacher's lounge. Almost forgot her pumpkin spice latte from Starbucks, too.

Wow you look tired, Mel.

Long night?

What did you do all night?

Hot date?

Are you seeing someone new?

Dang, she had nosy co-workers. *Other* than Em and Kara, that is. No doubt Val had run her mouth immediately upon arrival at Richland Elementary. Both second grade teachers flashed knowing smiles before she could even say hello. Mel didn't have to tell them about her torrid night with Jared.

Not that she was going to announce it to anyone but Val, and that was only under the duress of needing a ride.

She usually *tried* be a private person, despite her bestie's prodding for details. Her temples throbbed and she rubbed her eyes. Of course, hangover would hit her now when she had to maintain control in a room full of five and six year olds.

Mel forced herself to remain pleasant and greeted the few parents who walked their children into the room.

She'd even helped Shelby hang up her jacket when the kiddo had missed her hook. That was before she'd glued her butt to her seat. If only she could sit behind her desk all day.

You only have to last until noon.

Thank God morning organization was eating up the last moments before the bell rang. If morning announcements could just last the first few hours of the school day, it'd sure help a lot.

"Miss Nash."

Mel looked into a pair of very blue eyes, and didn't have to fake a smile for the little boy who was holding an apple in his small palm. "Hi, Ethan. Thank you."

Ethan grinned. "My mama says teachers like apples."

She laughed and set the Red Delicious on her desk. "Your mama's a smart woman. Go ahead and take your seat. We're going to start something fun for Thanksgiving."

The little redhead nodded, dashing to the second table on the left in front of her desk.

Her kids sat two to a table instead of the desks

they'd graduate to in first grade.

Her classroom was open and welcoming. The walls consisted of their many art projects, as well as the Birthday Board behind the door. When one of them had a birthday, they got to pick a present from the treasure chest that rested next to the classroom's fish tank. Everyone got a turn to feed their dozen goldfish, too.

There was a primary colored woven rug they all sat on for story time, as well as bright bean bags in the back the kids got out when they watched a monthly movie.

God, why can't it be movie day today?

She chided herself. This job was her calling—her life. It wasn't her kids' fault she'd had a drunken night of sex.

With a stranger.

Mel frowned.

Stop thinking about it. Stop thinking about him.

Jared was a constant in her mind. Which was pretty crappy, since she'd already decided to forget about him.

She distracted herself by looking at all her kiddos. No parents in the room, and her count told her everyone was present—even though they were not all seated yet.

"Two minutes 'til I need y'all in your chairs," Mel called.

Kids shuffled, and the little boy who'd given her the apple caught her eye. He flashed an adorable grin she couldn't help but return.

Ethan Lucas would be one of her favorite students,

if she was allowed to have favorites. Both his parents were detectives for the Antioch Police Department.

Hmmm, Community Helper Day is soon.

First Friday in December. She'd have to call in a favor. See if either of Ethan's parents would be willing to talk to her kindergarten class about kid-friendly police basics.

She already had her dad, Antioch's Public Works Director, and Dr. Butler, the town pediatrician and one of Val's student's fathers, coming. All she needed was a firefighter and a cop, and she was set.

Not to be stereotypical or anything.

Mel rolled her eyes at herself and pushed her chair back. Her head throbbed and she ignored it. When her stomach jumped, she tried to talk her hurried breakfast of a bagel and a glass of OJ into backing down on their rebellion.

The last two children found their chairs.

Showtime.

She cleared her throat and twenty-two sets of little eyes settled on her. Innocent, open, trusting gazes. Mel smiled and came around to the front of her desk. "Good morning, class."

"Good morning, Miss Nash," they said in unison.

It was about as formal as she got with the kids, but it was a part of their daily routine. Her day wouldn't be right without the ritual.

"As soon as morning announcements are over, we're going to do something fun. A special art project for Thanksgiving. How does that sound?"

She received a few 'yays!' and the kids exchanged

grins.

Good.

They were excited about the project, so they'd be cooperative and — hopefully — productive. Maybe she could stretch it out until it was time to leave?

Who cares about curriculum?

"Can we draw a turkey?" one of the boys asked, his small hand shooting up at the same time he spoke.

"Sure, Gage." Mel nodded. "But we going to pick one thing we're thankful for, too."

That resulted in a few 'ohhs.' Like they were fascinated by the prospect. Also good news.

Please guys, be easy on me.

The bell rang, making her head spin. The beeping tone indicating Principal Edwards coming on the overhead made her wince. Mel cringed and changed her mind about morning announcements. The echo was killing her.

Pumpkin spice wasn't cutting it this morning.

Crap. Hurry the heck up, bossman.

It was going to be a lonnnng half-day.

Chapter Five

T he morning was a daze of questions swirling in his head.

What the fuck was Joe thinking? lead things off.

Something didn't sit right in Jared's gut. His brother wasn't a killer.

He knew it to his core.

The auto-theft ring thing didn't shock him. Joe had always kept their sporadic phone conversations shallow and all about Jared. Never said what he did for a living or where he lived when they'd talked.

The cop in him had long suspected illegal activities, but if his brother had ever been in trouble, or in jail, he'd done a great job of keeping it on the down-low.

Joe *knew* Jared was Antioch PD.

Shit.

He hadn't physically seen his older brother since he was a teenager. They'd been raised in the foster system, shuffled all over Texas, until coming to the Mannings' in Antioch. He'd been eleven to his brother's sixteen.

Joe had always been the one to get into trouble, at school, at home. Rebellion galore. Unfortunately, as great as the Mannings were, the guy hadn't been able to adapt or cope. He'd split after he'd turned seventeen.

Jared had been devastated. He'd been a little boy whose only sibling was his stability — his constant in the life of a nomad. Family after family, until he'd lost count.

Until Jason and Amy Manning.

They adopted him, raised him. They were his parents.

If only Joe could have felt like their son, too.

Jared needed to talk to his brother. *Now.* But the cell number in his contacts was no good.

Go. Fig.

"Jer, you okay? You got quiet."

His gaze collided with his partner's.

All he could read was concern in Cole's steel eyes.

Jared left his cubicle and perched himself on Cole's desk. His partner's workspace backed up to his. "I'm good." The affirmative came out fragmented and he had to clear his throat.

The guy frowned, but didn't call him on his bullshit—yet. With his partner of two and a half years, it was always only a matter of time.

He broke their eye contact and surveyed the CID room—Criminal Investigations Division, where all the detectives officed at the PD.

No one else was around.

Andi and her partner had already headed out. They were meeting an informant about a burglary case, but Pete had said he'd put some feels out to see if any of the theft ring—Jared's brother and friends—had been spotted by Antioch riffraff.

Jared and Cole had already checked in with dispatch before heading to their desks. No cars had been reported stolen in the last two days.

Then again, Joe wasn't stupid. He wouldn't jack an expensive ride if he was on the run.

Damn, Joe. Where are you? Now would be the perfect time to reach out to your little bro, the cop.

Preferably *before* Special Agent Carrigan came to town.

"What's with the secretive phone calls?"

Shit.

"Uh. Just trying to get a hold of someone." He took a breath. It was the truth, but his delivery made it seem a lie.

Double shit.

"Seriously, are you okay? No offense, but you kinda look like shit, partner."

"Gee thanks, buddy."

Cole shrugged. "Call it as I see it."

"I met someone last night. At *McAuley's*, after you hit the road."

His partner reclined in his chair, worry gone from his face. The info given to them by the FBI was spread out on his desk, but suddenly discarded. "Oh?"

Renee's crystal blue eyes flashed into Jared's mind, chasing worries about Joe away. He smiled genuinely. The distraction was welcome. He relaxed his shoulders and nodded. "She's…hot. And great…and…"

His partner chuckled and shook his head. "Another one-nighter, Jer?"

"Not this time…she's different."

I fully intend to see her again.

"What's her name?"

"Renee." Jared hoped it'd escaped his buddy's

notice that her name had exited his lips on a frickin' sigh.

"Renee what?" Cole smirked.

"Dammit."

A bark of laughter greeted his ears, and his partner shook his head. "I thought as much. Geeze, kid. You gotta stop the flavor-of-the-week thing. You're wasting your good years. Find a real woman. Settle down. I'm tellin' ya, there's nothing like—"

The phone blared, interrupting the lecture—thank God.

Cole grabbed the receiver and plastered it to his ear. "Antioch Police, Detective Lucas."

Kid. Really?

Right, 'cause you're so much older.

The guy only had about seven years on him.

Renee *was* different.

If he tried to explain it, he'd come off as defensive, and Cole knew all about Jared's prowess. Back in the day, his partner had been just like him, or so Cole had told him.

What was the big deal?

He liked the ladies—and they liked him.

Just because Cole had Andi didn't mean *he* needed a wife.

Wife?

Hell no.

Couldn't even remember the last time he'd had a steady girlfriend.

Renee's smile beamed into his head and he frowned. Different didn't mean…

What the hell does it mean?

Never mind. Don't overthink it. Besides, you got bigger problems.

Jared had to find Joe.

He reached down, grabbing the five-by-seven photo of his older brother off Cole's desk. The shot was half-profile—Joe was looking off to the right.

Jared clenched his jaw when unwanted emotion took him by surprise. He dragged two fingers down the picture, grateful his partner was absorbed by the phone call.

Cole's deep voice faded as he stared at the side of his brother's face he could see.

Strong jaw. Five o'clock shadow, messy dark hair in need of a good cut. Brow knitted, his mouth set in a hard line, like he was pissed about something. He was wearing a white A-shirt. Joe's shoulder and biceps were covered in tats, but the shot wasn't close enough to make any specific design out.

"He look familiar or somethin'?" Cole asked.

Jared jumped, cursing himself. He met his partner's eyes. "Nope." His stomach flip-flopped. He'd never lied to the guy before.

"You sure? You're starin' hard, like you know him."

"Not sure I know him at all. Phone call something I need to know about?"

The gaze on him still appraised, and he fought the urge to fidget.

His partner was former FBI. Had been with the Bureau for seven years. Had a built-in lie detector.

"You're weirdin' me out. What's up with you today? You gonna be okay after I go?"

"Nothing. Had a long night. But she was great. Maybe she scrambled my brains." Jared's gut churned.

Please drop it, partner.

He couldn't say it.

"What'd ya mean, go?" he asked after a subtle breath.

"I'm out at a quarter to twelve. Early release at school today. Andi asked me if I'd grab E-man and get the little one from day care. She needs to wrap up some case shit before Turkey Day."

"Ah. Yeah, I'm good. Big boy and all."

His partner smirked, but that gray stare didn't waver.

Cole Lucas was more than his partner. Over the last two and a half years, they'd grown close. Become friends. More than friends. Pretty much best friends. Actually, the guy was like an older brother.

Joe.

"Kinda surprised you're out. We just caught a case. Times change, huh?" Jared teased, crossing his arms over his chest. He often jacked with Cole about his steadfast *over*-dedication of years past. Truth was, since he'd been with APD, he was '*family-first*'.

Besides the lectures about women Jared didn't need or want, he admired Cole for being a great husband and father, as well as a hell of an investigator. Enjoyed working with him. He was the first partner that'd stuck.

Since he'd been a detective, he'd had four other

partners. No matter how he'd tried to mesh, Jared could never make it work one hundred percent.

One guy had quit, another had gone back to patrol, and a third had taken a job with the county sheriff's office. The last one had been halfway decent, but he'd been promoted and now ran a shift. Still, he'd never been as close to Jay Conner as he was to Cole.

His partner shrugged. "I studied the case file. Pete's putting the word out on scum-radar, and no one has spotted Joe Pompa and his gang *in* Antioch. Rumors of being close to town need to be solidified by a lead. It'll hold a day or two. The whole department's been briefed, it's not like we won't get a call if they surface. Hell, it's two days to Thanksgiving. I'd rather be home. You do your homework on this after I go. Lemme know what you think."

"Alrighty then. What was up with the call? Anything I need to know?"

He grinned, flashing dimples. "Like I said, do your homework, Detective Manning."

Jared arched an eyebrow.

"We're gonna have company. Special Agent Taylor Carrigan's coming to town."

Shit. I gotta find Joe.

Joe paced, cursing under his breath and glaring at the disposable cellphone. Rick had missed check-in, and he had no clue where Moose and Bran were — scratch that, he just didn't want to face it.

Moose and Bran were fucking. She'd probably

dragged the big oaf behind the old trailer, or maybe even inside one of the others on site.

Just treat her right, big guy. God knows I didn't.

Their hideout was quiet so far, but if he didn't get them out of town—and quick—the more likely they were to get caught.

Prison.

Not like that was new, but this time it was for something they—no, he—*didn't* do.

Moose and Bran had both refused to leave him, even after he'd been forced to run.

Joe knew who was trying to frame him—and he had the FBI on his ass. Funny, that tended to happen when one of their own turned up dead.

When he found the fucker, he was going to beat the living hell out of Carter Bennett. Or maybe he'd kill the asshole.

Whaddaya know, then I'd be guilty of murder as accused.

He was far from an angel, but he wasn't a killer.

Thief, yes.

He'd stolen, stripped and hawked more cars than he could count. Built a nice cushion doing it, too.

No one in his gang was a killer.

He wouldn't stand for that shit.

Besides, John Donovan—Murray, as it'd turned out—had been his buddy. Joe hadn't known he was FBI, of course—at first.

John had talked him into cooperating. The rest of the team was going to get slaps on the wrist, so he was going to do it. No one knew. He'd been trying to protect them—especially Bran.

The FBI guy had promised he could go to prison alone for them. Joe was the ringleader, anyway. He'd picked up the rest of his gang over the years. One by one, raised them up, trained them all to be savvy thieves. For years, they'd never even been on law enforcement radar.

When that little fucker, Carter, had found out, he'd accused him of being a traitor.

John had convinced Joe to run.

Carter betrayed him. He'd beaten the agent within an inch of his life before killing him.

Joe couldn't prove it.

He'd fled.

Coward. Fucking coward.

He should've stayed. Fought beside John Murray. He couldn't have risked Bran's life like that, though. Stubborn woman would've insisted on staying.

Moose, too. The big oaf saw him as an older brother.

Hiding in Antioch, Texas—where he'd spent about a year as a teen—was reckless, though. His brother was a cop. Like, locally.

Considering he'd abandoned the kid with foster parents number one-hundred-forty-seven, Joe wouldn't blame Jared for arresting his ass.

When he hadn't been able to deal and had split, he'd been seventeen to Jared's tender twelve. He made sure his brother was safe—protected—and he'd left.

They kept in touch from time to time. No details. Just a quick *'How the hell are ya?'*

Joe dragged his hand over his new buzz cut. "Fuck me."

None of his crew knew he had a little bro, let alone the fact he was a blueblood. Not like he went around announcing it.

The phone rang and he jumped. "Yeah?"

"Boss." Rick's voice was low.

Something's wrong.

He gripped the crappy twenty-dollar throwaway cell tighter. "Talk. Quick."

"In Cali. Carter's setting up a score. Train break."

"Fucker. He get in touch with my contact?"

"Yeah, we're going forward. Four million in Ferraris and Lamborghinis."

"Foolish asshole. That's too much to go after at once, especially down three men. Not to mention the Feds are watching."

If confronted, Carter would shoot his way out. Putting the remainder of Joe's family at risk. They might've sided with the asshole, but they were still *his.* He cared about them.

Not to mention if the punk was apprehended, he'd agree to testify that Joe killed John Murray. He felt it in his gut.

Rick snorted. "I know. He won't listen to shit. Rowdy and Mack are totally in, though."

"What about you, Rick?"

"I gotta lay low. Can't run my mouth." Joe's number two paused. "I'm going."

"Cover your ass."

"Will do. Don't tell me where you're at, but you

safe? Moose? Sweet Bran?"

"For now."

The guy sighed. "Good. Carter said after he moves the new rides, we're coming after you."

Joe laughed, but the sound was bitter. "I wish you could tell that fucker I said, bring it."

"Stay safe, boss. I gotta go."

"You too, Rick. Call me when you can. If I ditch this phone for a new one, I'll text you the number." He ended the call. Rage made his blood boil. He sucked in a breath, fighting the urge to toss the cell across the shitty trailer. With his luck, the impact would make the wall collapse or something.

He scanned the place they'd been crashing for the last few days. Wallpaper no longer recognizable, but was probably floral or some shit. Peeling in all the corners.

The carpet was missing in some spots. The counter in the kitchen was whole, but had seen better days. Two of the cupboard doors hung by hinges. The place had a rotted out couch and a broken recliner with a huge hole in the seat.

It was the better of the two they could get into on site, though. There were a few other trailers, but they hadn't approached them. One had yellow crime scene tape surrounding it.

Joe didn't want to know what'd happened in there.

Piles of new blankets they'd grabbed at Wally-world were piled in the corner. He'd cringed that Bran had had to sleep on the dirty floor, but she hadn't even flinched.

They had cash money—and a lot of it—but they couldn't risk staying at a hotel or motel.

Not close to Antioch anyway.

What if he ran into his brother?

"Fuck me. We have to get out of here."

Feminine laughter made Joe glance toward the trailer's entrance and he tried not to scowl as Bran and Moose tumbled into the piece of crap mobile home, arm-in-arm.

So they were done hiding their *'relationship'* from him.

Waking up that morning on the shitty carpet only to see Moose's arm flung across her body like he owned her had been bad enough.

His gut tightened. "Rick called," he barked.

The smile on Bran's pretty face faded. Her blonde hair was tousled. Her lips swollen, cheeks still flushed pink.

Joe knew that look. Had been the cause more times than he could count.

Her glow didn't fade even as her brown eyes became solemn.

Dammit.

Moose dropped her arm and squared his huge shoulders. Bald, and with more muscles than three guys needed, he always looked harsh. Normally a grimace passed for a smile. But the look on the guy's face when he'd entered the trailer gazing at the woman Joe still loved had been tender.

They have feelings for each other.

He was trapped with them.

It just gets fucking better and better.

"And?" Her question made his heart flutter.

Joe squared his shoulders and scowled. "Carter's making a move."

Chapter Six

M el gave a sigh of relief when the last bell rang and she lined her kids up to go out to the — hopefully — ready cars of parents and caretakers. She caught Val's eye as her bestie walked with her own class.

Val flashed a smile and winked.

Chaos ensued, breaking up lines of kids as people headed into the school. Not all parents always waited in their cars outside the building.

She sighed and pressed into the wall. Her temples pounded with every happy yell or exclamation. The older kids valued the break more than the kindergarteners and first grade classes — the little ones still *liked* school.

"Daddy!"

Mel heard Ethan Lucas call for his father, and straightened.

She'd been planning to call Detective Lucas, but why wait?

He didn't usually pick up his son, so she should take advantage of seeing him.

The very tall man laughed and scooped the little redheaded boy into an embrace before setting him back to his feet and taking Ethan's small backpack. He threaded his arm through the straps. "Hi, buddy."

She smiled when he ruffled his son's copper hair. "Detective Lucas," she called, trotting over to them.

Gray eyes met hers. He smiled, flashing dimples. "Miss Nash."

"I was going to give you call."

His expression sobered. "Is everything okay?"

"Oh, yes. I was going to ask you for a favor, actually."

His huge shoulders loosened. "What can I do for ya?"

"Well, I'm sorry for the short notice, but next Friday is *Community Helper's Day*, and I was wondering if you would be willing to come in and talk to my class about being a police officer."

The detective nodded. "I'd love to."

"Yay, Daddy! You get to come to school with me." Ethan jumped up and down, clinging to his father's hand.

Mel grinned.

"What time, and do you mind if I bring my partner?"

"About nine-thirty, and two perspectives would be awesome."

"You got it."

"Thanks, Detective. I really appreciate it." She stuck her hand out for a shake.

He took it, flashing those dimples again. "No problem, Miss Nash. Thanks for being a great teacher to my kid. Ethan talks about you constantly."

Mel beamed. Couldn't help it. That was about the best praise a teacher could ever get. She'd adored Ethan Lucas from the first time she'd talked with the little boy. "Thank you for the compliment. I mean it when I say;

Ethan's a delight to have in class. I'll miss him next year."

"I'm sure his mother will be pleased to hear that. And hey, maybe my other one will end up in your class in a few years."

"My little brother's Micah," Ethan said. He enunciated the word *brother* as if was still working on it.

She smiled. "I hope I meet him!"

The little boy nodded and grinned.

"All right, buddy. Let's hit the road. We gotta get Micah and go to the store for your mom."

"Have a good Thanksgiving, Detective. Ethan, be sure to show your dad your thankful picture from today."

"Thanks, Miss Nash. You do the same," Detective Lucas said. After one last wave, he grabbed her student's hand and guided him down the wide corridor.

"Can we put my picture on the fridge, Daddy?"

Mel smiled again as they walked away, the detective's deep cadence melding with his son's much higher one. She waved to other parents and children, and wished several more 'Happy Thanksgivings'.

Fatigue threatened and she swallowed a yawn. Dang, she was tired. Ready to go home.

Maybe a nap was in order after she stopped at *Marty's*. She still had to pick up a few things for Thanksgiving dinner at her dad's.

"Who the heck was *that*?" Val sidled up to her, and Mel rolled her eyes.

"Married."

"So? I'm just alookin'."

She shook her head at her best friend. "I swear, you're a hormone."

Val laughed. "Am not. It's just that not *all* of us have only recently had the best sex of their life."

"Will you hush? There are still little ears around! Geeze. We *are* at school."

"I wasn't shouting." Her bestie stared, unrepentant. "So who was the guy? Why the heart-to-heart?"

"One of my kids' dads, obvi."

Val cast her eyes upward. "Um. I get that. Everything okay?"

Mel studied her friend, trying to determine if she was concerned or just curious. "He's a detective. I snagged him for *Community Helper's Day*."

"Niiiiiiicccce." Her best friend flashed two thumbs up and grinned.

"Let me get my stuff, then I'm outta here. Thank God Edwards canceled the meeting. I'm whipped and I still have to go grocery shopping. You still coming over for dinner?"

Val's parents were gone and so was Mel's mom, so for the past few years, they'd spent holiday dinners together with Mel's father.

"Sure! I wouldn't miss a day with you and Jack for the world. What do you need help with?"

"Wanna make a few pies? Apple? Pumpkin?"

"You got it."

They headed back toward their classrooms. Her

friend had farther to go, as the third grade rooms were down the hallway and around the corner.

"Hey," Val called when Mel had one foot inside her room.

"Yeah?"

"I can tell you one thing for sure."

She arched an eyebrow. With the mischief in those blue eyes, her best friend wasn't about to comment on Thanksgiving dinner. "Oh, I can't wait."

Val flashed a grin. "If you didn't notice how hot that cop was…welllllll, I guess Jared-from-the-bar did his job."

"Shut. Up. Valerie Hart."

Jared hit *McAuley's* after five in hopes of running into Renee.

No juice.

Disappointment churned his gut and his head whipped around every time the door opened, but his lover didn't magically appear.

Dammit.

He was waiting for a call from Special Agent Carrigan anyway, so relaxing at home was out until he heard from the FBI chick. Hopefully she didn't mind meeting him at a bar.

He still wanted to wait for Renee.

Besides, he had a feeling Carrigan was going to be a pain in the ass. The way Jared saw it, they were in a race to get to Joe.

He had to win.

"Hey, Bri."

Once again, Brian McAuley was tending bar. He was in the corner by the double doors leading into kitchen, mopping up a spill. The guy swept the last of the broken glass into a dustpan and dumped it in the trashcan. The tall redheaded man offered a head nod. "Detective."

"Can I ask you something?"

"Sure." Brian trotted over. "You need a drink?"

"Nah, not stayin' long. Just wondered if you'd seen the woman I was with last night?"

He shook his head. "Not today. The one with three other girls, right? They left together, 'cept for her?"

"Right."

"Never seen her before. Not a regular."

"Damn." But it made sense. He was a regular, and had never seen her before. "You know her name?"

The bartender arched an eyebrow. His eyes asked, '*you don't?*' "Nope."

"Thanks anyway, man." He dug out a business card and slapped it on the bar. "If you see her, can you tell her I'm looking for her?"

Why the hell had she snuck out of his apartment—his bed—that morning?

He *knew* he was a considerate lover. She'd had a good time. He'd made sure of it. The sex had been…awesome.

Jared didn't even know her last name.

Damn. It.

"Will do." Brian grabbed the card and thumbtacked it to the corkboard on the wall behind the bar.

You have a case. Stop thinking about her.

"Can I ask you one other thing?"

"Shoot."

He grabbed Joe's picture from inside his jacket and flashed it before the bartender. "Have you seen this guy around here?"

Brian gripped the picture and studied it. Then he shook his head.

Relief mixed with a second dose of disappointment washed over Jared. All day his thoughts had zoomed from Renee to Joe and back. Chaos in his head. He couldn't make sense of either of them.

He'd read the FBI case file — twice. Stared at all the pictures. A few more shots of Joe. An oversized bald guy — Michael 'Moose' Gentile. A pretty girl named Brandelyn Willis, who didn't look much like a car thief. According to the files, she was the gang's computer genius. It also said she'd been involved in a romantic relationship with his brother.

Four more guys, Richard Wilkins, Eric 'Rowdy' Vargas, Sean McKinley, who went by 'Mack', and lastly, a blond guy named Carter Bennett, who was cited to be Joe's second in command.

Report after report from the dead agent, John Murray. Detailed dossiers on all of Joe's gang. Crimes, contacts, the works. Even things they were suspected of, but there was no proof they'd pulled off.

His brother's gang wasn't average car thieves. They were organized, did their research, and were most definitely high tech, like those Vin Diesel movies.

They were allegedly responsible for the theft and resale of millions and millions of dollars' worth of every luxury and sports car brand imaginable.

Bottom line — they were *good*. More than good.

Rarely did anyone get hurt. No one killed. Which only solidified that Joe Pompa wasn't a killer.

So who killed the FBI agent found in their midst?

The rest of the gang was suspected to be out west, Nevada or California, but Joe was said to have fled with the girl and the bald guy, Michael Gentile, after the murder.

John Murray's body had turned up on a riverbank on the Texas-Oklahoma border. Several hundred miles from the location of the gang's last job — and the last place Murray had checked in from.

"On second thought, this guy does kinda look familiar, Detective."

Brian's speech jarred him, and his fingers shook when he accepted the photo back from the bartender. Jared made his eyes graze the picture before sticking it back in his pocket. "Yeah? So you've seen him?"

Has Joe been here after all?

Casual. Just act casual.

"Hmmm, maybe. But if I have, I don't know if it was here or somewhere else. A lot of people come and go, not always regulars."

He forced a smile. "I get it. If you see him again, or remember anything, can you give me a call? My cell's on that card I gave you."

"You bet, Detective. You sure you don't want a

drink?"

"No thanks, I'm actually working."

Brian nodded. "Lemme know if you need anything."

"Will do."

A guy slipped onto the barstool two down from Jared and ordered a beer.

With one last head nod, the youngest McAuley left to do his job.

It was happy hour until seven-thirty, so people were pouring into the place.

Still no Renee.

Give up on that, think about your case.

Saving your brother's ass.

Jared stewed in his seat.

Where the fuck is Joe?

Why did the FBI suspect he'd headed toward Antioch anyway? Had they connected the dots to Jared?

Did Special Agent Taylor Carrigan know they were brothers?

His heart tripped and he shook his head.

No way.

He'd been adopted, his name legally changed from Pompa to Manning at age twelve. He hadn't had a middle name that Child Protective Services had known about, so he'd taken his dad's first name, Jason, as a second name. So Jared Pompa to Jared Jason Manning would be even harder to match up.

Unless someone knew to look, sixteen-year-old court records shouldn't even come to light.

Joe had been gone at seventeen. Their calls had been sporadic. Not even Jared's parents knew he'd had contact with his brother.

He'd never mentioned it because he couldn't stand the disappointment in his mother's eyes if his brother's name was said aloud.

Amy Manning saw Joe as the boy she'd failed to save.

They would've adopted him, too. They'd tried so hard with Joe the year he'd spent in their home. Jared didn't remember too many specifics since he'd been so young, but his brother's time with the Mannings had been filled with rebellion, truancy and a few police reports.

"Fuck me." He fought the urge to close his eyes and glanced at his watch.

Twenty after six. He'd told Cole he'd handle Carrigan's advent, but he regretted it.

He'd rather troll any likely hideouts for his brother and friends. There were a few places in Antioch he could look. The old warehouse district, and the decrepit trailer park came to mind. Or Homeless Row.

How well did Joe know the small city? His year in Antioch had been a long time ago. The place had changed.

Jared's cellphone blared from his pocket and he jumped. "Manning."

"Detective, this is Special Agent Taylor Carrigan. I spoke to your partner earlier. He told me to contact you."

Her voice was deep for a woman's. Direct, like her

words. Maybe she had a low bullshit tolerance.

Is that good or bad?

"Yes. If you want, we can meet now. Where are you?"

"Stuart and Main." Carrigan's answer was without hesitation.

She's prepared. Definitely doesn't do BS.

He smirked. "Hang a left on Ash. You'll see *McAuley's* on the right."

"All right. I assume I'll see you in a few minutes."

Jared ended the call and shook his head. "If first impressions mean anything, let's hope *efficient* doesn't mean *hard-ass*."

"Did you say something, Detective?" Brian McAuley asked, as he filled a frosty glass from the tap in front of him.

"No, sir. Just talking to myself."

The bartender flashed a smile. "That's just fine unless you start answering yourself, too."

"Thanks. I'll keep that in mind." Jared chuckled, and ran his hand through his hair. His stomach was in knots.

Chapter Seven

Taylor set her cell in the cup holder in lieu of trying to bury it back in her jacket pocket while driving. She passed a large blue reflective sign with white lettering that read *Antioch Justice Center* and had an arrow pointing toward on Precinct Drive.

Where she'd assumed she'd be heading after leaving *The Covington.*

Not so much.

Her GPS hollered that she was being rerouted when she made a left on Ash, as the detective had instructed.

When she saw what had to be a bar's parking lot, she made a face.

So much for hoping it was a restaurant.

The word *McAuley's* was on the front of the building, posted high and in blue and red lit-up letters. The colors made her think of a police cruiser's lightbar, but the place wasn't the police station.

First time in the small city of Antioch, Texas, and Taylor had never imagined meeting local law enforcement—temporary co-workers—at a place that served alcohol.

She didn't want to deal with Manning anyway. Her boss, Special Agent Matthias Baker, had told her to cooperate with the local PD.

That wasn't going to be a problem, but she wanted to deal exclusively with Cole Lucas. He was former FBI.

He knew his way around an investigation, *and* how things would have to work. He was off grid, or so his text message had said.

My partner's around. Jared Manning. Told him to expect your call. See you in the a.m.

Then Manning's number.

So Taylor didn't have a choice.

Lucas was married, so she didn't blame him, really.

A picture of John's smile, his kind brown eyes and handsome face flashed into her mind. She'd loved the cleft in his chin most.

Sorrow caught in her throat and she swallowed so she wouldn't sob. Taylor clenched her jaw until pain shot into her teeth.

Emotion is weak.

Her father's mantra teased her brain. Besides stupid feelings she didn't need, she was working.

Get it together.

She tried to banish the circling chaos, with little success. *She* was supposed to have been married, too. John and Taylor had been planning their wedding for almost six months.

The date was inching closer and closer. February the fourteenth, in honor of the anniversary of their first kiss, as well as Valentine's Day.

That bastard Joe Pompa had taken it all away.

Taylor would get him.

Cuffs or a bullet, she hadn't decided yet.

Get that out of your head. You're not a murderer — like he is.

Prison.

Pompa needed to go to *prison* for a long time. She'd make it happen. No matter what she had to do.

Taylor pulled the Chevy Impala into the parking lot, but she didn't park up next to the building. She glanced at the clock as a few more cars and a truck pulled in and several guys headed inside.

Great, the place is busy.

She had no use for alcohol, let alone some stupid Happy Hour, which lasted until seven-thirty, according to the banner attached the building.

Taylor tried not to slam the car door. She trotted up to the place she had no desire to enter. Fought a shiver, even though it was warm for a November evening.

A tall guy with sable hair wearing a brown leather jacket and tight dark jeans, held the door open. He winked as she passed him and mumbled thanks. His demeanor screamed *'cop'* but she ignored him, including the lack of returning his pleasant smile. Doubted he was Manning.

When Taylor looked around the inside of the place, her frown deepened. It was like some deranged cop shrine.

The history of anything Police-Americana had vomited up all over the place.

No wonder the sign is red and blue.

The guy that opened the door hadn't gone away. "Can I help you find someone, ma'am?"

The Texas twang that still got to her sometimes rocked her a little bit. She'd grown up in Chicago, and had only been assigned to Violent Crimes, Special Investigations Unit, out of the Dallas office of the FBI for two years. Not many FBI agents were actually from Texas in her unit. Quantico shipped people all over the US after graduation.

Her gaze snapped to his face. She tried not to notice the unusual amber color of the man's eyes. Or that he was handsome and tall.

Still looks like a cop.

The need to clear her throat before speaking irritated her. "Actually, yes. I'm supposed to meet Detective Jared Manning. Know him?"

"Yup." He looked around, then met her eyes. "Black leather jacket, far end of the bar."

"Thanks."

Flashing a dimple in his right cheek, he nodded. "Anytime. Sure I'll see you around."

Taylor watched him walk away, her stomach jumping.

He shook hands with two men at a back table and took a seat.

She frowned again and smoothed the front of her blazer. Then she turned toward the detective and squared her shoulders.

Let's get this over with.

The longer the FBI agent took to arrive, the more his stomach twisted. She'd been about five minutes away when she'd called.

What the hell?

Jared whipped his head around every time the door opened. So far no female had entered, let alone a woman that fit the FBI-bill. He turned back to the bar with a sigh. Took a sip of the water Brian had put in front of him a few minutes before, even though he hadn't asked for it.

Water really wasn't cutting it. Maybe he should order that drink after all. A shot of Scotch, his normal. Or two.

It might calm his worries about Joe...and his longing for Renee.

"Detective Manning."

The deep, yet feminine, tones from the phone almost made him jump, but he chided himself to sit still. Plastered on a smile and swiveled on the barstool.

Carrigan was sizing him up, even before he stuck his hand.

"Jared Manning," he said.

She accepted his shake, her eyes landing on his face. Didn't smile, but offered a nod. "Special Agent Taylor Carrigan."

For some reason, he wanted to squirm in his seat.

"Last I checked, Antioch Police Department is down the street."

Jared smirked. "Yeah, well, it's after five. And if you take a look around, you'll find more than a few cops in here."

She arched an eyebrow. Still no smile. "A bar."

Guess it was too much to hope that she wasn't a

hard-ass.

Insisting on heading into Antioch tonight, despite the long drive, should've told him something.

"Right. A bar. Do some of my best investigating from right here. Have a seat. Take a load off. We can talk shop."

Agent Carrigan stared at him as if he'd sprouted wings. She wasn't very big for someone whom intimidation was currently rolling off. Then again, most women were diminutive to him, since he was six-three.

"I prefer somewhere more confidential. Like the police station," she said.

"Maybe in the morning. I'm here. Not there."

If Jared hadn't just met her, he would've told her to loosen up.

Her strawberry blonde hair was in a librarian's bun, not a strand out of place, even at six forty-one p.m. Her outfit was neat and tidy, too. Black slacks and a royal-blue button-down that was most definitely tucked in. She wore a black blazer that concealed the handgun instinct said was at her waist.

Even if he wasn't a cop, he would've been able to spot her as law enforcement ten miles away. Her demeanor screamed '*FBI agent*'.

Add *uptight* to that.

Not even the freckles strewn across the bridge of her pert little nose gave her an air of innocence. Kind of ruined her beauty, in a way. Because Agent Special Taylor Carrigan could've been gorgeous without the stick up her ass.

"Detective Manning, I don't think—"

"I read your case file. I have some ideas."

Her mouth snapped closed, but she didn't relax. Crossed her arms over her chest. Her hazel gaze was shrewd. "Ideas?"

"Of where to look for Pompa and his gang."

Damn it's hard to say 'Pompa' like the name means nothing.

"Ah."

"Do you have a place to stay tonight?"

The FBI agent straightened, as if she hadn't expected him to ask. "Yes, I checked into *The Covington* before I called you."

"Good deal. Well I don't know about you, but it's been a long day. And it's two days before a holiday. So why don't you head to your room and we'll meet in the morning? I'm sure my partner will want in on our discussion anyway."

Carrigan frowned. "I assumed we'd start tonight."

Jared stared. He wanted to ask if she was for real, but it was obvious. Not only was she a hard-ass, she was a workaholic.

Great.

He and Cole were no strangers to working their asses off for a case — all hours of the day and night until it was done. This time, it was a holiday week. His parents expected him at the table on Thanksgiving Day.

His younger sister, Jenna, was coming in from Corpus Christi where she went to college. It was a long drive — about ten hours — and she'd be in town tomorrow. Was bringing a guy — her new fiancé, actually.

He needed to be there to threaten the dude. If the guy hurt his baby sister, he'd kick his ass — or worse.

Wasn't Carrigan leaving family in Dallas for the holiday?

"My partner and I — our whole detective squad, actually — are up to speed with your case. I think our hands are really tied 'til we meet as a group, anyway."

Her frown deepened. "I'm not fond of wasting time, Detective. Especially my own."

Jared thought better of rolling his eyes — but he was tempted. "How about a compromise?"

She arched a fair eyebrow — again. "How so?"

"There's a corner table over there, I'm sure no one'll bother us. We can get a bite to eat and talk about the case. I'm sure you're hungry after your drive, and I'm starving."

Carrigan cocked her head to one side as if she was thinking about it. Then the FBI agent gave a curt nod.

When he stood from the stool, she amended her gaze to look *up* at him, and he bit back a smartass grin.

She was short — had to be about five-one.

"Hey, Bri," he called. "We're going to order food in a few."

"Sure thing, Detective."

That fair eyebrow shot even higher. "Come here often?"

Jared snorted. "Like I said, half of APD is here right now. This is the cop-bar in town. Thought it'd be obvious with the décor."

Carrigan made a disparaging sound, and pulled the chair out when he led her to the back corner. She touched it daintily, as if it was filthy.

Jesus, don't tell me she just added 'prissy' to workaholic hard-ass, too.

He plopped down across from her and tried not to look at the table just to the right; where he'd been seated with Renee the night before. "So tell me, what makes you think Pompa headed to my small, no-where city?"

The FBI agent studied him, but her expression was pleased, as if she hadn't expected him to dive right in, and liked not being put off again.

"It made sense. Considering where Murray's… body was found." She squared her shoulders and cleared her throat.

Jared watched her swallow — twice.

Hmmm…emotion?

Or had he imagined it?

Who was the dead agent, John Murray, to Special Agent Taylor Carrigan?

He appraised her until she averted her gaze. Surprise rolled over him. She didn't seem the type to admit defeat — even in a staring contest.

Carrigan was hiding something, and she didn't want him to latch on.

We'll just see about that.

She grabbed a menu. "So, what's good here, Detective?"

"You can call me Jared."

Her pretty hazel eyes widened and she shook her head. "Formality is better for me, Detective. No offense."

Jared gave her another onceover then let her

comment slide. He reached for his own menu from behind the rack of condiments, sliding the salt and pepper shakers out of the way. "I usually get a burger, but they have other tasty things if a hunk of beef isn't your style, Special Agent."

She paused, fingertips in mid-turn of the second page.

Speechless?

He bit back a grin and tried to school his expression, but she'd read him like a book if Carrigan's tight brow was any indication.

The appearance of one of Brian's two waitresses stopped the FBI agent from answering.

She ordered a burger after all. With bacon *and* cheese.

He tried not to smirk as she tucked into it with her pinkie finger sticking straight up. Like she was drinking tea.

Carrigan was dainty after all.

Jared glanced down at his plate and grabbed a few thick French fries. They were the best—carnival style. Damn good thing he and Cole would run off the bad food choice in the morning. They were supposed to meet at the track at five-thirty. Not like he watched what he ate like a chick, but he'd been tossing back too much grease this week and had missed one run already.

Although, vigorous, fantastic sex was exercise, too.

Do not think of Renee right now.

Carrigan didn't talk much as they ate, but he was okay with that.

However, it didn't escape his notice that her gaze kept darting to the left, to a table of three APD cops — Shannon Crowley, Mark Rodriguez and Joe Benton.

"Know them or something?" he finally asked when she looked that way the fourth — maybe fifth — time.

She jumped.

Jared arched an eyebrow.

The FBI agent cleared her throat. "No. The one on the left opened the door for me is all."

"Ah. They're all APD. Brown leather jacket?"

Carrigan nodded.

"His name is Shannon Crowley. Newly promoted to sergeant, he works the graveyard. Must be gearing up for his shift." He smirked. "Want an intro or something?"

She glared and Jared chuckled. "Let's get down to business."

He laughed again, ignoring her frown. He should back off anyway — he didn't know her well enough to jack with her.

The professional part of him thought it might be good to get her take on things, too. She'd been working this case for a while, so her familiarity wouldn't hurt.

You still have to get to Joe first.

Jared bit back a wince at the reminder and opened his mouth. He had to brief her on the layout of the city before they could get started.

Chapter Eight

Mel smiled at her dad from across the table.

He stretched and patted his midsection. "That was fantastic, Melody. And the pie! You're a baking genius, Valerie!"

Her bestie grinned from ear to ear and reached for her glass of red wine. "I'm glad you liked them. The melted caramel over the lattice weave crust on the apple is my special touch."

"I'll say," Dad said, grinning back.

They'd had a pleasant meal with funny and natural conversation, but Mel felt alone in the room with the two people she cared about most in the world.

Her mind refused to abandon thoughts about Jared.

It was a holiday. Where was he?

Was *he* having a nice day, a nice dinner with family?

Was he alone in that apartment?

Mel could seek him out. Head to his place, see him again.

"Hey, you okay?"

Val's voice made her jump, and she looked into her friend's blue eyes. All she could read was concern.

"Yup." She smiled, and patted her hand before looking at her dad. "Daddy, you want more pie?"

"No, sugar, I'm full. I can barely move. Too much turkey, mash potatoes, yams. You two outdid yourselves."

"Thanks, I'm glad you enjoyed it." Mel had been up early, had cooked all day. "Val, wanna help me clean up?"

"You know I will." The searching gaze didn't waver, but she smiled. "Then we can head to the tree lighting!"

Mel groaned. "No way. I don't want to go."

"Jared might be there."

She glared at Val and shot a glance at her dad, but he was already dozing at the table. "Daddy, why don't you head to the living room? The game's already on." She'd turned the TV on before dinner.

Her dad would fall asleep in the recliner as soon as he sat, like he did every time.

Mel always went to the house she'd grown up in for holiday meals. It was a sprawling ranch, the home her dad was most comfortable in. She missed her smaller house, two streets over. She'd bought it after a year of being a teacher.

It was *hers*. The place she was most comfortable.

Her dad's always felt like it was missing something.

It was.

Mama.

Anne Nash had been gone eight years, but it still seemed like yesterday that the breast cancer had taken her.

Dad was only fifty now, but her gut shouted that he'd never move on. Never date again, or remarry. He'd told her many times her mom had been the love of his life.

Jack Nash smiled and pushed back from the table. "You girls need help?"

"No, sir. We're going to clean up and go watch the fireworks," Val said, ignoring the shake of Mel's head.

She *so* didn't want to go out, despite the fantasizing about Jared. She wanted to go home. Curl up on her couch with a good book and a cup of coffee.

"Oh, good. I've heard they have a big event planned this year. It's free. Enjoy yourselves. It should be an unusually warm evening for it, too." He rounded the table and kissed Mel's cheek, then Val's.

"Jack, I wish I could find a man as sweet as you." Her bestie patted her dad's thick hand and flashed a grin.

"Sugar, you need a man who can handle you." He chuckled and Val beamed.

"Amen, Dad. A-men," Mel muttered.

Val winked, instead of being offended. "Still trying to see if he exists. Hey, I know. I might meet him in the park. Tonight." She waggled her eyebrows and Mel rolled her eyes.

Jack left the dining room, shaking his head and laughing.

"Not likely," she said.

Her friend jumped up from the table and started piling their dirty dishes. "You never know," she said in a sing-song statement. She was dressed casually, in jeans and a pink sweater, but as always, Val looked fantastic.

"Are you in a musical?" Mel grabbed the gravy

boat and an empty glass, following into the kitchen.

"Hmmm, already showing signs of withdrawal."

"What?" She looked up from the plastic container she was about to pour leftover gravy into.

Her bestie flashed a grin and dipped her head low as she loaded the dishwasher. "You're grumpy."

"Am not."

"I rest my case."

Mel frowned. "Usually I do speak fluent Val, but this time I have no fricking clue what you're talking about."

She laughed. "You're uptight. Showing symptoms of lack of great sex. Just once and you were obviously hooked. Sad, really. 'Cause you *could* run into him tonight."

Mel gasped. "My dad's here."

"In the living room. Two rooms away." Val pointed with a dirty serving spoon before setting it on the top rack. "You know he's probably already asleep in his chair, anyway."

She let the retort slide and left the room to get the turkey. Unfortunately, Val was on her heels.

"You know I'm right."

Mel sighed, both hands on the large platter. "About *what*?"

"You want to see him again."

You are right.

She'd cut her tongue off before she admitted *that* out loud.

Val giggled as she grabbed the mash potatoes and the container of sweet yams. "Your silence proves it."

"*Why* are you so concerned about *my* sex life anyway?" Mel asked when they made it back into the kitchen. She grabbed a knife to get the rest of the turkey off the bone so she could put it into a container. "You should get one of your own."

Scrunching up her nose, her bestie nodded. "I'm working on it, believe me. Hence, trying to get you to go with me to the fireworks and the tree lighting."

"You meeting someone?" She paused.

"Not really. I mean, I told this guy I might be there."

"Who? Are you serious, or just making something up to get me to go out?" Mel studied her.

"Some guy I met at *Marty's*, who constantly flirts with me. We've run into each other a few times. He hasn't asked me out. Dunno why, 'cause I'd go. So I mentioned I might drop by the park Thanksgiving evening, when I saw him looking at the poster in the store window."

"Hmmm…what's this guy's name?"

"Chris."

"Chris what?"

"How the hell should I know? We've only flirted." Val's eyes narrowed. "You think I'm lying?"

Mel shook her head. "Nope. But I don't think you're into this Chris-person."

She shrugged, hipping the dishwasher shut. "He's cute. There's potential."

"All right." The acquiesce came out on a sigh.

"You'll go?" Val's face lit up and she grinned.

"Yes, I'll go."

Her bestie cupped her face and planted a noisy kiss on her cheek. "I knew I loved you."

"It's kinda required."

Val laughed and kicked her leg up. "You bet. I'm gonna slip into something hotter. Be right back."

"Yeah yeah," she muttered, turning back to the bird.

Jared might be there.

The statement taunted. Mel ignored how her heart sped up, and her stomach flipped.

Joe gnawed on his thumbnail. He kept one foot moving in front of the other, like pacing was his new favorite past time.

Although she said nothing, Bran's eyes tracked him from where she sat on a blanket, her back against the crappy trailer wall.

Her gaze burned and his stomach flipped.

Moose had gone to get them something to eat, and she'd refused to leave Joe alone, despite her lover's urging to go with him.

He winced at the word in his brain. Bran with someone else…

God, it hurt like a bitch.

Still.

"Why don't you sit down?" Her voice was low, but she was matter-of-fact, not trying to pacify him.

That would've just pissed him off, and his ex knew him well.

"Rick hasn't called."

"I know." Same unruffled tone.

"It's been two days."

"Joe. Breathe."

His heart skipped, but he obeyed, sucking in air until his head spun. "What the fuck are we going to do?" He closed his eyes and stilled.

Looking at Bran hurt, but he did it anyway. She might not be with him anymore, but her presence still calmed.

Grounded him, like she always had.

"We're going to be fine."

"What happened to us?" Joe blurted.

Her mocha eyes widened and she straightened her shoulders.

Fuck.

He'd never meant to say *that.*

Bran looked as surprised as Joe felt. Pain flickered across her beautiful face, and she averted her gaze.

His gut tightened. "I'm sorry."

She shook her head, her blonde locks jumping with the movement. "I'm not."

"What?"

Bran met his eyes, her jaw clenched. "I waited for you to ask me that for a year, Joe. A whole *year.* You pushed and pushed until I broke. I...couldn't wait anymore."

"I know." He made a fist. "I made you give up on me."

"I never gave up on you," she whispered.

His heart stuttered at the tears in her eyes.

Joe glued his boots to the tattered carpet. If he

didn't, he'd rush to her side, pull her into his arms and take her mouth.

He couldn't. Not anymore.

Bran belonged to Moose.

"If I gave up on you, I wouldn't be here."

Her statement washed over him like caress and he wanted to sob like a pussy.

I screwed everything up.

"Happy fucking Thanksgiving." Joe buried a hand in his hair. The feel of the new, much shorter cut startled him with its unfamiliarity.

Bran's dry laugh had him meeting her eyes. She shrugged and the some of the tension lifted.

His chest still fucking burned.

"We're together, aren't we?" she asked.

Not like I need us to be.

Joe forced a nod. Silence descended and he sighed as he took a seat next to her on the pile of blankets that served as their bedding.

"Why are we here?" Her head was cocked to one side.

"What d'you mean?"

"You never said, why this place…Antioch, right?"

His stomach jumped and he cleared his throat. Wasn't about to reveal Jared. "I dunno. It's far from New Mexico. Small, unassuming."

"Nah." Bran's brown gaze scorched as she studied him. "Didn't you say you spent some time in Texas as a kid? Is this the place?"

Shit.

He hadn't told his gang about his past, but *she'd*

always been different. Pillow talk over the years with the woman he loved had elicited secrets—without revealing Jared.

The only exception was Rowdy. He had a sister no one knew about, so when he'd found about Jared, his buddy had shared with the class about Cami.

Their siblings were a secret between them—not even Bran knew.

"Not the same place," Joe said.

"Bullshit."

He crushed his eyes shut and blew out a breath. Never had been able to lie to Brandelyn Willis.

"Why don't you tell me the truth? Before Moose gets back?"

"My brother's here." The confession fell from his lips unwanted. He looked away from the love of his life.

"Brother?"

Her soft grip on his cheeks made his mind go all sorts of forbidden places. Joe didn't fight her when Bran tugged the two-day beard, and their gazes collided.

"You never told me you had a brother."

"I can't think when you touch me." Confession number two made him wince as much as her wide-as-saucers brown eyes and her fingertips fell away from his face.

Regret roiled his gut. If he'd kept his thought in his head, maybe her hands would still be on him. Hell, maybe he could've held her again.

Bran looked confused—and hurt. "Joe, I'm with Moose."

"I know."

"I'm happy with Moose." Her whisper was clear. Honest.

Like a gut shot in a dirty fight.

Fuck. Me.

"I know." His repetition was a pained croak and his throat started to close. He swallowed — twice.

What the fuck is wrong with you, anyway? You have bigger things to worry about than your headfuck over Bran and Moose.

"He...loves me."

Jesus.

"You don't have to explain yourself to me."

Her face fell at his hard tone, but Joe had to pack it all away, focus on the *problems* at hand.

Rick hadn't called.

Bran was asking questions about Jared.

"You wanna know about my brother?" He pushed to his feet, unable to look at her again.

She didn't answer as he restarted pacing.

"He's a fucking cop."

Chapter Nine

Despite Carrigan being on his ass that morning—frickin' *Thanksgiving* morning—Jared hit his parents' porch *almost* on time.

His partner was taking one for the team and had invited the FBI agent to his and Andi's house, so she didn't have to spend the day alone in her hotel room.

Carrigan had said she wasn't heading back to Dallas.

When Cole had asked her about family, she'd shut him down, but his partner had strong-armed her into agreeing to his place.

Poor Andi. Carrigan's a bore.

Jared glanced at his watch.

Quarter after twelve, not too shabby.

When he opened the front door and stepped into the foyer, no one was there to greet him. A mixture of delicious scents tickled his nose, and he heard voices in the kitchen as well as commentary of a football game coming from his dad's giant TV in the living room.

He smiled as he slipped out of his leather jacket and hung it in the coat closet by the door.

Home.

Nothing ever made him feel like *this* place.

The shallow bark of a dog sounded at the same time he heard the *click click* of his dad's elderly basset hound's nails on the hardwood floor.

"A little slow on the uptake, old man, aren'cha? If

I was a burglar, I woulda cleaned out the place."

Ranger wagged his tail in response and Jared's smile widened to a grin as he kneeled to pet the dog his parents had gotten when he was in high school.

Solemn brown eyes met his and he gave the little guy a good scratch behind the ear. The dog groaned and pressed into his hand.

"Jared!"

Jenna's shout had him grinning again.

As soon as he'd straightened, his sister launched herself at him.

He chuckled, having no choice but to catch her or they'd both fall on their asses.

"Jenna, let your brother breathe," their mother said, but there was amusement in her admonition.

His sister ignored her, hugging him tighter and tucking her blonde head under his chin.

"Oomph. I need to breathe there, kiddo."

When light blue eyes locked onto his face, it dawned on Jared she wasn't a kid anymore, not really.

At twenty-two, Jenna was a beautiful woman. Long flaxen locks, pink cheeks, expression exuding happiness. She was petite and slender as always, but her blue top and jeans were both too tight for his liking—her body was on display.

When did this happen?

He suddenly wanted to stomp the fiancé he had yet to meet.

"I missed you, big brother."

"Missed you, too."

She flashed a grin and stood tiptoed to plant a

noisy kiss to his cheek.

"Are you done accosting your brother so I can hug him?" Mom asked, but she grinned.

"Gimme a break, Mom. You see him all the time. I live far away."

"Oh, I love when women fight over me. Carry on." Jared winked and pulled his mother into a hug.

Amy Manning kissed him and patted his chest. "Hi, baby. So glad you could make it."

He smiled and met her blue eyes.

She'd gotten a haircut since the last time he'd seen her. Her naturally fair hair was in a bob, making her look younger and beautiful.

"I wouldn't miss Thanksgiving for anything."

Jenna beamed when he caught her eye and Ranger circled them, wagging his tail. Although his younger sister could pass as Amy's biological daughter in looks, his parents had adopted her as an infant. She'd been five when Jared and Joe had come into their household.

Joe.

Damn, his brother could be here right now, sharing this holiday with family, if he hadn't been an idiot. He'd never understood his brother's need to get away. The Mannings had loved him, too.

Jared had never asked him why, either. He'd left the past where it lay, but next time he talked to the guy, he should push for an answer.

God, life woulda been different.

Did his parents know something he didn't?

Cole had told him to relax with his family, and they'd meet up that evening. His partner was probably going to be jonesing to get rid of Carrigan by then—or at least give her something case-related to do. There was no way she'd actually relax and enjoy the day.

He had a hard time picturing her playing with the boys, even if it might do her some good.

Carrigan obviously preferred his partner. Maybe not ever being FBI made Jared a redheaded stepchild in her eyes.

"Dad! Jared's here! Derek, come meet my brother!"

Their mother winced when Jenna yelled, and he had to laugh.

Like old times.

His sister's nickname as a kid had been '*Mouth*'.

Jared's dad, Jason, pulled him into a strong embrace.

"Hey, Dad."

"Why are y'all standing in the foyer? Is the boy leaving or something?"

He laughed again, meeting his father's hazel eyes. "No, sir. Jenna attacked me."

"Did not!"

"Oh, here we go. They're suddenly children again." Their mother rolled her eyes and Dad chuckled.

"Well come in. Sit down," Jason Manning said, gesturing to the living room behind him. A lieutenant with the fire department, his dad was still broad and tall, pretty much in shape for fifty-seven, but the years and his wife's cooking had filled in his midsection a bit.

He'd been eligible to retire for a few years, but Jared didn't see his dad quitting work any time soon.

He still got in there and led his shift when they fought fires. His father loved being a fireman like Jared loved being a cop.

"You got the game on?"

"You bet. Want a beer?" his dad asked.

"Maybe later. Mom. You need help with anything?"

"No, baby, relax with your father. For living in the same city, we don't see you nearly enough."

"Good job, Mom. Cut right to the guilt." Jenna winked.

He smirked.

"Jenna Marie," Amy admonished.

A fair-haired guy hovered under the archway into the living room, and Jared supposed he couldn't pretend his sister hadn't brought someone home any longer.

When she slipped her arm around the kid's waist, he had to bite back a scowl.

Jenna smiled sweetly up at him and when the guy looked back at her with the same adoration, Jared chided himself to calm down.

They weren't *just* dating.

His sister had a ring on her left hand.

If the yuppie hurt her, he'd kill him.

The couple came forward and the dude met his eyes. He was tall, nearly Jared's height. Blue eyes. Blond hair. Had the body of an athlete.

Held Jenna tight to his side, rubbing her back.

Jared wanted to bark for him to get his hands off her.

Be real. They're engaged. Probably does a lot more than touch her back.

He cringed.

Not like I can ask, 'You boning my sister?'

He didn't want to know, anyway. It'd just make him want to pound the guy's face harder…or ask, *where would you prefer the bullet wound?*

"Jared, this is Derek Harris. My fiancé." She practically glowed. "Baby, this is my big brother, Jared."

Baby?

He forced his hand out, chiding himself to be polite. "Nice to meet you, Derek."

"Likewise." The guy accepted his shake, returning it with the same strength.

Jared gave him a grudging ounce of respect.

"Jared's a detective, like I told you before. Derek's a second year, like me."

His sister was in to school to be a doctor. She'd sailed through her pre-med in three years, valedictorian of her class.

"Ah, we'll have two doctors in the family."

Jenna beamed and Derek bent down to kiss her cheek.

"When's the wedding?" He tried not to narrow his eyes.

"Next spring, I hope." His sister radiated joy as she stood at her man's side.

Jared frowned when Renee's smiling face popped into his mind.

What the heck?

He still burned for his onetime lover.

"Your father and I feel they should wait." Mom crossed her arms over her chest.

Jenna's smile fell. "Mother, I don't want to go into this again."

"Jenna, I don't—"

Derek shifted on his feet when his sister broke their physical contact and glared at their mother.

Jason cleared his throat. "It's Thanksgiving, guys. Not often Jared and I get out of work, so let's relax as a family. That discussion is for later."

"Sorry, Mom," Jenna muttered.

Their mother's expression softened and she patted his sister's cheek. "I have things to do in the kitchen if we're ever going to eat."

"I'll help," Jenna said.

As the two women disappeared into the kitchen, Jared looked at his dad and shrugged. "Our family's not sexist or anything. Women in the kitchen, men in the living room."

Derek laughed.

Jason chuckled. "You know she'd just shoo you out as being in the way if you ventured in there."

"You're probably right. But I *can* cook!" He grinned.

By the end of dinner, Jared could halfway stand the kid his sister was in love with, and intended to marry.

Derek Harris was funny, kind and the way he

looked at Jenna at least convinced him the guy loved her.

He'd cornered him in the living room for his obligatory verbal, *'You hurt her, I'll crush your balls'* talk, and Derek had taken the physical threat well. Hadn't even asked if Jared was serious.

Smart. He knows I mean it.

No matter how many laughs and old stories Jared's family swapped—even with Jenna trying to embarrass him—he couldn't loosen up. Kept looking around the dining room at all the pictures on the walls then in the living room—hell, even in the hallways.

His mom had tons of photos of Jenna and Jared as kids, amongst the family shots of the four of them. Even a few baby pictures of him she must had wheedled from a former CPS worker.

But the one on the mantel rocked him to his core.

It was taken here, right outside the house. A tiny towheaded Jenna sitting on the porch steps between two dark-haired brothers. Each of them held one of her small hands.

All three of them wore grins.

Happy siblings.

Damn, even Joe looks like he belongs here.

My family.

Jared didn't remember the *when* of the picture, but he and Joe couldn't have been with the Mannings very long. They both looked so damn young.

Innocent.

Nothing like the shots of the angry tattooed man from the FBI file.

Unexpected emotion roiled his gut and he gripped his beer until the condensation-dampened label ripped.

He wanted to pick the photo up but didn't.

"Son? You okay?"

Jared jumped as the man's hand landed on his shoulder.

"Yeah, Dad. I'm good." He cleared his throat and blinked. Plastered a smile on.

Jason Manning didn't buy it, if his expression was any indication. "You were awfully quiet today."

He forced a smile. "Well, yeah, it's Jenna's show. Her man is here for the first time."

"Well, I don't buy that, but if you don't want to talk, I get it. No pressure."

Guilt bit at him and he shook his head. "No, Dad, it's just…" He looked around the large living room.

The TV was on, volume low, and they were alone, except for the dog. Ranger was napping on his plush bed next to the fireplace.

"Just you and me, kid."

"Where's Mom? Derek and Jenna?"

"You mother's upstairs reading. Jenna took Derek to the park for the festival. They're lighting the city Christmas tree tonight."

"Already? It's Thanksgiving."

Dad shrugged. "It's only a few days early, actually. They're making a big deal this year. Fireworks, a concert or something."

"Yeah, I guess I saw the poster on the board at work. Just didn't think about it." His freak out about Joe warred with memories of Renee for the hundredth time. He could've taken her to the lighting. Them, wrapped in a blanket, watching the fireworks and the Christmas lights.

Damn, I wish I could find her.

Monday felt like a year ago.

He missed her. Every night he crawled in bed he thought of nothing but Renee, remembered her lips, her taste, the delectable curves of her body. Them moving together—

"Come sit with me. Talk to me, son." Dad's imploring voice jolted him from sexual fantasies he *so* didn't need right now.

Thanks, Dad.

Jared clenched his jaw but nodded.

His father cracked open a new beer and grabbed the remote. He switched off the TV and their gazes met.

As he took a seat on the edge of the couch next to the man who'd raised him, he wanted to squirm.

He could never lie to Jason Manning.

Dad sighed and dragged his hand through his thinning dark hair. "Haven't been over in a while. You mom doesn't like it. Have to admit, neither do I. I know you're an adult, but come see your ol' mom and dad once in a while, okay? With Jenna all the way in Corpus, you're all we got, kid."

"I know, Dad. Sorry. I caught a tough case." He cracked like a kid, and Jared winced.

"That's what has you upset?"

Yes.

"Do you ever talk to my brother?" He cursed the inquiry as soon as he'd blurted it.

Technically he couldn't talk about the open case with anyone but APD.

Dad's hazel eyes sharpened, and he set the cold bottle down on the end-table, leaning forward. "No. Do you?"

Jared sighed and closed his eyes. "Yes. Occasionally.

"Is he somehow involved in your case?"

Yes.

"Dad, this is an open investigation—"

"Son, I know the drill. What you tell me stays between you and me. I'll leave the rest up to you. You tell me what you want; don't tell me what you don't. I won't even tell your mother."

"I know." He dragged his hand down his face. "Fuck. Me."

Amusement rippled across his father's face, then faded. "That bad, huh?"

"Yes, sir."

"Jared, this is tearing you up. I don't like it." He slid closer on the couch.

He didn't pull away when his dad squeezed his forearm. "I don't like it, either. Believe me, Dad."

"What's going on, son?"

"The FBI is convinced Joe killed an undercover agent."

Chapter Ten

Taylor's phone rang and she scowled at Detective Jared Manning as she dug it out of her pocket. The call had saved her from the temptation of marring his handsome face. She was so sick of being *questioned* by him. "Carrigan."

"Tay, it's me, Vasquez."

She straightened her shoulders as shock rolled over her.

Eddie Vasquez was FBI, but out of the LA office. He'd gone out to California after a two-year stint in her unit.

They'd never been directly partnered but had worked many a case together as a part of a team. Despite his annoying tendency to nickname people, she respected him. Hadn't talked to him in a long time.

"I don't have much time, so I'll dive right in. I'm so damn sorry to hear about John. He was good people." Her former co-worker was sincere, statement thick.

Her eyes smarted and Taylor turned away from the curious detective's dark stare. "Thanks, Eddie. I appreciate that." She cleared her throat.

"Listen, I heard somethin' the other day that might help; I know you're still working this. I know you'll get the bastard that killed him."

"What's up?"

"I'm working my own auto theft ring over here,

and my CI ran into someone you know. Someone who had plans to hit a train for some high dollar cars. My guy helped him set it up."

Her heart sped up. "Carter Bennett?"

"Yeah, that's the guy. Anyway, my CI was in the wrong place, wrong time, or the right place, right time, depending on how you look at it. Bennett went from needing a secure large-capacity fence to get rid of fancy rides, and was putting out feels for a hit. Said he had two guys to knock off and didn't want to do it himself."

"Go on..."

"I told my guy to agree to the hit, and as soon as money changed hands, we'd bring Bennett in. Well, the ass musta been impatient. When my CI got to the place it was supposed to go down, all he found was two warm ones."

"Bennett killed them?" Taylor's mind spun.

No way.

Out of all Joe Pompa's guys, Carter Bennett was the mild-mannered one, according to John's field reports. He was quiet and unassuming—even though her fiancé had said Pompa treated him like his right hand.

John's reports said Bennett was cunning and smart, but with a side of naivety, and no stomach for violence. Could his take on Bennett have been wrong?

If so, *how* wrong?

"That's what we're assuming as of now. Bennett's not in town. My CI asked around, since he'd already agreed to help Bennett ship the cars out of the country."

"What happened to the shipment?"

"Nothing. The crew never hit the train. The Lamborghinis and Ferraris got where they were supposed to go."

"So they didn't go through with it?"

"Nope. The dead guys might have something to do with it. He was two men short."

"Wait. He wanted to kill his *own* guys?"

"Yeah. My CI said Bennett was talking about being double-crossed."

Taylor sucked in air. "Were you able to ID the bodies?"

"Richard Wilkins and Sean McKinley."

"No. Way. Pompa's elite," she breathed, ignoring the sharp look from Detective Manning as he slid around to catch her eye.

Or they had been.

Until he'd killed the man she loved and fled.

Obviously the gang—and their loyalties—had been split.

That, she'd already figured, since the girl and the guy nicknamed Moose had been the only ones to accompany Pompa, according to their intel.

Is there more to it than that?

Could one of the guys who'd stayed with Bennett have been contacting Pompa? *Why* did it matter?

Taylor had assumed half of the gang had stayed out west so they didn't lose their hold on the area—or potential jobs.

Pompa needed cash, even on the run.

"You're sure it's them, Eddie?"

"You bet. Positive IDs. It's them. I'll email you my

initial report and photos."

"Thanks."

"So, besides Carter Bennett, there's one missing."

"Rowdy—Eric Vargas. Not including Pompa, Willis and Gentile."

"Right. After my CI called, I contacted Dallas for your case file. I've reviewed it all."

Since his info was helping, and Eddie Vasquez had a keen eye, Taylor didn't bother being annoyed that her boss had read her old co-worker in on her case. Having him on the lookout in California wasn't a bad thing.

"I know Pompa was close to these guys. If my informant hadn't run into Bennett seeking a hit, I'd say maybe Pompa came back to finish them?"

"We don't have anything to support any kind of falling out. Do you know something I don't?"

"Nah, just a theory. My informant didn't ask questions about Bennett being double-crossed. Wish he would've."

"At any rate, I don't think Pompa went west." She swallowed a sigh.

Her gut told her Joe Pompa had headed to Texas.

He'd been spotted about an hour from Antioch by a reliable source—according to the agent she'd got the info from.

Taylor had been in New Mexico, searching one of Pompa's suspected houses when she'd received the call and hightailed it back to Dallas.

After she'd studied Antioch's demographics and seen the wealth, she'd agreed to check out the small north Texas city. There was money and some nice cars, not to mention BMW, Mercedes, Cadillac and Hummer dealerships within twenty miles.

Pompa had never been so obvious, but she was going to sniff him out if he was here.

Wouldn't leave until she'd scoured the place.

She *would* catch the bastard.

"I tend to agree." The LA agent's acknowledgment sucked her from her thoughts.

What?

Oh yeah, Pompa. Out west.

"But I read John's reports," he continued, "and I don't think this Bennett guy is who John thought he is."

"Meaning?"

"Are you sure Pompa's your mastermind?"

"Yes." Taylor bit the affirmative, her gut roiling.

He killed John.

"Well, if you're sure."

"I am." She couldn't help but notice Detective Manning's frown.

He was close enough to overhear the call. He wouldn't move away, despite the fact she kept stepping back. Jared just came with her.

She wanted to glare, but turned away again instead.

It didn't last.

Taylor could feel the heat of his body at her back.

He was definitely trying to listen in and not hiding it.

"Well, my guy says Bennett—and Eric Vargas—if he's alive and well, are going to be headed after Pompa and the others. Bennett didn't confirm what for, but if he killed the other two, we can surmise it's not for a hug and a high-five."

"What the hell am I missing?" Her question was more to herself than Eddie or the detective that was giving her the stare-down, but her former colleague laughed.

"Whatever it is, it won't be long 'til you figure it out."

"Thanks."

"Just be on the lookout for Bennett. I have eyes peeled over here, and I'll give you a call if I hear anything new. My CI is pretty worldly. He knows most of the organized car theft gangs in the US. He's made some calls. So, if I don't hear something first, he will."

"What's *his* take on Bennett?"

Eddie laughed again. "He said, and I quote, *'Carter's one crazy motherfucker'*."

Taylor frowned. "Great." She ended the call and pocketed her phone, trying to ignore her temporary detective partner.

Was John wrong?

Her fiancé had always had good instincts about his cases.

This didn't add up.

"What was that about?" Manning asked. He stepped closer, his linebacker frame blocking her way to Lucas' computer.

She wanted to sit down, send some emails and make some calls. "A colleague with some new info."

"Like what?" His dark gaze burned her and she bit back a scowl.

There was something more to that look than curiosity about the case.

What does Manning know?

Stop. Now you're being paranoid.

"Where's Lucas?" she asked.

It was the detective's turn to frown.

He crossed his arms over his broad chest, but Taylor wasn't intimidated by him.

"You know, I'm sick of being treated like chopped liver. Cole is my *partner*. I don't need his permission to be read into this case. We're supposed to be working *together*. All. Three. Of. Us."

Pain washed over her, and telling herself emotion was weak did nothing.

John had been Taylor's partner — at work and home.

"I just don't want to repeat myself." She cursed the fragmented sentence, and she didn't care for the way he appraised her.

"Right. That's it."

"I need to make some calls," she snapped.

"No. You need to tell me what the hell's going on."

"When Lucas gets back, I will."

Jared glared at his FBI agent *'partner'*.

This was only the hundredth argument he'd had with Special Agent Taylor Carrigan for the day — and it wasn't even nine-thirty.

She wouldn't tell him shit.

Her call had been work — case — related.

He'd heard the name, '*Carter Bennett*', and '*CI*' a dozen times. Not to mention the word '*bodies*'.

Why the fuck did she think she needed Cole there to come clean?

He was more than sick of her *secrets*.

Every time he thought they might get somewhere on finding his brother, Carrigan would add insult to injury by making a snide remark — with a straight face, no less — about his investigation skills. Like an innocent observation, and of course, she meant not offense.

Or feed him a line of bullshit about wanting to make sure Lucas was in the room so she didn't have to '*repeat*' herself.

Screw that.

He wasn't a second-class citizen. It pissed him off that he had to *wonder* her intent. He was a damn good cop, and she could kiss his ass.

A week had come and gone, and he still had nothing on Joe's location.

Guess the good thing about that...neither does Carrigan.

Nor had he been able to find Renee, no matter how many times he'd stalked *McAuley's*.

Double frustration had him wound tighter than a ball of twine.

He needed to get laid.

Jared didn't want anyone but Renee.

Movement caught his eye over Carrigan's shoulder. His partner was crossing the CID room, wearing squeaky boots. Like they were too shiny or too clean.

That's new.

Irritation with the FBI agent lifted momentarily and he smirked. "What the heck are you wearing?"

Cole ignored him and picked a piece of non-existent lint off his navy blue Class As.

His partner was in full uniform. Dressed for a ceremony — or a patrol car. Duty belt and everything. Complete with radio, Taser, two pairs of handcuffs, in addition to the normal forty-caliber Sig at his waist.

Jared exchanged a look with Carrigan, but her expression was as implacable as always.

However, like always, his partner's presence loosened Carrigan's lips and she launched into details of her phone call — from a California FBI guy, as it'd turned out.

They both listened intently, cataloguing the new information about Carter Bennett.

His heart kicked up a notch.

Someone could be after Joe?

Shit.

He wanted to save his brother.

Carrigan wanted to arrest him.

Bennett wanted to kill him?

Double…triple…shit.

Jared *really* needed to be the first to find Joe.

"Manning and I have some place to be in about ten anyway, so we'll leave you to make your calls. You can check your email and search our stuff, too."

One of Carrigan's fair eyebrows shot up at the same time as Jared said, "We do?"

His partner grinned, flashing dimples. "Uh. Yeah.

Did I forget to mention we're gonna talk to Ethan's class today?"

"Jesus," the FBI agent muttered.

Lucas' smile faded. "Hey, I'm doing my kid's teacher a favor. We won't be gone long, and I'm sure you'll be fine on your own. You seem to work best alone."

She ignored his partner's jibe, but her hazel eyes flashed, and her mouth set in a hard line.

Jared groaned and dragged his hand down his face. "Seriously?" The last thing he wanted to do was chat up a bunch of kindergarteners. Although, Carrigan was getting what she wanted, so there was no reason for her panties to be wadded.

"Yes, seriously. No, you don't get to pick, thanks for asking."

He reclined into the wall of Cole's cubicle as he watched his partner show the FBI agent how to access their database software and reports—and their collective confidential informant list.

She'd said she wanted to see if any names jumped out at her.

His mind spun with new chaos. He'd wanted to find Joe to confront him—get the truth about John Murray's murder. Now he had to contend with not only the *good* guys chasing his brother, but bad ones.

A dude who wished Joe harm.

Had possibly killed two people.

Fuck. I really don't have time for a buncha six-year-olds.

His frown stayed locked into place, even after Cole

finished with Carrigan and gestured for them to head out of the CID room.

The FBI agent took Cole's seat and started to work on the computer, muttering thanks.

"Besides, getting out of the office will get you away from this sexual-tension-thing you have going on with Carrigan," his partner said.

Jared reared to a stop in the corridor before they rounded the corner. The back doors leading to secure parking weren't yet visible. "You're smokin' crack."

The guy laughed. "Am I? Kinda seems like you're into her, partner."

He snorted. "No. Way."

"Then you need to get laid."

"Won't argue with that."

God, don't remind me.

He didn't have room in his brain to think of *her*, too.

Not only had he *not* found the woman he sought, Jared hadn't spotted even *one* of the other women Renee had been with the night they'd met.

He'd not responded to any of the girls who'd hit on him during his nightly trolling at *McAuley's*. All he could do was sit at the bar and stare at the door. Of course, ignoring the sympathetic looks he got from Brian McAuley. Dude didn't seem to believe Jared was working.

"So what's the deal? Did you finally listen to me and lose the chippies?"

He groaned. "Let's just go to the school."

"Wait." Cole's hand shot to his forearm; Jared's

leather jacket made a creaking noise. "You're brewing and stewing. For…like over a week. All joking aside, what's going on?"

Oh, my brother's a big time criminal at the center of our case and I can't find the girl I want.

"Nothing. I'm good."

His partner's gray eyes stared him down until he fought the urge to back away, break their physical contact.

He made himself stand still and looked right back him. A tease about Cole's shiny badge pinned to his uniform shirt would've diffused things, but it wouldn't form.

"Really? You know you can talk to me, right? About anything."

Cole scanned…studied him.

Irrational panic threatened to swallow him whole.

Shit. Has Cole made the Joe-Jared look-a-like connection?

There were more photos of Joe in that FBI file than any other members of his gang.

Fuck. Please, God, don't let it be that.

Jared cleared his throat. He was going to have to give his partner something. Just not Joe. Until he had to. "Absolutely. You're like my brother, dude."

The man's big shoulders loosened and his fingers slipped from his arm. "I feel the same. Now, you wanna tell me what's going on?"

No.

"Remember that girl I told you I met? Last Monday night at *McAuley's*?"

One of Cole's dark eyebrows shot up, as if that was the last thing he'd expected to come out of Jared's mouth. "The one-nighter?"

"That's the thing. I want it to be more than that. But—" He sighed, throwing his palms up. Unexpected emotion roiled his gut and he frowned.

Is it Joe or Renee?

"But what?"

"I can't find her. Been looking since last Tuesday. Was the reason I met Carrigan there, 'cause I was Renee-scouting."

"Ah. So you *do* need to get laid." His partner smirked.

He ran his hands through his hair and laughed. "Yeah. I guess so. I need to find her."

"And no last name, right?"

"Right. Unfortunately."

"Well, maybe when we get back I can help you figure it out. Antioch's not that big."

"You wouldn't think so."

"We'll have to put Carrigan on something. No doubt she'd frown upon losing focus on Pompa twice in one day."

"She's kinda one-track-minded like that." Jared still hadn't figured out what *she* was hiding.

His partner agreed there was something there, though.

They'd figure it out, in time.

Cole patted the back of his shoulder and offered a slight smile. "We'll find your girl, buddy. I'd hate to have your balls implode from lack of use."

He shook his head when his partner laughed at his own joke.

Chapter Eleven

"All right class, it's *Community Helper's Day* and we have some awesome grownups here to tell us all about what they do in our city to help us. Without them doing their jobs, our community wouldn't be what it is. So make sure you listen, ask a lot of questions, and later we're each going to share something we learned."

The kids clapped and Mel smiled.

They were all sitting at their tables, little faces attentive.

Her dad, Doc Butler and Captain Turner from the fire department hovered near the chalkboard, each looking fresh and interested in speaking to her kids. They had tools of their trades and ready explanations.

Good.

The detectives weren't there just yet, but she wasn't worried they wouldn't show.

Ethan Lucas had already told the whole class his dad was coming today.

Maybe police work had delayed them. If they were busy, she appreciated even more that Detective Lucas and his partner would take time out of their day to come to her school.

She grinned and nodded to her dad.

Jack Nash had been the director of Public Works for Antioch for fifteen years, but he'd worked for the city almost thirty, two years longer than she'd been alive.

Mel had cautioned him not to gross her kids out; some of his sewage and water crisis stories were vomit-worthy.

He was up first. The plan was to have the cops go last. Usually her class thought they had the coolest job, of course. They always seemed to enjoy Captain Turner, or one of the other firefighters that'd come in the past, too.

"Has anyone ever heard of Public Works?" Her dad opened with the same question every year, and Mel tried not to roll her eyes.

Of course they hadn't, except when she'd tried to explain who was coming to talk to them.

She stepped back to let her father be front and center, flashing a smile when Captain Turner winked at her.

He was a good-looking older guy. Single, too. Hazel eyes, light brown hair, just starting to go silver at the temples.

She didn't know much about him, but had heard he was divorced. Two teen kids. Mel had politely turned him down when he'd asked her out in the past, as well as last week when she'd called to see if he'd speak.

Not that she had anything against divorce, but he wasn't the guy for her. Besides, he had at least fifteen years on her. She didn't see herself dating an older man.

Jared.

He had to be about her age.

Knock it off.

No matter how hard she'd tried, she'd been unable to get her one-night stand out of her head. It'd been over a week now.

Mel dreamt of him nightly. Could remember his scent, the feel of his kiss and his hands on her body. How he'd made her feel. *Vividly.* As if it was only that morning she'd snuck out of his bed. Her limbs warmed and her belly flipped as heat licked her neck and cheeks.

Seriously, knock it off.

Nothing worked.

She was Jared-obsessed.

Self-deprecation and scoffing wasn't curing her. She didn't *want* to crave him. Even if she'd known his last name and could find him, it wasn't like he'd actually want her again.

Hot guys didn't do fat girls more than once.

You're not screw-buddy material, anyways.

Mel winced and fought the urge to close her eyes.

Get over yourself. You're at work. Today's important.

Her dad said something to make the kiddos laugh.

A light knock had her gaze shooting toward the door.

Detective Lucas opened it a crack and she smiled, then stepped out into the hallway. He was wearing a uniform, like any other cop.

She was surprised, since he was a detective. The few times she'd seen him picking up his son, he'd been in jeans.

Detective Lucas smiled back. "Sorry we're late."

"No big deal—" Her whole body flushed when

she saw the tall, dark-haired man standing behind her student's father.

Jared looked just as shocked to see her; gorgeous midnight eyes as wide as possible. His lips parted and Mel couldn't help but stare...and recall how it was to kiss him. "Renee..."

Her middle name fell from his mouth on a whisper that jolted her.

His voice was just like she remembered.

Being in his arms at *McAuley's* danced into her mind, how his warm breath had tickled her forehead and made her knees wobble — then and now. Her heart flip-flopped and her insides were suddenly made of mush.

Seeing him was worse than simply *thinking* about him.

Detective Lucas watched them like a tennis match. "Um. So, I guess you two know each other?"

"No," Mel said.

"Yes," Jared at the same time.

Detective Lucas crossed his arms over his chest and flashed dimples. "Well..." He cleared his throat and looked at her. Then at the man who had to be his partner.

Jared's a cop?

You were *at McAuley's, idiot.*

"This is Ethan's teacher, Melody Nash. Miss Nash, this is my partner, Jared Manning."

"Melody?" her onetime lover asked, his brows knitted.

"Mel, I go by Mel."

Why the heck did I say that?

One corner of Detective Lucas' mouth shot up.

Jerk. He thinks this is funny?

She shifted from foot to foot, then glanced over her shoulder. "Well, ah…" Mel had to clear her throat.

Be a teacher. Do not look at him.

She forced her eyes on Detective Lucas. "Thank you for coming. The Public Works Director is speaking now then Dr. Butler. Then Captain Turner from the Fire Department. I'm going to have you guys go last, since the kids tend to have the most questions for the police."

Her student's father nodded.

They stepped into the classroom quietly, just as her dad was wrapping up his speech.

He'd given the kids each a little yellow foam hardhat with '*City of Antioch Public Works*' and the city's logo printed on it.

"Class, let's give a hand to Director Nash, and tell him thanks for the gift."

Her class beamed and clapped. "Thank you, Director Nash," they said in unison.

Her dad gave a bow that set them into a fit of giggles, and even Captain Turner chuckled.

Mel dove right in, introducing the doctor and letting him do his thing. She walked her father to the door; he'd told her he had to get back to work. "Thank you for coming, Daddy."

He kissed her cheek. "No problem, sugar. You know I love talking to your class every year."

She smiled. "Good. I won't stop asking then."

"Have a good rest of the day. Glad the cops finally

made it in." Her dad winked.

Her heart stuttered and she refused to look over her shoulder, but she could feel Jared's eyes on her.

"Melody, are you okay, sugar?"

"Absolutely. Thanks again. I'll see you tomorrow for dinner, okay? I'd better get back in there."

Her father studied her, then nodded. He pulled her in for a parting hug and she kissed his cheek like he had hers.

When she made it back inside, Doc Butler was talking about bones.

Captain Turner and Detective Lucas were whispering to each other, but not disturbing the doctor.

She *felt* her onetime lover's presence. Her body warmed and she commanded herself to ignore his stare.

Jared's dark eyes tracked every move she made, like she was a beacon.

Mel rounded her desk, standing on the far side, arms crossed over her breasts so she wouldn't fidget.

Ten feet wasn't enough distance.

Jared — Detective Manning — still watched her.

She contemplated having the detectives speak next so they could get it over with and she could get them out of her classroom.

Too bad you already told them the order.

Unfortunately, *he* made his way over to her.

She couldn't exactly run from him.

Dang it.

"Renee, huh?" Jared's question was low, amused.

She wouldn't — couldn't — look at him. "It's my middle name." Mel winced at her defensive tone.

He said nothing, and she still didn't dare spare him a glance.

"People lie to me every day. Guess I just didn't think you would."

What the heck am I supposed to say to that?

Is he hurt or something?

She cleared her throat. "Please be quiet. You're going to disturb Dr. Butler's speech."

"Sure. You can ignore me. *Now*. But just so you know, *Mel* Nash. Now that I've found you, I'm *not* going away."

The starburst of red spread out like seeking fingers, covering her whole chest before his eyes.

Bran uttered a shocked shriek and collapsed to the trailer floor, her baby browns wide.

It was all slow motion, like some sick movie.

This was *real*.

Moose roared, whipping out a huge, chrome-plated Desert Eagle handgun to return fire.

The wall of the mobile home was dotted with holes now, but they couldn't see their assailants. Besides, it was dim inside, the only light coming from the three camping lanterns they'd bought from Wally-world.

It wasn't quite four in the afternoon, so it was probably lighter outside. The shooters must've been too impatient to wait until it was fully dark.

Joe dove for his ex's side, gathering her onto his lap. He should grab the gun under his pillow, but he didn't give a shit if he died.

Not now.
Not if Bran —
No!

"Boss, get out of here! I'll cover ya both. Take her to safety."

One look at Bran told Joe it was too late for the woman they both loved. He ignored the big man who'd been his friend—more like a brother—and stared into her dark eyes.

The huge *boom* of Moose's fifty caliber weapon made his ears ring, but he focused on the bleeding woman in his arms.

The only woman he'd ever loved.

"Bran. Babe. Stay with me."

Her cheeks were sallow. Blood soaked her shirt.

She was hit twice he could see, and the darker—almost black—stain on her lower abdomen told him her liver was nicked.

Her chest heaved as she struggled to breathe, but her eyes zoned in on his face. "J-J-Joe."

"Babe. Don't talk. It'll be okay," he choked.

Pop, pop—over and over—joined the heavier sounds of Moose's gun, reverberating in Joe's head, but he didn't care.

"Joe…" Her hand shook, but she managed to drag two fingertips down his cheek. "Joe…"

"Bran, please." He grabbed her hands, kissing bloody knuckles. Joe started shaking and bit down until pain shot into his gums, but he didn't give a shit. Wasn't hurting as bad as *she* was.

"I love you. Always…loved…you…" Her eyes

drifted closed. Bran's body went slack in his arms, on his lap.

Tears streamed down his cheeks. He was crying like a pussy when he should've been trying to save his own ass. He couldn't move.

A gurgled grunt took his attention and Moose's huge form landed in a heap next to the L-shape kitchen counter.

His buddy didn't move.

Blood started to pool beneath him, half on linoleum and half soaking into filthy, torn carpet.

"Moose!" Joe gently pushed Bran off his lap at the same time the door of the trailer exploded.

Wood splinters flew through the air like the bullets that still hadn't stopped.

"There you are!" Carter Bennett's voice grated down his spine. "Lookie lookie, I got two traitors outta three, the first try. Go me."

The bastard was amused.

Rage boiled up from Joe's gut. He grabbed his forty out from under his pillow. Aimed straight at Carter's chest. "Yeah, here I am." He pulled the trigger of his Glock. Kept pulling it until the asshole dove behind the ratty couch in the living room of the mobile home. "Fucking. Coward."

God, I hope I hit him.

His gaze darted over his fallen lover and friend.

Joe had to leave Bran and Moose.

Now.

Carter was alone, as far as he could tell.

At least—there were no other guns being fired.

He sprinted to the door his former right-hand-man had kicked to smithereens. Pain in his chest threatened to cripple him, but he forced one foot in front of the other.

Bran would want him to survive.

Due to his ex-friend's perpetual limp, he had a chance to get away. Joe would always be able to outrun Carter.

The man's shout didn't give him pause, but more gunshots did.

He tucked and rolled, sprinting low around the edge of the crappy trailer they'd been staying in. Needed to move.

Faster.

The old mobile home park might be abandoned, but it wasn't far from civilization—the gunshots would be heard.

Police would be called.

Jared.

Joe ignored his brother's name bouncing around in his head. This game was called *survival.*

He needed to disappear.

Away from Carter *and* Jared.

Heavy footfalls made a tremor shoot down his spine until his teeth chattered. He cursed the quake in his limbs.

"Joe-Joe! Where are you, Joey-Joe? I know you couldn't have gone far." The bastard whistled as his boots crunched the gravel. The step was slow, meticulous. Carter sounded jovial, as if he hadn't just killed Bran and Moose.

Joe's throat started to close and his gut clenched.

No.

He couldn't think of her blood covering his shirt and jeans. Or the light fading from her dark eyes. How her weight had become heavy in his arms.

Fuck.

His heart thundered, threatening to pop out of his chest, while his pulse rushed against his temples, making him dizzy.

She's dead.

Maybe he should call to Carter, turn himself in.

Beg for the asshole to finish him off.

Bran would want me to live.

The sound of Carter's boots picked up speed, sprinting by.

He still only heard *one* set.

Where're Rick, Mack and Rowdy? Did the fucker kill them, too?

If Carter had overheard Rick and Joe on the phone — or discovered it later, it didn't bode well for his friends.

It also explained his appearance in Texas.

Joe hadn't told Rick exactly where they were. Obviously his ex-right-hand-man had figured it out.

God, please don't let that be the reason Rick didn't call.

"I'm gonna kill this fucker," he muttered. He slid under a ratty trailer that had a gap in the aluminum skirting big enough to fit his body.

Carter hollered a few more times, but each call of his name faded, as if he was moving farther away, instead of closer.

Good.

His *'friend'* was retreating.

Joe waited, knowing better than to come into view before he was *sure* Carter had left the area. However, he didn't have much time.

No doubt sirens — and uniforms — were imminent.

He crushed his eyes shut and lay on the cool concrete slab in the dark. Bounced his head off the rough surface a few times. All *that* resulted was a resounding throb in his brain.

Joe couldn't calm his racing thoughts or his heart. His whole body still shook.

He *hurt* more than he ever had in his life. Even worse than when that bastard foster father had molested him at age fourteen.

He'd gone to the fucker over and over so *Daddy Dearest* would leave then nine-year-old Jared alone. That had been their deal, and the son-of-a-bitch had agreed.

His little brother had never suffered like that at the fucker's hands — thank God.

He'd never told a soul — not even Bran.

Refused to accept that *particular* headfuck was one of the reasons he hadn't been able to take the Mannings' love and hold it dear. He'd had to get out of dodge. At least he'd made sure Jared was safe with the people who'd eventually adopted him.

With a curse, he pushed himself up, splaying his hands. The concrete bit his palms, but Joe clung to the sting.

All his cash was in that POS trailer.

He could go back, right?

Grab the black duffle, hightail it away.

Bran's…*body*…was in that shitty trailer.

Moose, too.

Guilt ate at Joe's gut.

He'd gotten her killed.

Gotten his long-time friend killed, too.

He inched out from under the old mobile home, sticking to the far end and listening until his head hurt even more.

No Carter.

No gunfire.

He had seconds. Needed to go grab the money.

The wail of one siren, then two more, coming closer, changed his mind.

He couldn't see the cruisers yet, but he wasn't about to wait around so they'd see *him*, either.

However, Joe was able to spot the refection of red and blue lights making the tree canopy look like it was spinning.

"Son of a bitch!"

What the fuck am I supposed to do now?

Chapter Twelve

H er stomach fluttered when she saw the tall figure leaning on the huge black Ford truck, arms crossed over his impossibly broad chest.

So, he'd meant it when he said wasn't going away. Crap.

Mel tried to ignore him, but stole a glance at his long muscular legs encased in dark jeans.

Bad idea.

It only made her remember them naked and entwined. Something she'd been trying to forget about since last Tuesday morning.

Em and Val gasped collectively behind her. Rapid clicking of high heels shouted as they hurried to their vehicles.

Traitors.

Not even a goodbye as tires squealed their way out of the parking lot.

Jared cleared his throat when Mel hit the unlock button on her fob by driver side door, but she did her best to pretend he wasn't there.

Of *course*, his truck was next to her SUV.

"Mel."

Her real name on his lips made her whole body flush. She sucked in a breath and tried to glare. "What are you, a stalker? I'm gonna call the police."

Their gazes locked and her heart stuttered.

Even the smirk on his face was gorgeous. She

melted a little and couldn't look way from the dark brown depths in front of her.

"Baby, I *am* the police."

"Seriously? Is that your idea of a pick-up line?"

He was at her side in seconds. Grabbed her hand and kissed her knuckles. "Thought we'd established I didn't need one of those with you." His expression was sincere, despite his playful words. "Go out with me."

"No." A tremor shot down her spine.

"Why not?"

Because I'll end up in your bed again.

She'd *never* admit that out loud. Not when he was looking at her like that. "We have nothing in common."

His eyes bored into her until her core warmed and throbbed.

She *knew* what he was going to say before he opened his mouth.

"I think we both know how wrong you are about that. The night we met proves how good we are together."

In bed.

He didn't have to add those words. Mel shivered anyway. "There's more to life than sex."

"Right." Jared nodded. "Which is why I want you to go out with me." He snaked an arm around her waist and pulled her into his chest.

She squirmed, but her traitorous body moved into him instead of away. "No." The stupid denial exited on a half-moan.

"I can't get you out of my head, Mel," he whispered into her hair and her stomach flip-flopped.

Don't say my name.

The demand was never born, and his confession alone was enough to turn her into a puddle and make her beg for him. She resisted. Wiggled for him to let her go.

When his mouth crashed down on hers, she stilled—her hands on his hard pecs—and kissed him back without hesitation. Couldn't help it.

Her whole body tingled, warmth spreading down her limbs and settling low in her belly. Her sex pulsed, pleading for him.

Their tongues danced, twined and dueled. She wrapped her arms around him when her legs wobbled, but Jared held her closer, pinning her to him.

He kissed her harder, making her head spin. Desire melted her, and Mel squeezed her arms around his neck, needing to meld into him.

What is this man doing to me?

She'd never reacted like this to David's kiss. Breathing was difficult, but she didn't want to stop kissing him. *Couldn't stop.*

Jared reached down, squeezing her bottom with both hands, rocking his hips. His erection ground into her pelvis, and it wasn't nearly enough.

She wanted to lift his shirt and run her hands over his defined lines like she'd done the night they'd been together. Touch him, kiss him then have him inside her.

Wait.

That'd been the alcohol, right?

She'd been upset about David and had had too much to drink.

No.

So it wasn't the alcohol.

Jared's kiss was just as potent sober.

Oh, crap.

Mel was in trouble.

She yanked away and slipped out of his arms, swiping her hand across her mouth. Tried to glare. "No, Detective. *That* is all you want from me, and it's not going to happen again. Forget it." She couldn't bring herself to declare being with him was a mistake, because it hadn't been.

Darn it.

He shook his head and reached for her, but she scooted back until her ass hit her SUV's door. His wide shoulders drooped, expression fell, but she refused to fall for it.

"That's *not* all I want from you. I want to spend time with you, Mel."

"No." She didn't buy it for a second. He was *hot.* He could have anyone he wanted. Jared was a cop, for God's sake.

Mel wouldn't be *anyone's* booty call. David had made her into that, cheating. *On* her, but *with* her, too. He'd married someone else. Had a son and another child on the way.

She'd been *the other woman* and hadn't even known.

"Yes. Seriously, Mel. I wanted to kiss you, and I won't apologize. But I didn't mean for things to get carried away like that."

"Stop saying my name."

"Why?" His dark eyebrows drew tight.

Because it melts me.

"Just…leave me alone. I won't go out with you. What happened between us was a mistake. I-I-I won't do it again." She wrenched the Kia's door open and climbed inside, not even taking a moment to fix her bunched skirt. She averted her gaze from the hurt in his eyes.

Hurt?

She shook her head as he stood, facing her car. Sucked in a breath and started the SUV, then drove off without hesitation.

Mel didn't look back.

Jared watched her go, his stomach twisting. His cock throbbed, but he ignored it. Something that suspiciously felt like hurt washed over him.

She'd turned him down.

Since when does a woman turn me down?

Especially after he'd rocked her world the night they'd been together.

Mel.

Not Renee. Mel. Melody Renee Nash. Kindergarten teacher. His *partner's* kid's teacher.

"No wonder she seemed innocent."

He was torn between feeling like a skeeze for taking her home that night and aching even more because he still wanted her. More than he'd ever wanted a woman. Especially one he'd already had.

Was her rejection the appeal?

No.

Jared was dying to be around her. Not just for sex.

He shouldn't have kissed her like that, but he hadn't been able to help it.

When he'd seen her in the classroom doorway, he'd wanted to knock his partner out of the way to make sure his eyes hadn't deceived him.

His onetime lover, whom he'd *just* discussed with Cole, was right before his eyes?

Ethan's teacher?

No. Way.

Antioch wasn't that big, after all.

She doesn't want you, so it doesn't matter.

Why did his gut ache?

Why do you care?

"You need to get laid." But Jared didn't buy the whisper even before it greeted his ears.

There were tons of numbers in his cell. Old lovers he could call if he needed a quick romp. If he'd wanted that—*really* wanted that—he would've dialed already.

For some reason, he wanted to empty out his contacts. Hit delete on every damn female name. He wanted to *add* one number he certainly didn't have.

Her kiss was just as sweet as before.

Mel's body fit his, like they were lost pieces from a puzzle.

Jared closed his eyes, took a deep breath, forcing clean chilly air into his lungs. Maybe it would cool his ardor.

October and November had been unseasonably warm, but Mother Nature had embraced December with a vengeance. Unusually frigid for North Texas.

His cell phone screamed from his pocket.

"Fuck." He jumped as he swiped his thumb across the touchscreen and put it to his ear. "Manning."

"Hey, it's me." His partner's voice was even, but had an urgent edge to it.

Jared was familiar with that tone after working with Cole Lucas for the past two and a half years.

"What's wrong?" He squared his shoulders.

"Meet me and Carrigan at the old trailer park."

"What happened?"

"We got two warm ones."

"Okay, on my way." His hand shook as he ended the call and dumped his cell back into his jeans.

God, please, don't let one of them be Joe.

At least work would distract him from Mel.

Maybe.

Chapter Thirteen

ared was twitchy the whole drive over to the old trailer park, and it had nothing to do with stolen kisses from a certain teacher he couldn't get out of his mind.

What am I walking into?

He should've pressed his partner on the phone.

Then again, he didn't want to know.

He clenched his jaw and sucked in the hundredth fortifying breath of the last few hours. It did nothing to calm him.

Get it — and keep it — together.

Carrigan and Cole were standing outside the trailer closest to the dilapidated old office, chatting with Sergeant Shannon Crowley on the small front yard.

Weird. Crowley's not supposed to be on for another two hours.

Maybe he'd relieved the day sergeant because working a murder scene would take a while.

Jared half-expected the shift lieutenant to show up, unless Cole had called Lieutenant Chloe Stein off. She'd been recently promoted and was in charge of the evening shift.

It was always up to the on-call detective — or whoever was working the case — to decide who ran the scene.

Crowley was capable, and his partner knew that.

He pulled his truck up next to Cole's blue Dodge

Challenger, parked in front of the former office building. The modern-day muscle car was between two cruisers. There were two more marked police cars in the perimeter of the trailer lot.

Jared didn't see Carrigan's Impala.

She musta rode with Cole. Poor guy.

He frowned as he took in the rotting door of the office's small structure. It was falling apart. It resembled a cabin, but the faux-wood façade was cheap siding and missing in multiple spots.

Pieces even lay where they'd fallen on the sidewalk surrounding the place. The two small windows were boarded up, destroying any sign of welcome that might've once been there.

He stared at the curved, decorative door handle.

Has someone tampered with it?

It was too dim to tell, but the door looked as if someone had forced it open.

"Probably wasn't recent." He snorted and filed the info away for later. Doubted it was pertinent to the murders.

Although he and Cole hadn't caught a case out here in a while, two of his fellow detectives—Sully and Jamison—had chased yet another small-time meth dealer off the property a few weeks ago.

They'd only been able to catch and arrest two guys, but the thugs had given them dirt on a bigger fish out of Dallas, so who knew. Maybe they'd be able to keep the trash out of here this time.

Nah. Wishful thinking.

The trailer park had been vacant since Jared was a

teen and most of the homes had been removed. There were still eight or nine on site. Decaying on their cement slabs, with various interlopers the police always ended up running off.

Over and over.

If the place could reopen and new homes were brought in, it'd help Antioch as a whole, forcing the druggies to find a new base, but the guy that owned the property was bankrupt.

Why he didn't sell was a mystery, but it didn't really matter. Even if the bank owned the trailer park, APD would still have to stick to it like glue.

Scum wasn't concerned with who held the papers.

Jared shut off his pickup and slipped out, wincing when the unintentional slam of his door rang in his ears.

His partner's head shot in his direction.

A cool breeze chilled his cheeks, but he had to convince himself *that* was also the reason for the tremors chasing each other down his spine.

Something's wrong.

His gut said it had everything to do with his brother.

"You okay, partner?" Cole asked.

He forced a nod and cleared his throat. "What've we got?"

"Brandelyn Willis and Michael Gentile are dead," Carrigan answered.

Shock washed over Jared and he squared his shoulders. "From Pompa's gang." The statement came out slower than planned, and he swallowed.

They are *in Antioch. Where's Joe?*

Cole's sharp gray gaze told him his partner had caught the shake after all.

Fuck.

"No sign of the man of the hour," Sgt. Crowley said, "but there's blood on the floor behind a sorry excuse for a couch. Hopefully we'll get some DNA."

"Let's go inside." Jared's knees wobbled, but he locked them in place.

"Waiting on Crime Scene," Cole said.

"Rather process it myself," Jared said.

Once again, his partner studied him. "No hurry. They're not going anywhere." Cole's mouth twitched, but the attempt at humor was lost on him—the FBI agent, too, if her glare was any indication.

Stop looking at me like that.

He always preferred to process his own scenes. Carried an evidence kit in the back of his truck as well as the white Ford 500 he usually drove when he was working. Cole knew that. It wasn't unusual. Jared had always helped the CSIers out anyway he could over the years, as well.

"I'm with Manning. I don't trust this to anyone but me." Carrigan's even statement had his partner smirking.

"You sound just like me when I got here."

Jared snorted. He remembered.

Cole had been irritated with *everything* APD had done regarding his case at the time—catching human trafficker and murderer, Carlo Maldonado.

"Our team really is awesome," Jared said. "Neil

and his guys know what they're doing. As does our lab. I just usually like to get in there on my own. Assess it with my own eyes."

One of Carrigan's fair eyebrows shot up. She wasn't convinced. "Right. I'll have my own look, if you don't mind."

Sgt. Crowley didn't look impressed with the FBI agent—his mouth was set in a hard line. He stared hard at her, not moving, even as a frigid wind shifted his hair.

"Of course." Cole tone was dry, and he gestured toward the trailer. "After you then, I guess."

She turned without another word, his partner on her heels.

Crowley let out a low whistle. "That one's a piece of work."

Jared laughed. "Oh, buddy, you got *no* idea." He slapped his co-worker on the shoulder and jogged after his two partners.

He'd seen several bodies in his career, both as a patrol cop being first on scene then as a detective, but for some reason, sadness washed over him at the sight of the young blonde woman's body.

According to the FBI case file, she was only twenty-five, and a virtual tech-genius. Brandelyn Willis should've used her talents in the real world, instead of joining up with his brother's gang.

The intel also reported she'd been involved with Joe, so who knew?

Maybe that was what'd kept her on the wrong side of the law. She'd had a rough life—not unlike Jared and his brother. Grown up in the system and had done juvie time for hacker jobs about five times before aging out of Child Protective Services in California. She'd also taken the rap for selling information and goods she'd obtained illegally.

Like Joe, since reaching adulthood, Brandelyn Willis had managed to stay out of jail. So, she'd refined her skills and not gotten caught, because she obviously hadn't changed her ways.

Photos in the file showed a pretty girl with fair hair and big brown eyes. Slender and petite, she looked too delicate for car theft.

He didn't want to look at that form marred with bullet holes, her life stolen by her choices.

"What a waste," his partner said, as if Cole had read his mind. He hovered over Brandelyn Willis' pale body.

Jared sighed and threw Cole a nod. He surveyed their surroundings like he was supposed to, being observant. Memorizing the scene.

He'd always been good at this part of investigation, catching things other detectives hadn't. His partner always liked to get his impression, no matter what case they were on.

Too bad Carrigan thinks otherwise.

The place had seen better days. Wallpaper peeling, the carpet torn and pulled up from the floor — missing in some places. Only two of the kitchen cupboards had a door, and one of the sinks was missing. Someone had gutted the single-wide.

The gray countertop was complete at least,

currently spattered with blood. A shell casing sat at the edge, but Jared couldn't tell what caliber from where he stood.

Someone—probably Carter Bennett—had kicked the door so hard it was completely gone, ripped from frame and hinges. It lay in two pieces, one in the kitchen and the other in front of a ratty dark green. Wood fragments were scattered from the threshold to the kitchen.

"Bloody footprints over here," he called, as soon as the evidence caught his eye. "Big." He compared them to his own size thirteens on the filthy linoleum.

"Smeared or clear?" Cole asked.

"Pretty clear, actually. I can see brand imprint. It's something to go on, anyway."

"Good deal." His partner didn't look up from the female body. His small flashlight's beam darted around her bloody clothing. "Looks like she's been hit twice."

"Damn, I guess it counted." Jared kept his sentence low.

Carrigan took ginger steps, looking around the crappy trailer, notebook in hand, pen poised. She stared and jotted in rhythm, standing still for only a few seconds as she cataloged, but her movements had a confident care. She was making sure not to contaminate the scene.

Still, Jared tried not to roll his eyes when he observed her stiff back and hard expression.

Game face, I guess.

Her wavy strawberry blonde hair was in its normal librarian's bun. Navy blazer firmly in place, as well as matching dark slacks.

When she smiled, she was rather pretty. Too bad the stick up her ass ruined it.

"It's getting dark." Cole stood next to the other body now, a huge man lying on his side by the L-shaped bar in the kitchen. Michael Gentile was built like a truck. Tall. All muscle. "Not much light coming in." He gestured to the two windows in the living room with his flashlight. One had been shot out, glass littered the carpet.

"Yeah, no electricity, so we're better off letting Crime Scene light up the place and get what they need to," Jared said.

Carrigan had a flashlight out too, shining it on the fragmented linoleum floor of the kitchen. "Shell casings," she said, as if Jared and his partner hadn't just spoken. "Looks like a forty."

"I'm sure there're a lot. Let's head outside and wait for Neil and his team," Cole said.

"Neil and his team are here." Neil's portly frame filled the doorframe of the ragged mobile home, the thick black strap of his case over his shoulder. He pushed his glasses up the bridge of his nose. The wind rustled his balding hair, and one side was swooped up like a wing. "And Neil doesn't need cops contaminating the scene." The lead tech's voice was dry.

Jared smirked.

"Special Agent Carrigan preferred to see things first-hand," Cole said, a smile playing at his lips.

Go, partner. Throw her under the bus.

She shrugged, unrepentant.

Neil gave a curt nod and gestured for Chuck, one of his guys, to enter the trailer.

The crime scene photographer, Marion, glared at Jared when she slipped inside, but she was already snapping pictures.

Amusement rippled across his partner's face and he didn't know whether to sigh or scowl.

The tall, slender Asian beauty was on the shy side. A nice, wholesome girl, and Jared had had sex with her once, about two years ago.

One-night stands were far from *her* routine, and he'd never called her after they'd gone out—and spent the night at his place.

Why she'd gone to bed with him was a mystery, but after the shouting lecture she'd graced him with a few weeks later, Marion had assured Jared she wouldn't suffer from *that* particular lapse in judgment again.

He had to admire her self-control. She *never* spoke to him. Not even about work.

Marion always went through someone else, rejecting his repeated attempt to smooth things over. He'd regretted how he'd treated her starting the morning after their night together.

He'd tried to apologize tons of times.

Marion wouldn't hear it—even two years later.

Jared had seen her struggling with heavy equipment a few weeks ago when he'd been dropping off some evidence at the lab, but she hadn't let him help. Even when she'd almost tripped. She'd just mumbled about him under her breath. '*First-class jerk*', she'd said.

She was right.

The photographer's glare or glower was the only look he ever received. Not that he'd ever expected a smile. Marion was sweet, reliable. The kind of girl who would do anything for the people she cared about.

Relationship material.

Mel's blue eyes danced into his mind. Her smile, the long, light brown waves of her hair. Her gorgeous curves.

Shit.

Jared had screwed things up with the photographer, and he was on his way to do the same with the teacher, too.

No.

Somehow, he had to convince Mel to go out with him.

She was different. Made *him* want to be different.

"Whaddya think, Neil?" Cole asked, yanking Jared from his chaos.

Thank God.

He was likely to depress himself.

The lead crime scene tech hovered over Michael Gentile's body. "Two to the chest. Probably dead for a few hours. But Max would know better than me."

Assistant to the Medical Examiner, Max Koto, had yet to make scene, but Jared didn't doubt he'd be there soon.

Marion sauntered past Jared and started snapping photos of the bloody footprints without so much as a look his way.

He winced against the bright light of her camera flash, despite Chuck having set up perimeter lights so the whole trailer was illuminated.

"Well, we'll get out of here so you can work. Gonna look around this place to see if anyone saw anything," Cole said.

"Doubt it," Jared answered. "I'm sure sirens set off all the scum-radar, if the gunshots didn't make the druggies scatter. This place is the ghost town it's supposed to be, 'cept for us."

"Sgt. Crowley said the 9-1-1 call was anonymous," Carrigan said.

The way she said the sergeant's name made Jared assess her.

She'd stared at the long-time cop the night they'd met at *McAuley's*. Did the snooty FBI agent have a thing for him?

He narrowed his eyes.

Another member of APD besides Cole she can halfway stand? Nah.

"Send you my initial report in the morning, like always."

"Thanks, Neil." Cole offered a nod and a thumbs-up that had Carrigan rolling her eyes.

Jared chuckled and followed them out, as the crime scene unit continued to do their thing.

Sgt. Crowley was speaking to Officer Nina Ricketts. He gestured to Jared, his partner and the FBI agent. "Ricketts says there's blood between this trailer and that one." He pointed to the mobile home sitting in the next lot, only about ten feet from the one where the bodies were found.

"There's a nice gap in the skirting and a smeared bloody handprint," Ricketts said. Her blonde ponytail whipped around with the winter wind.

"All right. Widen the perimeter," Carrigan ordered.

"You got it," Crowley said. He was still holding a fat yellow roll of *'Police Line. Do Not Cross'* barrier tape.

"I'll give CSI a holler to check it out," Cole said.

"Nah, got a kit in the truck. I can see if I can lift something," Jared said.

"There's also some nice boot prints in the dirt," Ricketts said. "Thanks to the rain we had yesterday."

"Awesome," Cole said. "I'll grab Neil to see if he can get an impression."

"I'll grab my kit." He jogged across the yard. When he hit the narrow roadway, gravel crunched under his combat boots and his leather jacket creaked. Frigid air burned his ears and he hunched his shoulders, hunkering down in his bomber.

Damn, it's cold.

Something made Jared pause before he reached his F-150. He tensed and flexed his right hand, hovering his palm over the Sig in his waistband.

What the hell?

His skin crawled and it had nothing to do with the temperature. He pressed forward, letting his eyes dart around the road, yard and buildings in view.

The streetlight on the far side of the former office was burned out, so he couldn't see much. It was fully dark now.

Someone was watching him.

It wasn't a cop.

There were only two uniformed officers left—Shannon Crowley and Nina Ricketts. Two of the cruisers had peeled off, the other cops back to patrol duties.

Max from the ME's office hadn't arrived yet, either.

The CSI van was parked on the other side of his truck, further blocking proper view of the whole office structure.

Jared's gut told him someone was right there, right out of sight. He'd left his radio in the truck, and if he shouted for help, he risked spooking his observer. He didn't know if whoever watched him was armed, and he wasn't wearing a vest.

Fuck.

He drew his weapon, muttering a quick prayer. After inching closer to his truck, he flexed his grip on his forty and concentrated on penetrating the dimness with sharpened vision. To no avail.

Double fuck.

A dark figure slid into view from the side of the decrepit building, both palms spread wide. "Don't shoot, little brother. It's me."

"Joe..." His brother's name fell from his mouth, the barest whisper, as shock washed over his whole body.

His heart galloped, but he didn't lower his gun.

Chapter Fourteen

He reholstered his weapon. Jared glanced over his shoulder, but none of his co-workers were in sight.

Thank God.

"J-man." Joe offered a small smile with the childhood nickname. "Look at you. All grown up. Taller than me. You look great."

Mixed emotions hit him in the gut. He rushed forward.

His brother braced his broad shoulders as if he thought Jared was going to clobber him, but he threw his arms around the man.

Joe returned his embrace with tentative arms.

When he pulled back, he noticed the blood. Covered the guy's whole torso. "Fuck. Are you hurt?"

"Nah, man. Not my blood." Sorrow rippled across his face, but his brother schooled his expression fast.

He pressed his truck key into his brother's palm. "Get in the F-150. Keep your head low."

"Jared—"

"Just get in the damn truck. I'll be right back." He exercised every curse in the book as he grabbed the evidence kit from the toolbox mounted in the truck's bed. He whirled away, even before Joe had shut the passenger door.

His instincts screamed to protect his brother, even if it was going to fuck Jared.

No matter what Taylor Carrigan thought, Joe didn't kill John Murray.

One look into his dark eyes confirmed what he'd already known.

His brother wasn't a killer.

And what're you going to do with him now?

Jared couldn't take him to his apartment.

"Fuck me." He rammed his hand into his hair, tugging it tight. His whole body shook as he headed back toward his two partners.

Sgt. Crowley was re-stringing yellow tape and Jared cursed some more.

You're damn lucky he didn't see Joe.

Or…you with Joe.

He ordered the inner monologue to go to hell and trudged on, joining Cole and Carrigan between the trailers.

Neil was with them, and Cole was lighting the area as the crime scene tech knelt, getting ready to pour plaster so he could solidify and lift the boot imprints Ricketts had found.

Probably Joe's footprints. Probably his bloody handprint on the trailer skirting, too.

Jared sucked in a breath, even though the winter air stung his lungs. It was good. A little pain would help him focus.

All this time he'd been dying to be the one to find Joe.

And he had.

Yay? Why didn't you make a plan?

Idiot.

Now that his brother had found *him*, he was lost. That little foster kid without a home.

Something whispered he owed his partner—probably both of them—full disclosure, but he ignored it. Cole would probably understand, maybe help him out of his mess, but Carrigan would take pleasure in snapping metal bracelets on his wrists and loading him in a cell right next to Joe.

"Uh. Gotta go." He shoved his evidence kit into the FBI agent's torso. She stood next to Neil and Cole, watching the crime tech work.

Scrambling to grab the boxy black case, she cursed and plastered it to her chest in lieu of dropping it. "What the hell, Manning?" Carrigan snapped.

"Yeah, what the hell, Manning?" Cole echoed, sounding half-amused, half-curious as he looked up from his squat next to Neil. His partner studiously ignored the FBI agent when she turned her glare on him. "What'd ya mean you have to go?"

Jared cleared his throat. "Family emergency."

Not really a lie.

Cole's expression sobered. He straightened, but made sure his light's beam was still on Neil's task. "Everything okay?"

"I think so. Or, it will be."

"Who is it? Your mom? Dad? Everything okay at FD? They have a big fire? Is your sister all right?"

Damn, Cole Lucas knows too much about me.

He didn't need twenty questions, regardless. "I'll call you later."

His partner gave a curt nod.

Thanks for not pushing me, partner.

Jared could feel Carrigan's burning glare all the way to his truck, even though she hadn't said another word. His hand shook when reached for the driver's side door and had to swallow — twice.

Joe had obeyed his order. Was slumped in the back seat of his extended cab. His six-foot-plus older brother looked super uncomfortable. He'd donned the black hoodie Jared had stowed after a run with Cole the other morning. His head was tucked into the hood.

Good.

"Where we goin'?" The guy's question jolted him as he stretched the seatbelt across his chest.

"No fucking clue."

His brother's laugh filled the cab, but there was a hard edge to it. "That's the story of my life, lately."

"I feel ya."

Silence descended, except for the chatter on the handheld police radio resting in one of the cup holders. The volume was too low to hear everything, but he recognized a voice or two.

Jared's heart rebounded against his ribs the whole drive down the tree-canopied road of the trailer park. He let his eyes dart back and forth, paranoia threatening to eat him alive.

When they got to the main road, he spotted the marked Chevy Tahoe driven by the shift lieutenant.

The big SUV sat in the middle lane of the main street, preparing to turn into the trailer park — signal on, waiting for traffic to move.

Chloe Stein wasn't running lights or sirens, and

she offered a wave as they passed each other. She must want to check out the murder scene, after all.

He had to force his arm up to return the gesture. He didn't slow so she could pull up next to him to chat, either. Hoped she didn't notice how he gunned it to dart through his right turn onto Anderson Boulevard, a main artery into Antioch.

Being nervous around cop cars was new.

So this is what being a fugitive feels like.

Jared exercised his cussing muscle. Now that he had his brother, what exactly was he supposed to do with him?

Knowing Joe was innocent—of murder anyway—and *proving it* were two different things. It wasn't like he could waltz up to Special Agent Taylor Carrigan and declare she was wrong. Demand she change her mind.

It's gonna take hard evidence.

Problem was, so far they didn't have shit.

Everything except that phone call from California pointed *to* Joe Pompa.

Not even Carrigan could surmise why Carter Bennett would turn on Joe.

Shit, now that he could ask *his brother* what was going on, he couldn't form a fucking sentence. Jared needed to get the hell over the shakes ravaging his body.

One of the homes the city owned—and APD used for a safe house from time to time—lay up ahead on the left. It wasn't the nicest place, but it was over a hundred years old. The former farmhouse was a leftover from when the area had been rural.

The historical society was restoring it. Was supposed to be a showpiece when it was done.

An idea bloomed and once it was locked in place he couldn't shake it. Even though it would involve a little breaking and entering. "I know where we can go, big brother."

Seeing his little brother — the *man* behind the wheel of the huge pickup — rocked him to his core.

Checking in with Jared on the phone every few months — most times even longer — was definitely different than *in person*.

He'd missed so much. Hell, he'd missed *Jared* so much.

Joe could still see that scared little boy, clinging to his hand from placement to placement. Even tears on his cheeks when Jared had been young enough to cry. Innocent, big brown eyes that'd been through too much shit.

The guy he'd become was a tall SOB. Broad and muscled, like a linebacker.

At the trailer park, seeing the gun in his hands, as well as the dropped stance, ready for action, had jarred him, even though he'd known his brother's chosen profession.

Jared was all cop.

Ironic.

The criminal and the detective.

Tied by blood.

It's good to see you, little brother.

I'm proud of you for making something of your life. God knows I didn't.

He'd like to say that to the man before him, but his tongue was thick, glued to the roof of his mouth. Words wouldn't form. Joe's emotions were all over the place.

He'd lost his woman but found his brother.

There was a slight tremor to Jared's tense forearms and hands as he guided them down a main street. "Joe?" Jared's voice was as deep as his own, but his name had been strained.

"Yeah, man?"

"Did you hear what I said?"

"I did. I don't know what the hell to say. It was never my intention—"

"Just stay low. I have to go to the PD."

Alarm washed over his body, and he hunched his shoulders. His heartbeat kicked up. "PD. As in Police Department?"

Was his brother going to turn his ass in?

Nothing less than you deserve, really. Bran's dead and it's your fault. Moose, too.

Joe slammed the vault door on that kind of thought and focused on what his brother was saying. He couldn't afford crippling agony and guilt at the moment.

"Yeah. Don't worry. My back windows are tinted. Just stay where you are and we'll be fine."

"What're you gonna do?" As much as he wanted to reconnect with his little bro, if Jared admitted to wanting to turn him in, he was going to have to run.

"I need to get a key."

"Key?"

"To a safe house."

What the hell?

"J-man, I can't do this to you. You're one of the good guys." *And I'm not.* "This is illegal shit, man."

"I've been looking for you for two weeks. Chill. I got this. Besides, what's a little breaking and entering between brothers?"

Joe paused. Smirked, even though his brother wouldn't be able to see him. "Is it really breaking and entering if you have a key?"

Jared laughed.

Despite the deep shit they were in, it was good to hear.

"Point taken," his brother said.

"Damn, man. It's good to see you," he whispered.

"It's good to see you, too, buddy. Seriously." Jared's answer was just as quiet.

Joe closed his eyes and sucked in breath. Bran dying in his arms and Moose dying while trying to protect them both played in his head like a sick movie he couldn't shut off, despite the vault door he'd pictured in his mind, and tried to shove them behind. "Jared, I can't do this to you."

"Joe. I know what I'm doing."

Right. His brother sure didn't sound like it.

"Fuck," he whispered.

"Tell me about it."

Silence fell again.

The only sound was the *click-click* of the big truck's directional signal as Jared continued on his *tour-de-*

Antioch.

Police. Station.

Joe's skin started crawling even before he saw the blue reflective sign with a helpful arrow. The text on the body of it shouted, '*Antioch Justice Center.*'

His brother turned the F-150 down the road and slowed.

Shaking started in his arms then his legs, and shivers raced all over his body when he read the sign that announced '*Police Department*'. It only got worse when he saw, '*Jail Entrance*' etched beneath it.

"Just chill. Stay low. We're going in the back, up to the sally port."

Could Jared read his mind?

That didn't make him feel better. '*Sally Port*' was a fancy was of saying, '*Jail-Driveway-Entrance*', usually. Joe nodded and yanked the hood forward. He slouched even lower in the kid-sized backseat. Gulped. Couldn't help it. "At least they'd never look for me here," he mumbled.

"Right. I'll be quick." As Jared spoke, he heard a beeping sound and the gate-arm in front of them lifted.

They proceeded slowly into what looked like secured parking and back entrances to the PD as well as the jail.

"Don't move. I'll be right back."

Joe didn't answer his brother as he left the truck. His gut screamed to run and he was twitchy all over. He squeezed his eyes closed and made himself breathe normally.

Just hurry, little brother.

Chapter Fifteen

Jared kept his head down, hands in his pockets as he headed down the hall. Like he was doing something wrong.

Yeah, you kinda are.

He passed by the break room. Anyone who saw him would assume he was going to CID. The Criminal Investigation Division's large room was right around the corner from Chief's office.

"Oh, hey, Detective."

His heart and stomach jumped simultaneously when he heard the familiar voice.

Calm the hell down.

He didn't—couldn't evidently—even when he met her brown eyes. "Hi, Jeri." He forced a smile for one of their two female jailers.

She must be on break, because she had a slice of pizza on a paper plate in her grip and a can of soda in the other hand.

"How are ya?"

"Good." *Liar.* "You? Must be dinner time."

"I'm great, and it sure is. We have a wild one though, so I'm going to eat at the desk." She pointed toward the hallway leading back to the Jail Employee Entrance, right next to Dispatch.

"Oh yeah?"

"Yeah, a DWI Benton brought in. She's a little nuts. Kept crashing her head into the bench in the cell. So, we had to put her in the restraint chair. Her blood-alcohol level was off the charts, too. She blew a point-two-four."

"Shit. And she's conscious?"

Jeri laughed. "Was when I left. She'll be fine when she detoxes. You're here late."

"Yeah, gotta grab something."

So, not a lie, but still…

"Take it easy, Detective."

"You too." Jared took a breath and continued down the hall. How on God's green earth was he going to do this?

Police department…cameras *everywhere.*

Nikki never locked the outer office door to her and Chief's executive suite, but he needed a plausible reason for going in there.

There were no cameras inside the two adjoined rooms — the only space in the PD besides bathrooms and locker rooms that lacked them.

Jared headed to CID, like he was going to his desk.

Like normal.

He flipped the lights on. Paced in front of his cubicle, thanking God — yet again — that no one was working late.

A pink sticky note was plastered to his monitor.

'Self-eval for Chief', written by his own hand. He'd been ignoring the reminder since he'd jotted it the other day.

Annual performance reviews were in a few weeks. The city's Human Resources Department had decided in their infinite — stupid — wisdom to change procedures this year and were making *everyone* form goals and outline them, along with the regular *'How am I doing?'* kinda thing.

It was so ridiculous. His was late—by like a week.

"Yes!" Jared had an excuse to go into the office, but he'd have to do the asinine paperwork. Be quick about it, too, or he risked freaking out his waiting brother even more.

Impatience didn't serve him well—he pounded on the keyboard to wake the computer up, clicked the mouse a hundred times when the doc didn't open right away then made his fingers fly over the keyboard.

"Hope the boss doesn't mind typos."

He stared at the first thing he had to answer on the form—*'Please summarize your professional goals for the upcoming review period.'*

Jared smirked, typed *'Catch more bad guys than anyone else'* then backspaced it. Didn't want to piss the chief off. Nor did he want to have to fill out this damn thing more than once.

He answered all the questions as quickly as he could, forming credible goals that would keep his boss off his back.

"Finally done. God that was painful."

He looked over everything he'd typed and clicked *'save'*. Tapped his boot on the thin industrial carpet when the printer didn't respond right way. Restrained himself from hitting *'print'* again.

When the stupid thing was *finally* in his hand, he forced a breath and squared his shoulders.

"Act normal. Calm the fuck down." His heart

wasn't obeying the command, but he turned on his heel and headed out of the room.

His hand shook when he turned the knob into Nikki's office. He flipped on the light and slipped inside, pulling the door shut. Stared at the closed entrance to his boss's office and fought the shakes threatening his body.

He was about to add *theft* to *harboring a federal fugitive.*

Jared swallowed and dropped his evaluation on Nikki's desk. Grabbed a sticky note from her pad and scrawled —

Chief, sorry this is late. –JM

He added his badge number, two-thirty-two, as an afterthought.

The box of keys was in the drawer on the bottom right side of the desk. He'd watched Nikki dig into it dozens of times.

He clenched his jaw and reached for the handle. The drawer slid open and he peered down at the gunmetal-gray lock box.

Please don't be locked.

It wasn't.

Jared scowled instead of breathing a sigh of relief. Was still doing something wrong. He crushed his eyes shut, forcing himself to ignore the guilt creeping up his gut and reached for the box.

Opened it.

Nikki was pretty organized, so he grabbed the set

of keys with a plastic tag labeled '427 *Montgomery Street*'.

The folded white paper—the key log—glared at him from the plastic sleeve on the backside of the door. The date the keys were checked out, the reason, and the officer who took them were supposed to be recorded on that form.

"God, I hope she doesn't check this daily or anything."

She might. Keys to police cars were housed in the box, too.

If someone had to switch out their assigned cruiser for any reason in the morning, would Nikki notice?

Did she inventory the keys?

Jared's pulse thundered in his ears and breath rushed from his lungs. He tucked the safe house key in his pocket and tried not to slam the drawer shut. Although, if he smashed his fingers, it was no less than he deserved.

It took all he was made of not to lean on the door once he was on the other side of it.

His text message alert sounded and he jumped even before he could sneak out the back door. He swore and dug his cell out of his jeans.

Scene secure. Heading home. Will start report. Everything okay with fam? Lemme know.

He screamed at himself to stand still and answer his partner's message.

S'all good.

Okay. Won't push. Meet me at the track in the a.m.?

Cole returned quickly.

Yeah. Thx.

Jared could use a good run — or five.

"Friends First? Are you crazy?" Val peered over her shoulder, her blue gaze intent on the screen of the laptop. She had a beer in her hand and set the other one down on the desk for Mel.

They were planning to watch a movie. Popcorn already sat on the coffee table.

"Why not? It'll be fun." Mel's voice was tight and her best friend's expression told her that her she'd caught on.

Great. She can tell I can't even convince myself this is a good idea. Fun? Right. Like swimming in shark-infested waters.

"A dating service? You have finally lost it, Melody Nash."

"Hey, I didn't invite you over for dinner and a movie tonight for ridicule!"

"Well, I'm spending my Friday night with you."

"We always do Friday movie night!"

Val smiled at the protest. "When I don't have a date."

Mel smirked. "Well, you're wrong."

"What?"

"*Friends First* is *not* a dating service." She pointed to the flashing banner on the website. "It's an activities club. For singles." She forced a smile and grabbed the frosty bottle, taking a swig, but she could still feel Val's stare.

"You're not single."

Mel frowned. "I am so."

Her bestie's blonde curls jumped with her head shake. "Only because you won't go out with Hot Cop."

"God." She scowled. "First off all, stop calling him that. Secondly, stay out of my business." She ignored the jump of her stomach that had nothing to do with the tiny bit of alcohol she's just put in it.

Val rolled her eyes. She'd nicknamed Jared '*Hot Cop*' when she'd called to demand news of what he'd wanted in the school's parking lot this afternoon.

Of course, against her will, the confession of that bone-melting kiss has poured out. Val wanted her to call him and renege on her refusal of a date.

Immediately.

Her heart skipped.

I just can't.

Mel had told Val over and over, but her friend wouldn't let it drop. She'd said *Hot Cop* about twenty times in the hour she'd been at her house.

Dang. It.

Ignoring the heat of her bestie's body at her shoulder, she scrolled through the ads and photo gallery of smiling, good-looking *Friends First* members.

"Look, they have a special right now. Join before the end of the year and it's half-off. The Christmas party mixer is free. It's next Saturday! We can check it out before we decide to join." Mel spared her a glance.

The blonde had one eyebrow arched. "We?"

"I want you to go with me."

"No."

"What do you mean *no*?" She swiveled her computer chair around, arching an eyebrow of her own.

Her friend crossed her arms over her ample breasts. "*No.* As opposed to *yes*. Just call Hot Cop and agree to go out with him. Boyfriend problem solved. No reason for this *Friends First* crap or dragging me along with you — three weeks before Christmas, to boot."

"Geesh. After all the places you've made me go over the years, you can't do me this *one* favor?"

"Did you hear *anything* I said?" Irritation laced Val's inquiry.

"I'm not calling Jared."

"Why not? He kissed you in the parking lot. Practically begged you to go out with him. Something tells me *begging* isn't something he normally does. Guys that look like him don't *have* to beg. He likes you."

Right. Sure he does.

"From now on, I'm not telling you squat about my life."

She snickered and perched herself on the edge of the desk. "Right. Let me know how that works out for you."

Mel sighed and cast her eyes to the ceiling of her

living room. "Thanksgiving Day."

"What?"

"You made me go to the tree lighting. I didn't want to go. You were meeting a guy."

"Who turned out to be a douche."

Mel met her best friend's eyes. "Not. My. Fault. *Please* do this with me. Because all the things you've made me do and go to over the years don't tip the scales on what I've asked of you."

Val muttered a few words that shouldn't be in the vocabulary of a third grade teacher. She frowned. Then took a gulp of beer. "Fine. I'll go."

Mel beamed.

"You can stop gloating. I'm only going 'cause there might be hot guys there, and *I* am actually the single one."

Chapter Sixteen

"**W**hy are you so jittery?" Cole stared, the water bottle plastered to his palm. When Jared didn't answer, he squirted liquid in his mouth, but his eyes didn't waver.

"I'm not, it's just cold." He jumped up and down.

"We just ran two miles. You're not cold. There's something else going on."

He shook his head. His spine tingled. Sensation spread down his biceps, forearms, wrists, and onto the run-tightened muscles of his quads. It was like spiders crawling all over his sweaty form, and he winced.

His partner was right. He wasn't affected by the temperature, even if they were having an unusually frigid winter. He could see Cole's breath as they both cooled down from their run. "I'm good."

But he wasn't.

Hadn't been for the last three days.

It's been a loooooooong fucking weekend.

Since Friday, when he'd taken the key to the big safe house on Montgomery Street from the lockbox.

After he'd got Joe settled that night, he'd had a copy made at the hardware store, but Jared hadn't been able to put the original back.

He should've stopped by the PD Saturday or Sunday, but he'd been paranoid there would be no logical reason for him to step into his boss's office a second time. So he'd chickened out and had stayed away from the station.

They'd worked a little, but hadn't accomplished much. Jared, Cole and Carrigan had gone back to the scene and gone over Neil and Max's two reports.

He'd have to put the key back this morning — if he could beat Cole to work.

Too much longer, and there was no way Nikki wouldn't notice.

Joe was alone in the place. Had promised he'd stay out of sight.

The guy was torn up, but wouldn't say about what. The first night — as well the following two — Jared hadn't been able to get a word out about what'd happened inside that crappy trailer.

His brother had paced the master bedroom and kept ramming his hand through his shorn hair.

Because of LA FBI agent's call, they had a pretty good idea who the shooter was, but Carter Bennett hadn't been found in Antioch.

They had a BOLO out with every neighboring department, as well as the County Sheriff's Office, and Carrigan, of course had spread the word to her contacts.

Joe was going to have to talk, but Jared was giving him some space — and a little time. He'd try again later today. It'd been long enough.

He'd gone to his apartment, although he'd not wanted to walk away from his older brother. Jared had stuffed clothing and toiletries in a bag and bought enough food for a week. He'd left his Ducati in the garage at the safe house for an emergency. If Joe had to leave and a cop ran the license plate, he was screwed.

What the fuck are you doing?

Brother or not, he was harboring a fugitive.

Day three.

Shaking like he had the DTs was becoming his norm, as well as the paranoia he'd get caught by Carrigan—or Cole—at any second.

Joe was only making it worse by thanking him profusely every time he'd gone to see him. As well as his constant asking if he was sure about this.

Hell no, I'm not sure about this.

He'd told his brother he was determined to prove he was innocent of murder. Joe still hadn't said anything about—well, *anything*—but the look he'd flashed was grateful.

Jared had managed to get Joe to promise not to take off.

That's something, I guess.

"No. You're not." Cole yanked him from his inner torment and he met his concerned eyes.

What? Oh, yeah. Me. Okay.

"I'm fine. Really." Nodded for effect, but his partner's expression shouted he didn't buy it.

"You need to let me in on whatever's going on in that head of yours. Is it Carrigan?"

"No."

"Okay, then." Cole tilted his head to one side. "How'd it go with Miss Nash?"

Jared frowned and ignored the urge to rub his chest. "It didn't." Another thing he'd been trying to forget about for the longest weekend of his life.

"Damn. She shut you down?"

He didn't answer as Cole took another swig of water before popping the lid shut and tossing his bottle into a black duffel.

The morning was chilly, and it wasn't quite six-thirty. Normally they saw a few other runners at the public track, but today they were alone.

For the second workday in a row, they'd met to run beforehand, but they normally tried to do so several times a week.

Cole was one of the few guys who could keep up with him and his workout routine. Jared had always enjoyed hanging with his partner on the track or in the gym. Even at the guy's house for a football game, or playing with Cole and Andi's two little boys.

The man was his partner, but he was also his friend...his *family*.

Which just makes this shit harder.

"I'm still blown away that my kid's teacher was your one-night stand. She doesn't seem the type."

She's not. I'm a sleaze.

Jared wiped his face with a towel and continued to ignore Cole. He reached for his bag, stuffed the terry cloth inside and yanked the zipper closed. He hefted the duffel, settling the strap across his torso.

"Not talkative this morning," his buddy muttered. "You sure everything's okay with your family?"

Not if you mean my older brother.

"Yeah. Seriously."

Doubt flashed in Cole's eyes, but he didn't push.

Thank God.

They headed to the parking lot in silence.

"I'll meet you at work."

"Jer." His partner's expression was concerned, but hard. "Do you trust me?"

Shock washed over him, and he squared his shoulders. Flushed to his toes. Forced a nod, because he couldn't say a damn thing.

Stop looking at me like that.

"Good. My gut says there's something you're not telling me." Once again, that concrete tone matched the look on his face.

This was definitely one of those times Jared didn't appreciate Cole's instincts. "There's not." He cursed the croak in his denial.

"Then what the fuck is up with you?"

He swallowed. Hard. Part of the truth fell out. "I want Mel."

Cole's big shoulders relaxed. He studied him for a few seconds then blew out a breath, which was visible in the air. "That's what this is about?"

He forced another nod. It wasn't a lie. Jared *did* want her.

His partner whistled, and a slow knowing smile curved his lips. "It finally happened."

"What?"

"You're screwed in the head over *one* woman."

Jared scowled. "Yeah. Thanks, partner."

"Try calling her?"

"She shut me down in the school parking lot Friday after we talked to her class. I don't have her number. But if I show up again, with my luck, she'll call Chief. She accused me of stalking her."

Cole laughed.

"I'm glad you're amused."

The guy shook his head. "I never thought I'd see it, is all."

"See what?"

"The one you want doesn't want you."

Jared's gut tightened. "Thanks for putting it so succinctly. I'll see you at work." With a sigh, he turned to head to his truck, but Cole grabbed his arm.

"I'm sorry, Jer. I won't jack with you about her."

He fought the urge to close his eyes.

Mel's rejection and Joe's situation had him tight, despite the refreshing run and relieving stretch afterward.

"It's okay. Serves me right."

"Serves you right? Nah. Give it a day or two, and try again. You're basically a nice guy."

Jared smirked. "Thanks. I think."

Cole flashed dimples. "You gonna be able to play nice with Carrigan? Speaking of the next few days."

"I guess so. Why?"

"I have to go to New York. Caselli's trial is underway, and they need me to testify. Leavin' in the morning."

The big-time human trafficker had finally been caught last year by Cole's previous partner—Pete's sister-in-law, Special Agent Selena Dawson—now Crane. Lee and her partner led Cole's old unit in New York City.

Caselli had killed his former attorney himself and they'd finally been able to get enough evidence on him for a warrant. They had video footage and everything.

Hopefully all the other crimes Caselli had orchestrated would be factors in the trial, and he'd pay for everything illegal he'd ever done—sex trafficking, money laundering, drugs, owning gambling establishments. The man had had his hands in quite a few bags, from what Jared understood.

He'd sent men to Texas twice in years past to go after guys who'd turned on him. First Carlo Maldonado then someone who'd left his organization, Alberto Carbone.

So, Jared was familiar with the bastard. Had assisted in the multiple investigations that'd resulted in the man's taint on Antioch. The trail of bodies was bigger than city council ever liked to admit.

"Wow. When? We're in the middle of a case," Jared said.

"I know, but I shouldn't be gone more than a few days. I'd like to stay for the whole thing, but I need to be here, play referee to you and Ms. FBI."

"Yeah, yeah. I can handle Ms. FBI. But she won't like being left with the redheaded stepchild."

Cole chuckled. "Hey now, my kid has red hair."

He grinned. "Right. Carrigan *would* probably compare working with me to hanging with Ethan. We're both six years old in her eyes. You know she thinks you're made of gold, and I'm a pile of shit."

It was his partner's turn to smirk. "She does have a little bit of a superiority complex."

"Now that you it put it *that* way, that's probably why you two get along."

Cole laughed long and hard. "*I* know you're a damn good cop, even if you were never FBI."

"That's what it is with her?" Jared arched an eyebrow.

"I'm thinking so, but I have faith in you, partner." He patted his shoulder, grinning from ear to ear.

"Yeah, yeah. I'll see you at work."

Chapter Seventeen

aylor sighed. She tried to ignore Manning, but she could feel his glare from across the cubicle. She was using his computer, and evidently he had no patience for *real* investigation.

Lucas had been gone for three days.

She'd been stuck with the younger detective, and neither of them was pleased.

He was twitchy.

She kept snapping.

They were getting nowhere on the case.

Which makes things worse.

There was no sign of Pompa, Carter Bennett, or the last unaccounted member of their gang, Rowdy Vargas.

Jared Manning winced every time she said the name *Joe Pompa*.

Taylor hadn't figured out why just yet, but something was there.

It was subtle. His shoulders would tense and a ripple of some unnamed emotion would traverse his handsome face.

She needed to contact Eddie to see if he'd heard anything new, but then again, her fellow FBI agent would've called, like he'd said he would.

"It's likely Bennett did his job and got out of town," Manning said.

Had the detective read her mind?

"Yeah, that would make sense. But where's

Vargas? Getaway car — or body yet to be found?"

He shrugged, lifting one booted foot and resting it against the gray fabric wall of his cubicle. "You're the FBI agent. You tell me." He smirked.

Anger flipped Taylor's stomach and she sucked in a breath so she wouldn't snap at him. *Again.* Or worse — smack the look off his face.

Damn the man.

She turned back to the computer screen, flexing her fingers that rested on the mouse.

"I've been a cop for eight years, you know. Detective for almost six. I didn't get promoted for nothing."

She frowned and swiveled the chair around.

His posture was relaxed, his shoulders up against the felt wall, but the expression on his face was hard.

"Your point?"

"I'm not an idiot. I know what I'm doing. I'm an *investigator*. A damn good one, too. If you need to pull my file, ask my boss. Look at my close-out rating. Even before Cole was my partner."

"Still not hearing a point here." Taylor reclined in the chair, ignoring how the tension rippled across his broad shoulders.

Manning crossed his arms over his chest. "Bullshit."

"Bullshit?"

"You know *exactly* what I'm talking about. And *why* I am saying it."

She didn't respond.

The detective pushed off the wall and glared.

"Since you've arrived, you've been treating me like shit. You show me zero respect, like I'm a gnat to be swatted. Meanwhile, you think Cole Lucas hung the moon. I gather it's because I'm a cop in a city of less than fifty-thousand people, and you think since he was FBI and I'm not, I don't know anything. Well, I might not work on the Dallas Violent Crimes Task Force, but I *have* worked a murder or two, and I *do* know what the fuck I'm doing."

She didn't want to respond. Because he was wrong — wasn't he?

His cellphone rang and Taylor jumped.

"We're not done with this," Manning barked as he palmed the phone and glanced down at the screen.

Yeah. Kiss my ass.

Taylor didn't say it. She'd never admit that he was even a little bit right. They'd met at a bar, and she hadn't been impressed from the start.

That's just an excuse.

Truth was, she'd been struggling to function since John died, and it was just easier with Lucas, since he'd been FBI. Less explaining.

Then again — so far, Manning hadn't required much, either. He *was* a good cop. Sharp eyes and mind. Good ideas. He'd shown her around Antioch.

She'd never admit she'd been wrong in the way she'd treated him. Manning would see her as weak.

He was a straightforward kind of guy, so it was a wonder he'd held his tongue and not confronted her before now.

Just apologize so you can get on with the case. You still

have to work with him.

She bit back a sigh and fought the urge to close her eyes.

Taylor scanned Lucas' work area. It backed up to Manning's, with only a short cubicle wall separating the two. Her eyes rested—against her will—on the picture of him and his family proudly displayed next to his computer monitor.

Lucas, his wife—fellow detective Andi MacLaren-Lucas—and their two kids. Four smiles for the camera that just made her gut ache with loss.

I'll never have that with John.

Although, she'd never planned on kids. The FBI was enough for both of them. Being together was what'd mattered.

Her mind slipped back to Thanksgiving Day—again, unwillingly. The day had been pleasant. More than just a hot meal.

Too bad she's spent the whole time skittering between envy, loss and having a good time. She'd ruined things for herself. Couldn't relax and enjoy—something else she hadn't been able to do since John had been murdered.

She hadn't run into Andi in a work situation. Manning had nothing but good things to say about her skills as a cop. As Taylor understood it, the detective and her partner, Pete Crane, were working a stolen property case-turned huge burglary ring. So they'd been out of the office a great deal.

She and Manning had passed them about ten minutes before, when they'd gone to CID to review some reports, but the other set of partners was headed to lunch.

However, what Taylor had learned from watching Andi Thanksgiving Day was all good stuff. She was a good mom and wife.

Taylor had apologized for adding an unplanned plate to their dinner table on the holiday, but Andi had been gracious and welcoming.

And those little boys…

Ethan and Micah were adorable. At almost six, the elder was charming and talkative. He'd reached for a handshake when Lucas had introduced her to him, and Taylor hadn't been able to bite back a smile.

The little one wasn't talking much yet, but when he'd reached for her, she'd frozen. Micah had tried to scramble onto her lap, and of course she'd had to lift him up. Which had ended with her holding him.

She hadn't wanted him to fall and get hurt, after all.

Micah had stared up at her with his mother's big blue eyes and a shy smile that'd only made his dad's dimples peek slightly.

It hadn't been difficult to relax then, even though she hadn't had a baby on her lap for longer than she could remember.

Ethan had talked her ear off, going on about school, and his teacher, Miss Nash. As well as his parents, Uncle Pete, and — she'd tried not to frown — his *Uncle Jared.*

He was a bright kid, and just as adorable as his younger brother. He, too, had Andi's eyes.

Normal had surrounded her.

And had just about killed her.

Jared tried not to roll his eyes as he glanced at Carrigan's stiff back. He put his cell to his ear. "Manning."

Someone cleared their — her — throat.

Mel?

His heart back-flipped.

"Uh…Detective?"

Not Mel.

"Yes, this is Detective Manning." He ignored the disappointment eating at his gut. "How can I help you?"

"My name's Valerie Hart. I'm a friend of Melody Nash." She paused, but he could tell she wasn't done talking. "Best friend, actually. She'll *kill* me if she finds out I called you."

Now his interest was piqued. "What can I do for you, Ms. Hart?" After all, his mother had raised him with manners.

"Val, please. And it's what I can do for *you*, Detective."

"Oh?"

"Have you ever heard of *Friends First*?"

Jared frowned. He'd heard radio ads for the company. "That activities club?"

"Right. For *singles*."

Her slight emphasis on the last word had him stilling. "*Singles* club…Mel… No way. She didn't…"

"Wow, I like that you're sharp. And oh yeah, she sure did. She didn't join yet, but she wants to check it out. Christmas mixer is free to attend."

"Hell no."

Val laughed. "That's what I said."

"When, and where?"

"I'm really glad you're on board."

"More than on board. I suppose it's no secret what happened the night we met, but… I want to take her out. Date her, hang with her. She won't give me a shot."

"I know. And I can't seem to yell sense into her. So we have to be sneaky."

Jared grinned. He had a feeling he was going to like this girl. "I can do sneaky."

"Good. Saturday at three. The new Antioch City Center. Can you make it?"

"You bet."

"See you there. Oh, hey, Detective."

"Yeah?"

"You happen to find a purple shoe at your place?"

"Yeah, actually."

"It's mine. Can you bring it?"

"Sure." He disconnected and pocketed his cell, grinning about the shoe. So it was her friend's? Jared had tossed it in his truck's toolbox when he'd found it, so he'd just have to remember to give it back.

His heart soared.

He was going to see *Mel* in a few days.

She'd probably just reject him again.

No. This time I won't let her.

This time was going to be different.

Merry Christmas to me.

Even though Christmas was still thirteen days away.

Jared was giddy, like a little kid, but his smile faded when he met his FBI partner's hazel eyes.

"Plans?" She had one fair eyebrow arched, displeasure written all over her pretty face.

Carrigan's presence in Antioch very well might ruin his holiday. God knew she couldn't loosen up. And like Thanksgiving, she'd already stated she wasn't heading back to Dallas.

He probably owed Cole one for hosting her on Turkey Day, but he sure as hell wasn't going to offer her a place at his parents'. Even if being alone on Christmas would suck.

Besides, the irritation on her face at that moment sucked his manners away.

"If you must know, yeah. For Saturday."

"We're working a case."

Oh? Now you want to work with me?

He swallowed his instinct to snap. It wouldn't do any good. "Right, and you'll survive without me for a few hours. Cole should be back by then, I hope. You can ruin my partner's Saturday instead of mine."

The insult rolled off her without response.

"I'm sorry." The FBI agent's apology was soft but her eyes unwavering.

"Excuse me?" Shock hit him but he squared his shoulders. He'd never expected an apology, despite his confrontation before Valerie Hart's phone call.

"You're a good investigator. I should take

advantage of your skills."

Jared harrumphed. *Of course* she'd ruin her apology by being a think-for-yourselfer. Calling her on it would make things worse. "We're supposed to work together. So let's do that. Find Pompa and Bennett. Put them away. Maybe we'll get something accomplished before my partner gets back." He cleared his throat. Like always, he'd had to force his brother's last name out with conscious care, striving for normal.

Her gaze sharpened and he tried not to squirm. Carrigan nodded curtly, but she still studied him from his own chair. "All right."

He forced himself to loosen his shoulders with the FBI agent's affirmative.

"There's been no sign of Bennett, as we've already discussed, but there is this." She grabbed a piece of paper off his printer, and Jared stepped forward to take it.

His eyes skimmed the report. "Well, will you look at that." He whistled. "A stolen BMW, last seen by the owner, right outside of town."

"And two miles north, a sheriff's deputy found a maroon Mercedes with Arizona plates. Reported stolen outside of Tempe the day before Thanksgiving. I bet if we keep going west, we'll find a few more dumped."

"We agreed Pompa didn't go west." Once again, Jared had to clear his throat and focus on being normal. He forbade himself from thinking of Joe.

"Yes. I think it's Bennett, coming this way. After Pompa. John's body was found in Oklahoma, but we know they went to California. They must be coming back around. Maybe Bennett figured Pompa didn't go west, too."

"Yeah, I see it. The cars are a trail."

"Could be. Do you want to go check out the Beemer? It's conveniently in the impound lot your department uses." Carrigan's expression didn't change, but Jared had to admire that she was reaching out to him for the first time since they'd met.

"Sure. Has it been processed?"

"Inventoried, but I requested they leave the processing up to me—us—when my office got the call."

He wanted to ask why her office got a heads-up when the sheriff's office in question was in *his* county, but Jared screamed at himself not to be territorial.

Carrigan probably had a contact she hadn't shared with him. She might've apologized, but they weren't besties. Never would be.

"All righty. I'll get my kit."

She nodded.

He smirked.

She was probably going to argue with him about who was going to drive.

Chapter Eighteen

The hair stood up on the back of her neck.

Taylor's gut screamed *something* was very wrong.

It wasn't the fact she was following her Antioch PD partner. That wasn't even offering guilt at the moment.

Jared Manning lived in an apartment here in town. His parents lived on Chestnut Street, also in Antioch.

So why was he heading into a house on Montgomery Street with grease-soaked brown paper bags from the bar she'd met him at?

Yeah, I checked up on you.

After all, he'd suggested it.

She'd pulled his file after he'd left for the day. Tried to convince herself mere curiosity had her looking at his pertinents.

Manning hadn't been boasting when he'd mentioned his closeout rate. The man was a machine — even before he'd partnered up with Cole Lucas, as he's claimed. The two had an unreal solve rate of ninety-five percent.

Her detective partner glanced over his shoulder as he entered the huge house.

There was no way he could see her from where Taylor watched, but she winced anyway.

Watching him pretty much confirmed she didn't trust him.

So much for the apology and praise of his skills earlier that day. As far as Manning was concerned, they were square now. She'd even assured him she'd take advantage of his investigation abilities.

Liar, liar, pants on fire.

"But something *is* wrong here." Maybe saying it out loud would make her feel better. "I won't apologize for being right."

Right? And since when do you talk to yourself?

She couldn't put her finger on it, but from the start there'd been something fishy about Manning and this case.

Taylor's gut was never wrong.

The door closed, and even though she was too far away to hear the sound, the *thud* resounded in her ears.

What are you doing, Taylor? Watching your partner?

She drummed her fingertips on the steering wheel of her FBI-issued Chevy Impala.

Many a co-worker had accused her of being the suspicious sort—even for someone in her line of work. It made her keen, sharp.

Something didn't seem right with Jared Manning. No harm in checking it out.

Investigating.

That was her job.

What if you're wrong?

No.

What if I'm right?

Lucas was still in New York City. He'd called earlier and told them he hoped to be home by the end of the week.

Could she share her suspicions with the former FBI agent?

He'd want proof of such a hefty accusation, and she only had what her gut was telling her.

Was she becoming paranoid?

She narrowed her eyes and focused solely on the big house.

It was a nice place. Someone took care of the outside. The hedges were trimmed and lined the walkway and the length of the porch. Unlike most of the homes in the neighborhood, it was a two story, instead of a ranch, and from the outside it looked huge.

There were two windows on either side of the front door, and no light was visible from the inside.

Manning walked into the dark?

Taylor could see no movement, but then again, every visible window had navy or black curtains that didn't even have a sliver of a gap. As if someone had taken care to make sure nothing of the interior was visible.

Weird.

"No. Not weird if you're hiding something."

Manning hadn't told her where he was headed after work—not that it was any of her business.

They'd had a long, arduous day with little progress, despite making contact with the deputy who had found the ditched BMW.

The evidence they'd collected was a positive, but only if the DNA was a match for Bennett or Pompa. Hell, she'd even take Rowdy Vargas at this point.

After she'd read up on her partner, she hadn't been able to force herself to leave the PD. The day had felt like a waste, and she couldn't stomach it.

What am I missing? played in her head on a loop.

Taylor had sat at Manning's desk, reading a few of John's reports for the thousandth time. Especially the ones that'd detailed dealings with Bennett.

Then she'd studied Bennett's dossier. Tall and blond, he wasn't a bad looking guy, but he was lanky and had a congenital defect in his back that caused him to walk with a perpetual slight limp. His brown eyes were deep and obviously held dark secrets.

Carter Bennett seriously didn't give off the impression of killer. Criminal mastermind, yeah.

But Eddie's guy—and Eddie himself—were convinced he was crazy, and responsible for the deaths of two members of his own crew.

Make that four deaths.

When she'd shared Brandelyn Willis and Michael Gentile being killed, Eddie had agreed Bennett was responsible.

The conclusion was bad and good.

If Bennett was responsible for the murders in Antioch, it confirmed Eddie's informant's info.

The man *was* after Pompa and the two he'd killed. *He'd* known they were in small-town Texas or had somehow traced them there.

Bad news was they had no idea where he was or what the hell had happened to Pompa.

The ringleader's fingerprints had been all over the trailer—along with Brandelyn Willis' and Michael Gentile's.

So, her prime suspect had been right under her nose and had gotten away.

Were Bennett and Pompa together?

Nothing like a little shooting to help along a reunion.

Maybe Bennett had Pompa against his will?

Her questions were endless and evidence quite the opposite.

It'd been almost seven when Taylor had finally left the police station. She'd spotted Manning's huge black F-150 leaving the parking lot of *McAuley's* when she'd driven by the place on her way to her hotel.

She hadn't meant to follow him — at first.

Even at a distance, his posture had been tight in the driver's seat. More so than she'd ever seen him — and she'd been with him all day.

Manning had turned into a neighborhood that was opposite the direction of his apartment complex, so curiosity had had her following.

It was a wonder he hadn't spotted her, with all the head movement she'd observed on the short drive.

She would've broken off and gone on to *The Covington*, but when she'd seen her temporary partner pull into Freedom Park and sit in his truck for a good ten minutes, her interest had piqued even more.

Then the detective had exited his vehicle and not walked into the small park, but *away* from it. He'd crossed the street and headed the direction he'd just driven in from, jogging down the sidewalk and then up the porch steps of the big house.

Taylor's instincts had started screaming and not stopped since.

She couldn't see anything. Didn't matter — it still wasn't sitting right.

Her stomach growled, reminding her she hadn't eaten anything since that morning, but she didn't move. Kept staring at the door. Wouldn't learn anything — to lend to or from suspicion — if she left.

She'd learned a lot about Jared Manning in the short time they'd been working together, as well as when she'd read his personnel file.

Am I being paranoid?

Maybe she'd been at this too long.

Taylor hadn't stopped to take a breath since John had been killed. Had had to beg her boss to let her work the case.

Conflict of interest floated around in her brain.

But it wasn't, was it?

She'd been working Pompa's theft ring *with* John long before the bastard had killed her fiancé.

Taylor was just being thorough. Wanted to finish things. Get Pompa for the murder as well as his other activities.

Now she had to get Bennett, too.

Had *thorough* slipped into *paranoid* where her temporary partner was concerned?

Anyone could live in that house.

Manning could have a girlfriend. Hell, a friend could live on Montgomery Street. Family other than his fire lieutenant father and librarian mother.

"No." Her instinct wouldn't let her believe that train of thought.

Something's not right here.

All Taylor could do for now was watch.

Observe.

Exonerate or condemn Jared Manning.
Question was…
For what exactly?
And who's in that house with my partner?

"Joe?" Jared shut the door as quickly as he could manage with the paper food bags filling his hands.

He'd stocked the fridge of the big safe house, but something told him his brother wasn't posing as Sally Homemaker, so he'd grabbed burgers to go from *McAuley's*.

Can I coax Joe into talking?

He needed to know what'd happened at the trailer park. Needed to know what Joe had seen and confirm Bennett was the shooter. Maybe even find out what team Rowdy Vargas was playing on.

How he'd explain the new information was a problem for the morning.

Carrigan was too suspicious of a person in general to believe Jared was that good a guesser. Sucked that he'd have to keep new knowledge to himself — at least for now.

The BMW had been wiped clean — mostly. They'd found some blood residue. Hopefully the small samples they'd been able to gather would be enough for DNA, *and* match the bloody boot prints from the trailer.

One look at his brother's sneakers confirmed the prints didn't belong to Joe. And they hadn't been Michael Gentile's, either.

His gut and logic agreed both belonged to Bennett. But if the guy was bleeding, how badly was he hit, and where the hell was he?

Trolling hospitals had got them nowhere, so he wasn't hurt badly enough to seek medical attention, yet anyway.

Carrigan and Jared had come to a small peace. He felt better about things—sort of. However, she still stared as if she *knew* he was hiding something.

What did she *think* she knew?

Had she looked at Joe's picture and put together how much they looked alike? If so, would she mention it to Cole?

Not like I can ask either of them.

Not like *he* was going to bring it up in case they hadn't noticed what was so obvious to Jared. He and his brother had the same strong jaw line. Same high cheekbones. Their noses were different but that made them look like the brothers they were, instead of twins.

"Joe?" His second call still went unanswered.

"In here!"

Jared set his keys and the food down on the kitchen counter and headed toward his brother's voice. He found Joe in the master bedroom, doing push-ups.

His brother wore a pair of his light gray sweats and a ribbed tank. The cotton was a darker color in spots and even from the doorway, he could see the shirt looked like Joe had pulled it out of the washing machine.

Soaked.

Sweat—like he'd been at it for hours.

More of a punishment than a workout.

What's that about?

"I grabbed dinner. You hungry?"

The guy popped up off the floor and their eyes locked. "I could eat."

"Good deal."

"Lemme shower."

Jared nodded and turned to go.

"J-man."

He glanced over his shoulder in time to see Joe's small smile. "Yeah?"

"Thanks, man."

A nod was all he could manage.

Even as a kid, Joe had always been the strong, silent type, but there was more to it now than just being like the quiet teen who'd kept to himself.

He certainly didn't scream *demanding crime boss,* but Joe wore what'd happened to him like a shroud—even if he hadn't said shit.

It made Jared's gut ache. He'd want to help any guy in his brother's sitch, but since it was so close to home, it was worse. Didn't matter he hadn't seen him in years.

Blood was blood and Jared *had* to fix this.

No pressure.

That was what his brother needed.

He busied himself with grabbing plates and setting the table.

"Mom would be proud of my manners." He smirked and grabbed straws from the brown paper bag, stabbing them into Styrofoam cup lids. Tried not to fidget while he waited. Made himself take a seat so he wouldn't give in to the urge to pace.

A few minutes later, his brother came down the hall wearing a pair of Jared's jeans and a plain black tee that clung to his pecs. Joe had shaved and he caught a whiff of his own aftershave.

He wore a thick silver or white gold chain around his neck. A fat cross hung from it. He'd been wearing it while doing pushups, too. They'd never really been the religious types, even as kids. Although, several pairs of foster parents had dragged them to one church or another.

Wonder what that means? Who gave it to him?

They didn't talk as they ate.

Jared's heart thundered harder with each passing moment, but he forced his attention on savoring the heart-attack-on-a-bun in his hands. It tasted damn good. The bacon *McAuley's* put on a burger was exquisite.

"I didn't kill anyone."

He paused, making eye contact with his brother, but Joe looked away, reaching for his drink. He stared as Joe sucked dark cola up the straw.

"I know."

His brother's broad shoulders loosened and he let out a breath. His mouth wobbled and he clenched his jaw as if the emotion was too much to handle.

Jared had told his brother he knew he was innocent, but this was the first time the guy had confirmed or denied.

No pressure, he repeated in his head. He needed

info, but it was okay if it was on Joe's terms.

"Just like that?" His brother's whispered.

"Yeah. I told you before. You're my brother, man. Not a killer."

He closed his eyes. "I might not have pulled the trigger, but I'm responsible for two deaths. Three, if you count John."

Jared dug for all the professionalism he could manage. Tried to pretend he wasn't with his brother. He needed to treat the man across from him like any other witness. Needed to be sharp as he absorbed everything. And damn straight needed to remember it. Something told him his brother would clam up if he grabbed a notebook. "Tell me what happened," he said, dropping his statement like Joe had.

"It's my fault she's dead."

"She? Brandelyn Willis?"

His brother's eyes snapped to his face. "Yeah. Moose, too. My fault."

Joe wasn't the kind of guy to buy *'no, it's not your fault'* as a manner of comfort, so he didn't bother. "Was Carter Bennett the shooter?"

All he got was a nod, but it was still an answer.

The guy didn't look the least bit surprised Jared had asked, either.

"Was he alone?"

Silence descended and he doubted his brother was going to say anything else.

His big shoulders hunched as he leaned into the table, his burger forgotten. His jaw was tight and emotion flickered across his face. A good two minutes passed before Joe met his eyes again. "Yeah."

"You shoot at him?"

"Yeah. Moose did, too."

"Someone hit him. We found blood in the kitchen that didn't match Brandelyn Willis or Michael Gentile. You're not hit, so I'm drawing a conclusion here."

One corner of Joe's mouth shot up. "How elementary of you, dear Detective."

Jared grinned. "I so didn't see you as a Sherlock kinda guy."

His brother let out a low chuckle and shook his head. "It wasn't really me. It was her. She liked that show, you know? The one with the girl Watson?"

"Ah. Never watched, but I know what you're talking about. You cared about her, huh?"

Undisguised pain made its way across his expression. He nodded and his Adam's apple bobbed, then his brother broke eye contact. Cleared his throat.

Jared let him regain his composure. He might've talked a little but they were far from done. He had so many questions, but he let them spin in his head.

Joe wasn't ready for any kind of police onslaught.

"I'm glad I hit the fucker. I didn't know, 'cause he didn't go down. But you gotta find him, little brother. He can't die. Gotta get him before he dies."

He pitched forward as every word his brother uttered picked up speed. "Joe?"

"Carter Bennett killed John Murray."

Chapter Nineteen

Val kept looking around, and she wasn't checking out guys.

"What's got you so jumpy?" Mel tried not to snap.

Blue eyes went wide when they met her gaze and her bullcrap meter lit up even before her best friend — possibly former best friend, depending on the answer — spoke.

"Nothin'. Lotsa scenery around here. Hot. Single. Guys."

She narrowed her eyes and scooted to the edge of the chair. "Right."

The round table held up to eight people, but no one was seated with them in the big conference room.

The Antioch City Center had just opened a few months before. It was multifunctional—snazzy with giant flat-screen TVs posted in every corner, and still so new the scent of fresh paint wafted. The tables and chairs were top-of-the-line, too.

A projector flashed pictures of events past and testimonials of *Friends First's* awesomeness on all the screens.

Currently, *Christmas* was draped all over the place. Lavish decorated trees in the center of the room as well as smaller versions in all four corners. Boxes wrapped like gifts in bright printed paper as centerpieces on the tables, and cheery seasonal music filled the air.

The banner announcing *'Friends First Fifth Annual*

Christmas Mixer' dominated the front of the large room.

Mel had always loved Christmas, but the atmosphere was a bit much.

Val flashed a million-watt smile. "I'm gonna go flirt. That's what we're here for, right? I might as well snag me one. Maybe I can get a cop." Her voice cracked on the last word and alarm bells went off in Mel's head. However, her bestie was up and off the chair in two seconds flat.

She looked around, frantically scanning the crowd. People were everywhere, forming small groups, talking, eating, drinking and laughing.

Some couples had formed and broken off, sitting at tables or in the many sets of two chairs put together to encourage conversion with an air of privacy.

The scent of smoked ham from the buffet tables tickled her nose. Should've appealed, but her stomach was in knots.

She'd come here to check out *Friends First* and possibly meet someone.

Yeah, someone other than Hot Cop.

Mel couldn't stop thinking about Jared.

Geeze, she didn't waste any time.

Her eye caught Val talking to some tall-dark-and-handsome, looking slender and gorgeous in her Christmas-red outfit. The skirt was tight and stopped at her knees, showing off her killer legs. Her hair was up, accentuating her slender neck, and Val's matching sweater hugged her breasts. She laughed at something the guy said, suddenly even more beautiful.

God, she glows.

Mel groaned and fought the urge to cover her face with both hands.

What the heck was I thinking? Val was right when she said I'd lost it.

Putting herself out there to the opposite sex had never been her ideal. She'd always been awkward at best. In high school, David had pursued her, after all.

Like Jared.

No.

David and Jared weren't even in the same universe.

Her ex had been safe—at the time. Jared certainly wasn't.

Would never be *safe*.

She blew out a breath and tried to smile when a cute redheaded guy caught her eye and threw her a nod-and-smile combo.

Don't come over here. Don't come over here.

He turned, as if he was indeed headed straight to her.

Mel shot to her feet and slipped behind a group of four singles, praying she'd blend into the crowd. When she thought she'd lost him, she blew out a breath. Her throat was dry. A soda was a must.

Halfway to the drinks table, she stumbled. Almost fell on her face, actually.

Stupid heels.

She needed to stop borrowing her bestie's outrageous shoes. These were red Louboutins. It was a wonder she'd trusted her with them, after the debacle with the purple ones.

Then again, Val had told her she'd get her shoe back—eventually. Her stupid smile had been smug, too.

Once again, alarm bells. I'm an idiot.

Mel's trip had *nothing* to do with Jared standing by the buffet, speaking to a petite slender blonde. She groaned.

Val called Jared—

"Are you all right?" A male voice jolted her, and she glanced into a pair of green eyes.

The redheaded guy had a hand on her forearm, trying to steady her, but his touch unsettled.

Besides, she couldn't concentrate on her would-be-savior.

Jared? Here?

She was going to kill her so-called bestie.

"I am, thanks." Mel forced her gaze to stay locked on his face. She refused to look over her shoulder.

He'd been facing her direction when she'd tripped but maybe—just maybe—Jared hadn't noticed.

Not with my usual luck.

Red was cuter up close, freckles strewn across the bridge of his nose. He had a dimple in one cheek when he smiled. "Good. I was afraid you'd fall." His fingers slipped away and his eyes raked her frame.

Right. He saw you, clumsy.

Embarrassment washed over her and Mel tried not to squirm in the red dress. It was a darker color than Val's, but in general, red had always been too flashy for her. It had pretty silver embroidery along the sleeves, waist and hemline, but it wasn't her normal sensible style.

Her friend had insisted she buy it the other day when they'd gone shopping. Citing, of course, the low cut neckline and how much cleavage Mel would have in it.

Why on earth had she listened?

The guy's gaze had been appreciative, but it just made her feel naked.

Her cheeks burned all the way up to her ears. She forced a laugh. "I'm good. Clumsy is one of my attributes."

He chuckled. It was a pleasant sound and made her relax.

"I'm Pat." Red shoved his hand out for a shake and she loosened her shoulders.

She reached for his hand and smiled. "Mel. Thanks for the rescue."

"Anytime." He winked, and she found herself grinning.

"There you are. I've been looking for you everywhere."

A tremor shot down her spine, and Mel jumped. "Jared."

He wasn't looking at her. Pat took a step back when Jared moved forward, putting himself between them. "Thanks for helping my girl."

She huffed and stomped her foot, but Pat accepted the detective's intentionally shoulder-jarring handshake.

Not only had he seen her trip, now he was acting possessive?

Damn him.

She was torn between wanting the floor to open her up to swallow her whole and the anger that crept up from her belly.

"Oh," Pat said, before Mel could assure him she was *not* Jared's girl.

Jared slipped his arm around her and pinned her to his side. His smile was easy, he looked genuinely grateful, but the threat in his eyes was obvious.

Her blood boiled.

Pat threw her an apologetic shrug and fled.

She elbowed his side, threw his arm off her and whirled on him. She glared, ignoring the *oomph* of air that slipped from his lips. "You scared him off! He was a perfectly nice guy!"

His dark eyes were intense, but he rubbed his ribs. *Good, hope it hurts.*

"*I* am a perfectly nice guy."

Mel perched her hands on her hips and glared harder. "Generally that's something you show, not tell."

Jared stepped closer, invading her personal space. He snagged an arm around her waist and pulled her close. "I will. If you let me."

She wiggled, but he was too strong. She was aware of every inch of her body touching his and lit up from the inside out. "Dang it, Jared." The whisper fell from her lips.

"Just give me a real chance, Mel."

"I'm going to kill Val."

"Don't kill her. She did us both a favor."

She arched an eyebrow. He'd not bothered denying Val was the reason he was at the party. Should that make her feel better or worse?

"How?"

"She wants you to be happy. Besides, she saved me from an assault charge later. Plus, my dad being mad at me. That guy's with the Fire Department. Pretty sure he's on my dad's shift." His sounded serious, but he shrugged. However, he didn't loosen his hold on her.

Mel rolled her eyes.

"I don't want to see you with someone else."

She stared into his handsome face. His sincerity burned through her. Her heart skipped.

He means what he's saying. Why?

"Jared—"

"You can't judge me without being with me first, Mel."

"I was with you."

"There's more to life than sex."

Mel blinked when he flung her words back at her. "Let me go." The order was weak, and they both knew it. She commanded her gaze away from his full mouth. Tried to banish the memories—the feeling—of his lips moving over hers. If she asked Jared to kiss her, he would.

"Promise me you'll go out with me."

"No."

"Mel." Her name was a plea.

Her stomach somersaulted. "How about we start with today? Now…" What slipped out surprised her, but his slow sexy smile made her heart skip.

"We *are* at a party," Jared said.

"Right."

He loosened his arms, but he didn't release her. Her detective dipped his head down to brush her mouth with his.

It was the barest of touches, but her belly warmed and she clutched his forearms. Mel's head whirled as desire made her dizzy, but he stepped back before she could yell at him for kissing her.

Or worse, crush her lips into his for a real kiss.

How could that little smooch affect her like this?

Jared took her hand and pressed a kiss to her knuckles. "You won't be disappointed."

That's what I'm afraid of.

Jared stared into the pale blue eyes that had haunted his dreams. He'd *begged* her, but he wasn't the least bit ashamed.

She'd *agreed* to give him a shot.

Well, hang with him at the Christmas party in the very least. It wasn't his idea of a date, but it was a start.

God, she was gorgeous. The tiny kiss hadn't been nearly enough.

He needed to calm down, and cool off. Somehow keep his hands to himself so she couldn't accuse him of wanting her only for her body.

Her dark red dress was loose but flowed around her when she walked. It had silver swirls sewn in at the neck, on one billowy sleeve and hem. The shape only hinted at her covered beauty. The design of the threading curled around her waist, hugging her perfect curves.

Made him burn for her.

He wanted to grab her up and hide her from all the male eyes in the damn room. Especially that stupid firefighter.

Jared's heart had dropped to his stomach when he'd seen her almost fall.

Then Big Red had put his hands on her.

Hell. No.

Jealousy had boiled up and he'd rushed over to them. Glared *'this one's mine, get your own'* at the guy.

"Stop looking at me like that," Mel barked.

He snapped to attention and met her eyes. "Like what?"

"Like I'm naked." Her cheeks went pink and his smile slid into a grin.

He dipped low, his mouth millimeters from hers. Ignored her sharp intake of breath. "I won't forget that. Ever."

She smacked his chest. "You're gonna make me change my mind. Don't you have something to go detect?"

Jared straightened and laughed. "I'm off today."

Errr, he was taking time off. He'd pay Carrigan back later. More likely, he owed Cole for giving up his first Saturday back from New York.

God knew the FBI agent couldn't take a day off. She'd pushed until his partner had agreed to work on the case with her.

He'd told Cole about his plans with Mel, and the

guy had flashed dimples and told him to have fun. He'd even thrown in a *'good luck'*. Said he'd handle Carrigan.

Joe had taken his plans in stride, but Jared hadn't really elaborated. The night before, they'd talked a lot about Bennett and what had really happened to Special Agent John Murray.

He didn't have a clue how to get his brother out of the mess without coming clean to Cole and Carrigan, and it wasn't the time. Didn't have enough evidence.

Jared had promised Joe they'd work it out, and they *would*. His brother — and John — would get justice.

He needed to find Carter Bennett.

For today….he refused to think about the case.

Today was for Mel.

He was going to make the most of it.

She huffed and crossed her arms.

Jared ordered himself not to stare. Her dress offered some nice cleavage as it was, and her arms pushing her breasts up didn't help his libido. He reached for his inner southern gentleman and offered her a half-bow. "I just want to spend some time with you. Did you eat yet?"

"No."

"Shall we?" He raised his elbow and Mel took a step toward him, her gorgeous eyes wary. However, she tucked her hand in his arm.

They both shivered as their skin came together and he threatened to lop his cock off when it twitched. He needed to prove to her he wanted her for more than just sex.

He *did*.

Even if he couldn't examine the *why*.

"I was too nervous to eat," she whispered.

Jared frowned at the vulnerability in her gaze. "Why, baby?" He wanted to comfort her. Wipe that look off her face.

She shook her head. "Never mind."

"Mel, I—"

"I'm fine, Jared." She smiled. It was slight. Tentative.

It still made his stomach flutter. "You can talk to me, you know. We can't get to know each other if we don't talk."

Mel studied him. "You're right." She blew out a breath and relaxed again his side.

His heart stuttered. Was she going to give him a real chance?

"I'm no good at these things," she said.

"What things?"

"You know, meeting…guys."

Jared kissed her. Quick and hard; couldn't help it. "You don't need to worry about that. You have a guy. Me." He thumbed his chest with his free hand.

"What if I don't want you?" She smirked.

"I'll either call you a liar or do my best to convince you otherwise."

She laughed and it had him grinning again. "Seems to me calling me a liar isn't the best way to win my affections."

"What is, then?"

"Well, you're not doing too well, since you started off with stalking me."

Jared chuckled and shook his head. "One time doesn't count."

"I'm not so sure about that." Her expression screamed skepticism.

"Well, with your scary threat to call the police, I had to curb my disastrous ways."

She looked as if she was fighting a smile, but finally her delectable mouth curved up. "Yeah, yeah." Mel patted his forearm and shook her head. "My guess is you were busy or something. My little *threat* didn't make you blink." Her dry tone was as endearing as she was.

He laughed yet again. Weight of the case, and worries about his brother lifted from his shoulders a little bit. His problems were far from solved, but Jared felt better than he had in days. "Thanks, Mel." He let out a breath and squeezed her hand.

Her fair eyebrows drew tight and she stilled at his side. "For?"

"Being you, baby. Just…being you."

She looked even more puzzled and he leaned down again, kissing her lightly. His heart tripped when she kissed him back instead of pulling away.

He needed her. Needed this day, this small date away from reality.

Jared was damn sure going to make the best of his time with her.

Chapter Twenty

Taylor watched Manning go into the big house on Montgomery Street for the fourth day in a row. She'd tried to convince herself that she wasn't actually following him.

Finally, she'd accepted she was.

As if Mondays didn't already suck.

She hated feeling guilty, but now she was just trying to be inconspicuous. Was dying to ask Lucas who Manning knew on Montgomery Street, but both males were sharp. Taylor wasn't ready to come clean about watching, and didn't want Manning to overhear, or worse, have Lucas ask questions she couldn't answer.

She'd even opened her mouth three separate times to try, to no avail. Had ended up muttering, "Never mind."

The former FBI agent had shrugged the first time, raised an eyebrow the second, and stared like he thought she was crazy the third.

Maybe you are crazy.

Her gut had never stopped shouting that something with the younger of her two temporary partners wasn't right, even if she still hadn't put her finger on the *what.*

Besides, he was rarely away from the two of them, so *discreet* had to be the name of the game. When she'd worked with Lucas alone last Saturday, Taylor hadn't managed to bring it up.

He'd humored her by spending a few hours at the PD in the morning, but she hadn't been able to keep him past noon. He'd said he wasn't working the day away his first weekend back from the Big Apple, and he'd been serious.

They'd made a few calls and checked out some new lab reports. He'd said he had plans with Andi and their boys, and had even invited Taylor along to the small city's Christmas village to see Santa, and ride the Antioch version of the Polar Express.

She'd declined.

"Suit yourself," the former FBI guy had said. "It'll be fun. Ethan likes you. He asks about you all the time."

She sighed and fought the urge to close her eyes.

Just focus on work. Find out what Manning is up to.

The oversized front door on the big two-story brick monster of a house was shut. It might as well have been a bank vault for all the good sitting there was doing. Dark drapes still completely blocked the windows from the inside. No view for nosy neighbors, let alone sneaky FBI agents.

"Not sneaking. Investigating." Taylor's vocal reassurance did nothing to make her feel better about watching the man she was supposed to be working with.

Her cell blared from its normal resting place in the cup holder.

She jumped. "Shit."

Lucas' name and number lit up the screen.

She scrambled to grab the phone and answer

before it went to voicemail. "Carrigan." Her name came out as a croak. She cleared her throat. It wasn't like he knew where she was.

Nothing to get excited about.

"You okay?"

His deep voice made her square her shoulders in the driver's seat.

"I'm fine. Thank you."

Lucas paused. "All...right."

"How can I help you, Detective?"

"Ah, there's the FBI agent I know and like."

Taylor smirked.

He'd said *FBI agent*, but he'd meant *hard-ass*. Or *pain-in-the-ass*. He was just too polite to say it. *This time.*

"You like me? I'm touched." She kept her statements dry.

Lucas was silent on the other end of the phone for a moment before a chuckle filled her ear. "Why Special Agent Carrigan, was that a *joke*? You're gonna make me think you're actually human. You might wanna stop that."

She grinned in spite of herself, and even though he couldn't see her. "Don't tell anyone."

He laughed again.

The house—a reminder of her current *task*—sucked the light moment away.

Taylor frowned.

Why couldn't she loosen up around Manning like she just had with his partner?

Lucas had made her crack a joke. She couldn't even keep the frown from her face when she worked with Manning.

She'd actually meant the apology she'd presented Manning with when he'd confronted her last week. So, why couldn't she follow through?

Trust him.

His record more than proved he was a good cop.

But what about all the little things that don't add up?

Her conscience ate at her. She should tell Lucas she'd been watching Manning and why. But the *why* was the daunting part.

She had nothing but a gut feeling.

Something is *wrong. Right?*

"Anyway, the reason I'm buggin' ya after five is a good one," Lucas said.

"Oh yeah?" It had to be. He was usually off-the-clock for anything but emergencies when the work day came to an end.

"Got a call from the county lab, and I figured it could hold for morning, but you wouldn't want to wait. If it was me, I'd wanna know, anyway. So this is me, being nice."

Taylor chose not to respond to his jibe about himself. "Must be good."

"DNA came back from the car you and Jared processed. Matches the third unknown blood type found in the trailer. The bloody footprints."

"Carter Bennett."

"Ding ding."

"Well, we suspected it all along. Confirmation is good. Now we just have to find the bastard — bastards, actually."

The ME's office had already confirmed the other two blood types found in the mobile home had belonged to the two victims. They hadn't found any blood matching Pompa's DNA.

The bloody handprints that'd been on the other trailer's skirting had also belonged to Pompa. The blood itself was Brandelyn Willis'.

Taylor suspected she'd died in Pompa's arms. John's reports had cited they were lovers—though the relationship had been over for some time. Part of her felt for Joe Pompa, but only a tiny part. The other part felt some—albeit sick—satisfaction Pompa had lost someone like she'd lost John. Assuming the bastard had cared about the dead girl.

She felt guilty about those immoral feelings, but she couldn't banish them completely. Her normally strong sense of ethics and justice threatened to jump out the window where her heart was concerned, despite her overwhelming struggle with emotion. Her father, a career navy man had raised her—trained her—to suppress her emotions.

"Emotion is weak," had regularly come out of his mouth when she was a child.

Lately, all she could do was *feel,* and she didn't like the taste of vengeance on her tongue. Was trying to deal with it.

She wouldn't cross the line where Pompa was concerned. But the temptation was there.

Taylor fought it every morning when the alarm went off.

"We did get good prints from the other trailer,

though. Blood made for some nice lifts," Lucas said.

They all agreed Pompa had fled and hidden from his attacker under the other trailer. How and when he'd escaped was the mystery.

The boot prints they'd lifted between the two mobile homes matched the bloody ones from inside the trailer. Assumed to belong to Carter Bennett, not Joe Pompa, because the impressions revealed an uneven gait.

"Well, it's good to know, but it doesn't tell us where the hell Bennett and Pompa are," she said.

"Right. But it won't be long now. I can feel it."

Instinct.

Lucas was known for his gut feelings.

Not unlike Taylor herself.

"Lucas."

"Yeah?" The surprise in his tone was evident.

What had he gleaned from the way she'd said his name?

Her heart skipped. She hadn't intended to open her mouth, but it was too late now. "Who does Manning know on Montgomery Street?"

The former FBI agent was silent.

She wished she could read his mind.

"What d'you mean?"

Shit.

Taylor had backed herself into a corner. She'd have to come clean. Have to tell Lucas what she'd observed and *how.* Admit she was still watching Detective Jared Manning.

"There's   a   big   house.   Four-twenty-seven

Montgomery Street."

Lucas laughed, but there was an edge to it she didn't miss. "There're a lot of big houses on Montgomery Street. The neighborhood was built by a northern builder, which is why they're huge and multi-story. Newer places; they've come up in the last ten years or so, I think."

"The address doesn't ring a bell?"

"Nah."

She imagined him shaking his head.

Taylor didn't believe him. Her gut said he wasn't being honest.

Why?

God, you really are a paranoid freak.

"Why're you asking?"

She focused on his question, banishing her instant disbelief. Had *zero* reason to suspect Cole Lucas had just lied to her.

Taylor cleared her throat again.

C'mon. Tell him. You had the balls to bring it up.

Follow through.

Now.

"Carrigan? What're you *not* telling me?" he prodded when she still couldn't find her voice — or her guts. "What does my partner have to do with four-twenty-seven Montgomery Street?"

"I was hoping you could tell me."

"Gotta admit, you lost me."

Despite his words, her instincts flared. Once again, she didn't believe him.

Was the former FBI agent on a fishing expedition

of his own? Playing dumb so she'd put her foot in her mouth?

"Something's not right," Taylor said.

Dead silence.

For a good thirty seconds.

"What're you saying?" His inquiry wasn't loud, but it was a demand. Hard and serious. As if he suspected what she was about to say, but dared *her* to speak the thought.

"I saw him go into that house."

"Saw him?"

"Yes. A few times."

Four, to be exact.

"A few times?" Lucas' question wasn't complicated, but his tone was deadly. "What're— Shit. You're *watching* him?"

"Yes."

Silence again.

Her heart beat so hard her temples throbbed.

She was actually going to say it.

Out. Loud.

"I think your partner's dirty."

Four missed calls.

From Cole.

"What the hell?" Jared whispered as he wrenched his truck door open and stared at the lit-up screen of his cellphone.

He'd spent the evening talking to Joe. Jotting his brother's statement finally. He'd told him to do what he needed to do.

So Jared had started a formal report.

Although, his brother had hedged when he'd brought up the idea of him testifying.

Joe wasn't keen on the idea of ratting out his buddies, but Jared hadn't told him about the two bodies found in California just yet. He would — when the time was right.

The guy was doing some serious grieving, even if he hadn't talked much about it. He hadn't had the heart to lump more death on him.

He turned the key his F-150's engine roared to life. Jared swiped his thumb across his cell's touch screen and hit his contact list. Selected a phone number.

It only rang once.

"Where are you?" his partner demanded without so much as a hello.

"On my way home, why?"

"From where?" This was a bark.

"What the hell's with you?" Jared reared back, bumping his head into the driver seat headrest.

"Where've you been? I called you four times, Jer." There was an edge to Cole's inquisition. Not exactly frantic, but definitely annoyed, with a side of...accusation? Anger?

"Geeze, sorry I didn't call and check in, *Mom*."

"You still haven't answered me."

"*McAuley's*," he said the first thing that came to mind. Then winced. He was lying to his partner — again.

Cole was silent, and the hair stood on the back of

Jared's neck.

He looked around the park down the street from the safe house—where he always left his truck. Couldn't see anyone under the streetlamps that lit up the place, but his gut churned, like something wasn't right.

No shit. Your life isn't right at the moment.

"McAuley's?" his partner asked—finally.

"Yeah, what of it?"

The guy didn't answer right away. "Nothin'."

"Everything okay? Something happen on the case?"

"Why didn't you answer your phone?"

"I guess it was on silent, sorry. It was in my jacket, and I didn't feel it vibrate." True. Still, he didn't usually miss calls from his partner.

"Were you with Mel?"

"No. Why? I was just chillin'. Long day with Carrigan, and all. What's with the twenty questions, partner?"

Cole muttered something that sounded like "yeah, partner" then cleared his throat. Didn't repeat himself. "Everything's cool."

"Doesn't sound like it. You have a fight with Andi?"

"Nah. Was just trying to get a hold of you."

"Right. I got that. What's up?"

He launched into new info from the ME's office about the third blood type from the trailer being matched to the evidence from the car Jared and Carrigan had processed. His voice evened out by the time he was done talking, but Jared's spine tingled.

Something's not right.

Damn if he could tell what.

"Awesome. But why so urgent? It would've held until the morning."

"Yeah, well, maybe if a dude answered his phone it wouldn't make his partner worry about him."

Jared laughed. "You were worried about me?"

"Didn't want you to cheat on the teacher. She might flunk my kid or something."

He smirked. "You don't gotta worry about me cheating on Melody Nash."

"Good, I don't wanna hafta to break your face."

His partner was back to normal, but something still didn't sit right. He pushed it to the back of his mind and forced a second laugh for Cole's benefit. "Yeah, that would be a pity. I'm basically a nice guy, remember?"

Cole's chuckle greeted his ear. "Right. How could I forget?"

"Well, I'm gonna head home. Had my fill of beer and smoke. Speaking of Mel, I need to call her. Have a good night. Promise I'll be a good boy and answer the phone if you call again."

"You do that, partner."

Chapter Twenty-One

Mel turned back the covers just as her cell rang from her nightstand. She glanced at the clock and frowned.

Ten minutes to eleven. Who the heck — ?

She plopped down on her bed and made a grab for the phone. Her heart tripped. Jared's name and number flashed, and she had to take a fortifying breath. "Hello?"

"I didn't think you were going to answer."

She could hear the smile in his words and her stomach quivered. "It is late."

"I didn't wake you?" This time concern greeted her ear, and she heard linens rustling, as if he was sitting up in bed.

Mel tried to ignore the memories of his bed…him in it — naked — as they danced into her head. "No. I was about to hit the sack."

"Sorry for calling so late. Got home late, and I just wanted to hear your voice. Even your voicemail would've done."

She smiled. "I'm glad you called."

"Good. What're you wearing?" Jared dripped sex now.

Mel laughed, praying it didn't sound nervous. Glanced down at her simple pink and purple plaid PJ boxers and matching pink tank. Despite the chill outside, she always slept in a similar outfit. Tended to overheat at night. "You can't ask me that. It breaks the rules," she managed.

He laughed, and the sound wrapped around her like an embrace. "Rules, already?"

"I told you I need us to take it slow. You said all right. That you understood."

"I know. This is me doing that. That's why I called instead of coming over. I can't stop thinking about you. How beautiful you looked in that dress Saturday. How cute you looked on Sunday when we went to Dixie's. I'm obsessed with how your lips taste when I kiss you."

Her heart skipped and she swallowed.

Jared at her doorstep didn't sound like such a bad thing, but she wasn't going to admit it aloud. Mel forced her shoulders to relax and slid into her bed. She gripped the phone tighter and pulled her covers over her legs.

He'd looked hot Saturday, too, *and* Sunday when he'd take her out to lunch. Both times in tight dark jeans hugging his thighs and rear. Sunday's pale blue polo had clung to his torso and made the darkness of his hair, eyes and skin tone even more prominent. Cowboy boots instead of the combat ones she'd seen him in every other time.

Irresistible.

Had it only been four days since he'd ambushed her at the party?

Four blissful, wonderful days unlike any other Mel had ever experienced.

Four days felt like four months.

It was funny—he'd not dropped her off at her

house until midnight, after the *Friends First* Party, but he'd called her when he'd made it back to his apartment and they'd talked until after three.

Then he'd taken her out to lunch at Dixie's — a local mom and pop diner that was an Antioch institution. They hadn't met up on Monday, but he'd called that evening.

This morning, the best Tuesday she'd had in a long time, he'd texted.

He'd explained he was working a case and wouldn't be home until late, but he'd talk to her if he could.

Mel had been disappointed at the thought of not talking to him. Was glad he'd called now, even if it was past her bedtime.

Getting to know him was easy. Natural. Fun. Talking to him, laughing with him. He was charming. Funny. Witty even. Turned out her detective wasn't shallow. Or self-centered.

He was…perfect.

Made her feel beautiful…giddy, and petrified all wrapped into one moment after the other. She was starting to crave him.

This could be bad.

She didn't like *vulnerable.*

Mel kept scolding herself to take it one day at a time. They were having fun. There was no reason it would change. Their relationship — if they could even call it that — was in its infancy, no matter how natural it felt.

No matter how *Jared* made her feel.

"Mel?"

"Here. Sorry."

"You okay, baby?"

A tremor shot down her spine. "I'm good. What are *you* wearing?" she blurted.

Way to keep it PG, Melody Nash.

He laughed again. "Guess."

She shivered. The man was talking to her on the phone naked; didn't have to say it. But neither could she. "Flannel pajamas."

"Nope."

"You gonna keep me guessing?"

Why are you playing along?

"I think you know, baby. You just don't want to say it. Why don't you go first?" Jared said. His voice dropped, thicker, sexier.

"Why?" Mel smiled.

"Are you gonna make me break the rules and come over? God knows I want to be with you right now."

Her heart sped into overdrive. "You'd have to get dressed first."

"I have a trench coat."

She giggled, relaxing into her bed. She lay down and tried not to admit — to herself *or* him — she wouldn't have a problem with him joining her.

If she told him, it'd be a dare he wouldn't refuse.

"Well?"

"Slow, Jared. Slow."

"I love when you say my name. Say it again. And tell me what you're wearing. You've kept me waiting long enough."

Mel's breath caught. "I'm wearing what I always wear to bed, Jared. Shorts and a tank."

"What's under it?"

"Nothing."

She heard his audible intake of breath.

"You're killing me." This was a half-groan.

"Me? Why?"

"Because I have a fantastic memory. That's not what you *always* wear to bed."

Heat scorched her cheeks and her limbs warmed. It had little to do with her comforter covering her. "Let's not talk about that."

"Why not?"

She shook her head, even though he couldn't see her. "Because. I—"

"Slow or not, I want you, Melody Nash. I can be a good boy and wait until you're ready."

Mel trembled and desire settled low in her belly. How could the man have her so hot and bothered?

Because you have a memory, too.

Closing her eyes, she tried not to picture his bedroom. His large bed covered by rich red and black bedding.

Jared lying naked as the day he was born, gloriously muscled. In her mind he was touching himself.

She swallowed a gasp as her thighs quivered.

No. Way.

Get that out of your head.

Now.

If she didn't, she'd beg him to get out that trench coat.

"I want you, too." The truth tumbled out. The confession unwanted. She cringed.

Jared groaned. "I need to respect you. But I want to come over. We're separated by a five-minute drive. What do you want me to do, baby?" A question, but it was almost a demand.

Say the word and he'll come over.

Mel looked down at her body and shook her head. Too-rounded hips. Overly thick thighs. Her belly was too soft, and her bottom too big. Despite desire warming her, she lost what little nerve his words had built up. "I need slow, Jared. Slow. Please."

"Okay."

If he was disappointed, he hid it well, but her stomach fluttered anyway.

"I'm sorry," she whispered.

"Don't be sorry for being honest with me. Always be honest. But if *I'm* honest, I wish to God I could have you in my arms right now."

Whatever she'd planned to say dissolved.

I want that, too.

She couldn't tell him. Being naked with him under the influence of alcohol was one thing.

Totally sober?

Mel didn't have the guts.

"When can I see you again?" he asked.

"When are you free this week?"

He paused, as if he hadn't thought she'd agree. "I'm pretty involved in a case right now. Can we play it by ear? I want to take you to dinner."

"Yes. My evenings are open."

"Good. I'll call you every night. Until you let me come over and hold you. I want to touch you. I need to kiss you again."

Her heart stuttered. Silence fell, but when he grunted, heat suffused her whole body again.

"Jared?"

"Mel."

He moaned her name and a tremor inched down her spine.

"Where's your hand?" The phone gave her some unknown courage, but she wanted to hear him say what she already knew. Mel's picture of him in that king-sized bed pinned itself to her brain. She remembered his erection, his pecs, his six-pack. Her core throbbed.

"Where do you want it to be?"

Jared groaned and she closed her eyes.

Of its own accord, her hand started at her neck and traveled downward. Her palm followed the curve of her breast then her belly. She stopped short at the waistband of her boxers.

No way. You're not actually thinking about doing this.

"Don't leave me hangin'. Where do you want my hand?"

"On me. Touching me. Fingers inside me." Rushed, the truth came out, as unwanted as her previous confession. Her cheeks burned.

"Shit, baby. Don't tempt me. I thought we decided I couldn't come over."

"Touch yourself, Jared."

The order shocked them both, if his silence was any indication. Then he panted, and Mel's breath hitched.

She could see that powerful body writhing on the sea of red sheets. His back arched, muscles of his wrist taut as he pumped himself.

Thinking of her.

Wanting *her*.

The pulse between her legs grew insistent, and her hand wandered. Her nipples strained against the soft cotton of her tank and her skin was hot, damp. She wanted to be naked.

With Jared.

"Baby," he grunted. "Where are *your* hands?"

"Where do you want them?" Mel shut out all her insecurities. It didn't matter that she'd never contemplated phone sex in her life. Had never even masturbated. Sure, she'd touched herself in the shower, who hadn't?

But this…

Jared.

This gorgeous man wanted her. The night they'd been together, he'd treated her with respect. Had been concerned with her pleasure, had been a fantastic lover.

One night and he'd showed her more care than David had over the *years* they'd been together.

She'd be with Jared like this for now.

Until she could work up the guts to ask him to come to her house and take her for real.

It wasn't going to be as good as the real thing.

It broke the *slow* rule she'd locked down.

Mel didn't care.

"Take off your shorts."

She didn't hesitate. "Hold on." When he said okay, she set the phone on her pillow. She shoved her boxers off her hips and down, kicking them across her bed. She whipped off her tank top and spiked it to the carpet. "Jared?"

He grunted her name. "Take your top off."

"I'm already naked."

"Oh, God," he groaned.

Her whole body was on fire with just those two words. She had the power to make his voice wobble and they weren't even in the same room.

"You're going to come for me. You're gonna scream my name."

Heat rolled over her body at his declarations, as sure as a caress. Her clit throbbed, begging for a touch. Grasping for courage and a clear head, she took a breath. "You're going to come for me, too, Jared."

He panted. "Oh, God."

The repetition made her even hotter for him.

Mel grinned. "Does that do something to you?"

"Fuck yes..." The rest of his statement was garbled, but her name was in there somewhere. Jared cleared his throat. "Baby, if I was there with you right now, do you know what I'd do to *you*?"

She remembered the play of his defined muscles as he rose above her the night they'd met. The feel of his skin under her seeking fingers. The ache in her loins shot up a notch. "No, tell me."

He moaned before he continued. "I'd kiss you. Deep. Until you begged for more. Then I'd kiss my way down your neck. Tease your nipples and suck them until you called my name and pulled my hair. Then I'd work my way downward, touch your thighs, kiss them before I have my first taste of you. You'll be hot and wet for me. Are you wet now?"

Waves of heat and need rolled over her, and she rocked her hips. Undulated and whispered his name. Her fingers shook as she parted her own folds. She was slick and her clit throbbed at the barest pass over it. "Yes..." Mel caressed herself and called his name, remembering the blunt tips of his fingers sliding into her. She inserted one finger and thrust, teasing the swollen bundle of nerves at the top of herself with her thumb.

"God, you taste so good. I remember it. I want more. If I was there, I'd suck your clit into my mouth. Rub my tongue all over it until you screamed. I'd shove my fingers in you and make you beg me to thrust. Then I'd lick you and suck you until you came in my mouth. All over my face. Are you touching yourself? Rub your clit, baby. Tell me what it feels like."

"Jared..." Mel threw her head back on a moan, adding a finger to her sex and thrusting both harder. "God...it feels good."

He chuckled, it was a satisfied sound that made a tremor slide down her spine.

"Baby, you have me so hot..."

"Are you hard?"

"Yes. Aching for you."

"Pump your hand and tell me what it feels like." She whimpered, circling her clit with her thumb again. She bit her lip to keep from crying out when she pressed down. Pleasure shot through her, and her inner thighs quaked.

"Mel," Jared breathed. "This is supposed to be about you."

"No," she whispered, still moving her hand. "It's about *us*."

"Oh, God." His breathing was strained, and she pictured his palm moving fast, the plump head disappearing and reappearing as he moved up and down.

Her breasts rose and fell as their conversation faded and she stroked herself to the sound of his panting.

She saw that huge, defined chest heaving as he struggled for normal breath. He worked himself and made her blood boil. Her body jerked as climax crested.

"Close," Jared growled.

Mel whispered his name when he called hers, closing her eyes and pushing her head into her pillow as orgasm roared over her.

"I'm coming for you, baby." The words were guttural, broken, and somehow made her burn even more.

"Me too. Now," she breathed. Her hips jerked up off her bed and she screamed his name.

"Come hard for me."

She couldn't find a verbal answer, but her core pulsed, as if his order made her body follow his command.

The intensity of her orgasm stole her breath as aftershocks of pleasure traveled down her limbs. Mel collapsed into her sweat-damp sheets, trembling. "Oh, God," she croaked.

He chuckled. "I wish I was there to see your face, baby. Your skin flushed. Glowing pink. Because of me. Your hair all over your pillow. Your lips begging for a kiss."

Mel whimpered and wiggled.

I want that, too.

The cool air of her bedroom caressing her naked body was a relief. Cleared her head. She shut down the embarrassment at the thought of what she'd just done. Focused on what Jared was saying. Sweet words that she clung to like a blanket.

"Holding my cell to my ear isn't as good as holding you. I want to make love to you again, Mel. Sleep with you in my arms."

She sighed as unexpected emotion hit her chest. Her heart skipped. She wanted to believe him. = What the heck was she supposed to say?

"Jared…"

"I won't push you, baby." The whisper had a touch of sadness that flipped her stomach.

"I can't wait to see you again." A new rush truth fell from her lips and Mel closed her eyes. Fear of getting hurt by this gorgeous cop warred with her desire for him.

Jared isn't David.

She chanted it, but insecurities about her body

chided.

Things her ex said over and over, then the blame she'd always brought upon herself for his choice to cheat pushed away Jared's praise.

Her detective told her she was beautiful. Could Mel believe he *meant* it?

She had the sudden urge to ask what his plans were for Christmas but lost her nerve.

Thanks to the countdown she was doing with her kids, Mel recalled that the big day was eight days away, and they'd been on two dates, not including talking on the phone daily. He'd think she was either nosy or clingy.

She didn't have to be an expert on men to know neither would work for a guy like Jared.

"I can't wait to see you either. Do you like Italian food?" He yanked her from her stupid brain, and she hollered at herself to talk to him.

Be normal.

"I do. How about Rizzoli's? I love that place."

"Sure."

Mel heard his smile again.

For some reason, she wanted to cry.

"Tomorrow night? Unless work changes it? I'll let you know as soon as I can," he said.

"Sounds good." She closed her eyes and took a breath. "Well, it's late."

"It is. I have to hop in the shower."

She shivered at the thought of what he had to clean up, as well as his beautiful body with rivulets of water running all over it. "Goodnight, Jared." She forced the closing out evenly.

"Night, baby."

Right when her thumb hovered over the *'end'* icon, he called her name.

"Yes?"

"Dream of me, baby."

Mel grinned. "Like I have a choice about that."

Jared laughed and her heart fluttered.

Chapter Twenty-Two

ole Lucas said nothing as he sat in the passenger seat of her Impala, but both of his fists were clenched tight on his lap.

Taylor licked her lips and took a breath. It wasn't often she was speechless, but what the heck could she say to the guy?

He'd said, "*Show me.*"

She had.

Lucas obviously didn't like it.

They'd worked all day together — Manning, Lucas and Taylor.

Eddie had called from California. There was buzz about Bennett gathering new cronies and organizing a big hit on another train carrying high dollar vehicles. The shipment was in a few weeks.

The FBI agent's CI was going to participate, and was ferreting information back to Eddie as it came. The only thing he could confirm was that Bennett wasn't back in LA — yet.

Her former co-worker had said he'd keep her in the loop.

They had to get through Christmas, which was a week away — from today.

Eddie had joked that even thieves took a break for presents.

So she and her two detective partners had spent the afternoon strategizing on where Bennett could be and how he was getting there. He was injured — they knew that. Just not how badly.

The new info made it clear he wasn't dead in a hole somewhere, but they needed more. Needed to find him.

They'd made contacts with local law enforcement and worked their way out, calling in favors from fellow cops to keep an eye out for stolen cars. All three had called every last cop, detective or deputy they could think of.

Taylor called every FBI offices between Texas and California to watch for Bennett, too.

It was a good day.

She felt like they'd accomplished something, though neither Bennett nor Pompa were in cuffs.

Unfortunately, in all the info Eddie had shared, Bennett hadn't mentioned Pompa, and neither had the CI heard anything.

Joe Pompa's whereabouts was still unknown.

Manning had been in a hurry to leave the PD when five o'clock had rolled around. Said he had a date.

Lucas had ribbed him about some kindergarten teacher, but Taylor had been poring over a report and only paid half-attention to their banter.

The younger detective had left then, and she'd finished up a few emails while Lucas hovered in his cubicle, suddenly sullen.

They hadn't discussed the phone call where she'd said the words since it'd happened — and somehow last night felt like a week ago.

Bottom line — Lucas had told her she was full of shit. He *knew* Manning, he'd sworn. Asserted his partner wasn't dirty. He'd even said, "End. Of."

However, she hadn't missed his watchful gaze all day. He'd been keener than normal. *He* watched Manning, too. Conversation might not have revealed his intentions, because he'd been pretty normal, but Taylor could *see* the suspicion. Hear the subtle questions — she recognized him analyzing everything. As a trained observer should.

"You ready?" His deep voice had been too close for comfort when she'd signed off the computer less than an hour before.

"Ready for what?" She'd whirled the chair around and met his eyes.

The former FBI agent had been reclined against the side of his cubicle, his posture appearing relaxed, but his jaw locked, belying the loose shoulders and the boot he had propped up. When he crossed his arms, his biceps bulged and forearms flexed. Tension had rolled off him. "You need to show me something, don't you?"

It only took her a half-second to get with the program. She'd nodded.

Now they sat in her car. The air was stifled and her chest hurt. She felt for him.

She really did.

Taylor had only known them for a few weeks, but Lucas and Manning were close. Their friendship went beyond partners. Beyond work. They were like brothers. Involved in each other's families — personal lives.

Manning had jogged down the street moments before, a brown paper bag in his arms.

They'd watched him head into the bar to pick up his order. First stop after leaving the station.

Then she'd driven a route that'd become familiar, except that Lucas' partner had rounded the block twice before he'd pulled into the Freedom Park. Being December, the place was deserted, with only one other car parked in front of the pavilion. No people in sight.

Taylor had slunk the Impala down the street and parked around the corner.

The big oak tree dominating the front yard of the house to their left hung over the sidewalk and offered some cover.

Following the younger detective was getting more difficult.

Manning looked around a lot, upping the observation of his surroundings.

Like a cop should.

She had to give him that. She hadn't been caught yet. Right?

Does he suspect something?

"So much for a date." Lucas spoke for the first time since his partner had left *McAuley's.*

Taylor didn't remark; didn't know what to say.

Silence fell again and she studied the wide porch, the front door. Scanned all the windows of the big house, even the ones upstairs.

Still can't see inside. Dammit.

"Do you know the girl he's dating?" she finally asked.

"Yes."

"Let me guess, she doesn't live at four-twenty-seven Montgomery Street."

He shook his head, an odd look on his face. Lucas opened his mouth to say something then sighed. He frowned.

"What do you know that you're *not* saying?" she prodded when the FBI agent-turned-detective didn't speak.

"Nothing," he said a bit too fast.

"Nothing?" Taylor cocked her head to one side and appraised him.

His expression hardened, but she couldn't read him. He was suddenly pure concrete. "Let's just not jump to conclusions."

"Who said we're jumping? I've been studying his behavior. There's a pattern. And more than one thing that doesn't add up."

"Great, you're profiling my partner," Lucas muttered. He rubbed his cheek. The five o'clock shadow made a scratching noise.

She narrowed her eyes. "I'm doing my job."

"No. Your job is to work this case. Find Pompa and Bennett. Bring them in. I know you're determined, and I respect that. But I think you're seeing something that's not here."

"Am I?"

"I know my partner a hell of a lot better than you do, is what I'm saying."

"I don't dispute that. Perhaps you're too close to see what's *here*."

"Me?" he scoffed, then pointed to her chest. "I think *you're* reading into something you *think* you see.

Which, by the way, you've yet to name. *'Something's not right'* isn't evidence. Besides, I'm not chasing the guy who murdered my fiancé. By the way, you've gotta tell me how you got your boss to let you stay on the case."

Taylor froze. "You checked up on me."

"Damn straight I did. You accused my partner of being dirty. I think you're too close to this case, Special Agent."

"Obviously you and I will never see eye-to-eye on that particular facet of the investigation," she said, intentionally ignoring Lucas' accusation.

He laughed — *laughed.*

She frowned.

"This isn't a *facet* of any investigation, Taylor Carrigan. Jared Manning is not a dirty cop. I'd bet my badge on it."

"Baby?" Jared kept his back facing his older brother.

Joe's head was in his hands, his whole form soaked in sorrow. Exuding it, actually.

The burger on the plate in front of him had gone long cold. One bite reshaped the bun. French fries were still in the Styrofoam container, untouched.

The guy hadn't even wanted a beer.

"Hi, Jared." Mel's bright, sweet — *perfect* — voice made him wince. "I'm almost ready. Are you coming to get me, or are we meeting at Rizzoli's?"

He closed his eyes and sucked in a breath. "I'm sorry. I hate to do this, but I'm gonna hafta cancel."

"Oh, okay." If she was disappointed she hid it well. "Everything all right?"

No.

"Yeah. This case is just killin' me."

"Will you be okay?"

Her concern had him smiling.

Jared just made sure to keep his back to Joe. "Yes, ma'am, I think so."

"You're…" she paused. Didn't continue.

"I'm what?"

"Making me worry about you." Mel rushed her words.

He laughed. "Sounds like you think that's a bad thing."

"Well, I don't want to be one of those clingy girlfriends."

Girlfriend?

She considered herself his girlfriend?

His heart sped into overdrive. Jared's limbs warmed. His tongue was thick in his mouth and he wanted to speak sweet nothings in her ear until she melted and moaned like when they'd had phone sex.

"Jared?"

"I'm here." He had to clear his throat. "And you can cling to me anytime, baby."

She laughed and it heated him even more. "Such a guy thing to say."

He grinned. "I *am* a guy." Jared heard the screech of wood against the linoleum and glanced over his shoulder.

Joe didn't look at him as he stood, but he did push

the chair in.

His heart plummeted to his stomach as reality made his head spin.

My brother needs me now.

He lost track of what Mel was saying. Guilt hit him in gut. His desire to be with her warred with where his head needed to be right now. With Joe. "Baby, I'm really sorry, but I gotta go."

"Oh, okay. I understand."

Of course she does.

Which made Jared feel even more torn. "Listen, I'll call you when I get home, if it's not too late."

"Okay. Be careful. Be Safe."

He managed another smile. "You know it. Always. I'll see you soon. Promise."

"You'd better."

He could hear her joy. See her gorgeous smile in his head.

Hanging up just about killed him. He pocketed his cell.

Joe was in the living room, but instead of reclining in comfort in on the couch, loveseat or one of the two overstuffed chairs, he was on the floor in the corner next to the entertainment center. Balled up, back against the wall, head bowed. "You should go be with your woman," his brother croaked.

"No way." Jared slid the ottoman close and sat a few feet away.

"Don't be stupid."

"I'm not being stupid." He tapped the guy's sneaker-clad foot with one of his boots. "I might be *with* stupid, though."

His brother smirked, but shook his head. "Yeah. You're right. I'm a fucking idiot."

He frowned. "Nah. Shit happens. We'll work this all out, big brother."

"This FBI chick…Carri-whatever, she's after me pretty hard."

"Carrigan." Jared nodded. "Yeah, she is. But I have your statement. I know what happened at the trailer. And if you turned yourself in, we can work it out. I promise."

"Fuck." He dragged his palm down his unshaven face. "Prison."

"I know. But it's better than death. Or being on the run for the rest of your life."

Doubt crossed his brother's eyes. The room was dim, but Jared didn't miss the pain darting across his expression.

He reached down and squeezed Joe's thick forearm. "I got your back, bro."

"So you keep saying," he whispered.

"You don't believe me?" Jared cocked his head to one side, and studied his older brother.

"I do. It scares the shit out of me. I don't want to jeopardize your job. Your life."

"Joe." He waited until his brother looked up at him. Held his gaze. "You're my brother. My blood. As my partner would say, end. Of."

One corner of his mouth shot up and he nodded. "Partner, huh?"

"Yeah. His name's Cole. He's a good dude."

"You're close?"

"Yeah. APD isn't that big, and we're like a family."

Again, agony dominated Joe's strong jaw line and high cheekbones.

He sighed. "Anything you wanna talk about?" Jared still hadn't told him two other members of his crew had been killed. He couldn't. His current expression—one he wore most often lately—discouraged it even more.

"I lost my burner phone."

"Not a shocker. Probably smart of you, actually."

"I haven't been able to talk to my guys. Rick's like a mother hen. I'm sure he's worried. Mack and Rowdy were Team-Carter when I left, but still. I wanna make sure they're okay."

Oh. Shit.

Jared forced a nod, but Joe eyed him with suspicion.

"What? Do you know something?"

"I didn't say anything."

His brother laughed. "Right. You have that look you always get when you're hiding something. Like you did when you lied about something as a kid."

He arched an eyebrow. "I have a look?"

"Yeah. Only someone who knows you well could pick it up. Spill it, little brother."

Shit. Has Cole seen 'my look?'

Jared shook his head. "Nothin' to spill."

"Bullshit." Now he quirked one dark eyebrow and Jared tried not to smile, despite the news he didn't want to share.

Like lookin' in a mirror.

The intense glare in his Joe's eyes made his thoughts sober. His stomach jumped.

"You have bad fucking news. Just hit me with it. Faster the better."

There was no reaching for police professionalism when Jared read the fear and dread in his brother's gaze. "I'm sorry." The apology came out as a croak.

Joe made noise in his throat.

"Richard Wilkins and Sean McKinley are dead."

"No." His brother slumped and buried his face in his cupped hands. His shoulders shook and Jared's heart broke.

He scooted off the ottoman and landed next to his brother on the carpet. Threw his arm around the guy.

They didn't speak, but Joe didn't push him away, either, so he took that as a good sign. He let his brother grieve in silence.

"Get off me."

The muffled order minutes later made him smile.

He did his brother's bidding. Dropped his arm to his lap and intentionally rocked into Joe's shoulder. "What? You're too old for a hug?"

"Fuck off."

Jared chuckled.

"You know I've never been good at that shit."

"What shit?"

Joe wouldn't meet his eyes. "Being comforted."

"Yeah, I remember. But you were always the one doing the comforting, anyway. To me. Your whiny little brother."

A ghost of a smile played at his lips. "A guy's gotta do what a guy's gotta do."

"Yeah, I wouldn't have survived childhood if it wasn't for you."

"Ditto."

"Why'd you take off? My parents—the Mannings—wanted you, Joe. Mom—Amy—grieved. Dad—Jason—looked for you. Hell, the cops looked for you. You just *poofed*. I think Mom was just as devastated as I was. Maybe more. She felt like she failed you. I missed you like hell."

An unnamed emotion flickered across Joe's face. He averted his gaze, staring at the blackout curtains on the closest window.

The wall between them was palpable.

Jared was startled. Not because his brother shut down—that he understood. He'd forgiven him for leaving years ago, even if he'd never had the balls to ask why.

Cold fury burned in his brother's eyes when their gazes finally met. Joe made two tight fists and planted them in his lap. "I left for you."

"*For* me?"

"So you could have a normal family. Normal parents. Cute kid sister. Without your fuckup of an older brother."

"You're not a fuckup." He was half-surprised Joe remembered Jenna.

"Was then, am now. Always will be. Thanks to that asshole."

"What asshole? What're you talking about?"

"Remember the Danvers family?"

Jared reared back. "Yes." They'd been removed from that foster family when the parents had been accused of physical abuse. He didn't remember much—had been too young—and the couple had never touched him, though some of the kids in the huge household had often worn bruises. "What about them?"

"Daddy Danvers."

"Did he hit you?" He frowned.

Why is this news to me?

"Sometimes, but that's not what fucked me up."

He stared into his brother's dark eyes.

Joe averted his gaze again and flexed his jaw.

Silence stretched.

"Joe—"

"He raped me, all right?"

Air whooshed from Jared's lungs. Damn good thing he was sitting or he would've fallen on his ass for sure. "What?"

"Over and over. I went to him so he'd leave you the hell alone."

"Joe—"

"I wasn't one of the ones he beat the shit out of, because I went *willingly*." His brother spoke in a monotone, and he still wouldn't look up.

The room spun and he reached for the ottoman to steady himself.

"So that's why I'm fucked up. *Why* I couldn't be normal. Why I couldn't stay in Antioch and the reason I couldn't keep my shit together for *her*."

He doesn't mean Mom.

Jared's heart pounded so hard Joe's words faded in and out, like he was about to pass the fuck out.

Silence fell again, because what the *hell* was he supposed to say?

Joe cleared his throat what felt like hours later. "I can't believe I fucking told you that."

"I can't believe you hadn't told me before." He pushed the statement out as his brother finally looked his way.

"It was a long time ago." Joe wore a sad smile. "What happened happened. It's okay. I'm so fucking proud of you, J-man."

Just like his brother move the spotlight off himself.

"Joe. We should talk about this."

"Hell no."

"Joe."

"Jared." He sucked in a breath and patted Jared's arm. "It was a long fucking time ago. I'm over it. I accepted my lot in life. I'm glad you got out." The guy's jaw was locked.

He sighed. "You're not over it. And *you* are not the choices you've made." He wouldn't get anywhere pushing him, but he didn't regret saying it.

"Just drop it," Joe growled.

Jared tilted his head against the living room wall. "Okay. Okay. But do me a favor?"

"What?"

"When you wanna talk, gimme a call. No judgment. You're my brother, and I love ya."

Silence greeted his ears for the third time, but

when he met Joe's eyes again, his brother's lips were curved up.

"I'm so damn sorry about your friends, Joe."

The smile fell off, but he nodded. "Carter killed them. That little fucker."

"Yeah, that's what the FBI thinks, too. I need to convince Carrigan he killed Murray, too."

His brother sighed, and helplessness darted across his face.

"We'll get him, big brother. I promise."

"Now I hope he bleeds to death."

He hadn't told him all the details to the case, but he had told Joe about the car with Bennett's blood in it.

"Hey, if Rick and Mack are dead, where's Rowdy?"

"Eric Vargas?"

Joe nodded.

"Haven't found him. We don't know if he's dead, or took off—with or without Bennett. Are you sure no one was with him at the trailer?"

His brother nodded. "I'm sure. Even outside, it was just Carter. God. Bran." The guy's Adams apple bobbed as he swallowed and he closed his eyes.

"I'm sorry for the reminders of that night."

"I loved her," Joe blurted. He grabbed the cross around his neck with white knuckles.

Ah, she gave it to him.

He didn't have to say it.

Jared snapped his mouth shut. It was the first time his brother had spoken of the dead girl since the night he'd mentioned the TV show she'd liked. "I knew ya'll were together."

Joe shook his head. "We weren't." Undisguised agony made his dark eyes shiny. "I fucked that up, too."

So Brandelyn Willis is the 'her' from earlier.

When he launched into the story of his heartache, Jared listened.

Unlike the childhood trauma, Joe seemed to need to talk about the woman he loved. With every sentence, the more fragile his tough older brother became. The more he started to fall apart.

"You have a woman," he croaked. He grappled for Jared's forearm, his eyes imploring.

"Yeah. She's great. Her name's Melody. Mel." He felt himself smiling.

"Don't fuck it up, J-man. Hold onto her."

Mel.

He needed to see her.

Now.

Chapter Twenty-Three

er eyes were frantic when she whipped the door open, and she clutched the short robe to her neck when a gust of wind blew by.

Jared shivered, but it had little to do with the weather. He clenched his jaw to keep emotion at bay.

"Jared. What—?"

He wanted to push her back into her small house and grab her up. Take her mouth, then take *her*, but he dug for manners. "Can I come in?"

Mel backed up, nodding. "Jared, what's wrong?"

He couldn't answer.

Just kicked the door shut and walked toward her in the living room.

Her robe stopped mid-thigh.

He tried not to stare, or imagine what she was wearing beneath it. Their phone sex session reminded him it wasn't much. Jared needed to hold her. Kiss her. Remind himself she was real. She was in his life.

Seeing Joe so broken over everything—childhood trauma that should've never happened. His friends being murdered. Losing the woman he loved.

It was affecting Jared's ability to deal with what was being thrown at him.

Nothing had rocked him to his core more than his brother's imploring dark eyes and urging to hold Mel to him. Not lose her.

Joe had given him his blessing to go to her.

As a matter of fact, he'd told Jared he needed some alone time after all the revelations.

With his frantic urge to get to Mel, he hadn't even made sure his brother was really okay.

Yeah, he's not. He's not gonna be okay for a long time.

Joe had practically pushed him out the door, and Jared had run down the street to get his truck from the park.

He couldn't seem to make his mind or his mouth work. Grabbed her wrist and drew her into his arms. Needed her against his chest. Needed to feel her body, her warmth.

She didn't fight him. Mel's arms shot around his middle and he pulled her closer.

He closed his eyes and rested his cheek against the top of her head.

"You're so cold."

He'd accidently left his leather jacket at the safe house. He couldn't tell her that. "I'm good. Now that I have you in my arms, I'm good." His sentences were thick, broken.

One lamp lit the room. The place was charming, homey. Totally Mel. Simple décor. Comfortable-looking overstuffed couch, loveseat and recliner, both dark blue. Nice sized TV. The room was set up for conversation, the small fireplace it's focus, not her entertainment center.

Worry creased her brow when she lifted her head and met his eyes. "What's wrong, Jared? I've never seen you like this. You're shaking."

"I just—"

"Did something happen tonight? After we talked?"

Jared couldn't talk to her about his case. His brother. "Work," he croaked.

Understanding softened her features and she squeezed her arms around him. "Okay. You can't tell me. It's okay. I get it."

"I broke the rules," he whispered, shattering the short silence that'd descended.

"What? Like the law?"

"Me and you. You wanted slow. I showed up here, I'm sorry, baby."

Mel offered a soft smile. "It's okay."

"I just…needed you."

"I'm glad you came. I'm glad you're all right." She rested her hand against his cheek. Her thumb moved back and forth against his stubble, and the light caress shot a tremor down his spine.

Jared groaned, turning his face to press a kiss into her palm. "I need you," he repeated.

Her crystal blue eyes widened, but she met his lips when he dipped his head down to take her mouth. When she wrapped her arms around his neck, he deepened their kiss. He was already hard, his zipper biting into his cock.

She moaned and his balls tingled.

"I want you," he said into the kiss.

Mel shivered, breaking the seal of their mouths. Stared up at him.

"I'm sorry," he croaked. "Damn, I'm pushing you." He released her with one last caress to her flushed cheek. "I promised you slow, so, I'll just go. God, I'm sorry."

She lowered her lashes. "Jared." Reached for his hand, and he let her take it, entwine their fingers. "I don't want you to go. I want to be with you."

He froze. His mouth was dry and a shiver racked his frame.

She tugged on his hand when he failed to speak.

"Baby—" Words dissolved when she finally met his gaze again.

"I'm ready. I don't want to wait. Phone sex isn't cutting it." A smile played at her lips.

Jared smirked.

Mel came back to him, standing tiptoed to press her mouth to his.

He groaned and plastered her to his chest, kissing her until neither of them could breathe.

They stumbled to her bedroom, neither able to stop their lip-lock for longer than two seconds.

Discarding clothing was a blur, and Jared panted her name when she was naked in his arms. They stood next to her bed. Her curves hit him in all the right places. Her full breasts flat against his pecs, her pelvis flush to his. His cock was pleasantly trapped against her warm flesh. It pounded, demanding he push her back onto the bed and get inside her.

He met her lips when she tilted her face up with another invitation, and he melded their tongues, tasting her while she plundered his mouth. He broke the kiss only because he needed to breathe.

Mel's hands were all over his back and ass, and his

blood was already boiling.

"Baby, let me look at you."

Her cheeks went crimson. She shook her head, snuggling even closer.

He chuckled, but she whimpered, and it wasn't in pleasure.

Jared lowered himself onto the edge of her bed and looked up at her, but she wouldn't meet his gaze.

Her face was turned to one side, her eyes squeezed shut.

His stomach flipped and he grabbed her hands. Tugged when she still made no move to look at him. "Mel, what's wrong?"

She muttered something that sounded like, "No alcohol," under her breath.

"What?"

Mel swung her head toward him. She opened her eyes but cast her gaze upward. Her teeth were biting into her plump, kiss-swollen bottom lip.

Jared tried to pull her down to him, but she straightened her back. Wouldn't come. "Mel."

When those pale eyes finally met his, they were shiny with tears.

His heart stuttered.

"You...I—"

"What, baby?" he whispered.

She was upset about something, and not knowing was about to kill him.

His gut tightened.

She looked at his naked body and shuddered, shoulders shaking. But she didn't look away from him — thank God.

"Talk to me, Mel. Please."

"You…" Mel pulled one of her hands free and motioned to his body then her own. "Me…fat." The last word was so low he almost missed it.

Alarm rolled over Jared.

She thought she was fat?

Jesus. Hell. No.

His woman was not about to feel that way about herself.

"Melody Renee Nash."

Her eyes snapped to his face when he said her full name.

"Damn good thing I'm not into spanking."

She startled, as if that was the last thing she thought he'd say.

Jared plastered kisses all over her knuckles, until she offered a small smile. "Look at me."

It took a moment to get her to meet his gaze again.

"I need you to look right here" — he gestured to his eyes — "when I say this. Because I mean *every* word." He paused to make sure she wouldn't look away. "You. Are. Gorgeous. With or without clothes on. The most beautiful woman I've ever seen. Definitely the best one I've ever been with."

Mel scoffed. Rolled her eyes.

He squeezed her hands. "So, you don't believe me. Looks like I have to show you."

She yelped when he yanked her forward. She scrambled for a grab on his shoulders so she wouldn't fall into him, but Jared wouldn't have given a damn if she had. He would've caught her.

He dragged his fingers down her shoulders, across her collarbone, and cupped her perfect breasts. Jared teased her nipples with his thumbs until hard peaks pushed back. He groaned, because he wanted to taste her, but he needed to make her understand first. "This part right here is fantastic." He pressed a kiss in the valley between her breasts. "Then this here, I can't get enough of." He laid a row of kisses down her belly until she squirmed. "Then there's *here*." Jared lightly gripped her waist, kissing his way across from one hipbone to the other.

He caressed her thighs, whispering praises between wet kisses.

She wiggled but didn't pull away.

Good.

Jared cupped her ass, turning her to the side to kiss one cheek then the other. "Here, too, I love. Flawless."

Mel's legs wobbled, but he held her up.

Turned her to face him again.

A deep blush lit her cheeks. Made her look innocent.

Adorable.

He flashed her a smile. "But here's the sweet part." He pushed his lips into her lower belly, right above her sex.

She moaned his name.

"I love the way your skin tastes. I love making you whimper and moan. I love making you scream. I love everything about your body, Melody Nash."

Mel wrapped her arms around his neck, kissing

him in answer and pushing Jared down onto the bed.

He chuckled against her mouth and pulled her on top of him. "Now that's what I'm talkin' about."

She smiled.

Finally showed him the expression he craved.

He rolled them over, rising above her. "Don't stop smiling, baby. Just one more thing about you I adore."

Her eyes went misty again but he made her moan when he slipped his hand between their bodies and stroked her already slick folds.

"No crying, unless you're screaming my name when you come."

Mel swallowed and he kissed her throat.

Jared teased her swollen clit and had to bite back a groan. She was so wet, so ready for him.

He'd missed this, missed *her*.

Their night together had been too long ago.

Phone sex definitely doesn't cut it.

Her intimate skin was silky under his moving fingertips. She writhed against him, her thigh grinding into his cock, but the friction wasn't enough. More torture than pleasure.

"I need you, Mel. I need inside you."

She moaned in response. Her eyes were closed, her head back on her pillow. The thick waves of her light brown hair were spread out, covering the floral printed case. Pale cheeks flushed pink, she panted under him.

It made Jared crave more.

He found her mouth again, pressing her down into the bed.

Mel was right with him, kissing him back hard.

Their tongues dueled and danced.

He rocked against her, finding a rhythm.

She moved with him, under him, mimicking the sex act, but all it did was make him scorch even more.

When he couldn't take being separated from her one second longer, he guided his cock to her center, thrusting forward to fill her with one long stroke.

Mel gasped and gripped his biceps with both hands.

He stilled. "Did I hurt you?"

She shook her head and lifted her hips, rubbing her pelvis into his.

He fell even deeper into her and Jared moaned. "God, you feel good. Tight. Hot."

Mine.

She felt too-good as her sex hugged his dick.

He thrust forward gently then froze. Intense pleasure rolled over him, shooting a tremor down his spine. His balls shook.

He felt Mel *completely*.

"Shit," Jared groaned. "No condom. Wait, baby." He started to ease back, pull out of her.

Mel's legs shot around his waist, stopping him. "I'm on birth control. It's okay." Their gazes collided.

"Are you sure?"

"I...I...want to be with you like this."

His heart skipped.

She trusts me.

Words tumbled out. "I usually don't...I always use one...I..."

"It's okay. I promise. I want you like this. Nothing

between us, Jared."

His name on her lips made him even hotter, if it was possible.

They stared at each other in silence, their bodies connected.

Mel reached for him, settling her hand at the back of his neck. "Kiss me," she whispered. "Be with me." She lunged upward.

Jared's spine tingled. He needed to move. *Now.* "Oh, God." His exclamation was lost against her lips as their mouths fused. He propelled forward over and over, driving into her as deeply as he could go, but it wasn't like the frantic movements of the first time they'd been together.

They stared at each other between kisses.

Meaning was in those heavy-lidded blue eyes as she gazed up at him.

His heart kicked into overdrive and it wasn't because of his pistoning hips.

When Mel pressed her lips to his and he tasted her again, feelings slammed into him. His body flushed, despite the sweat covering his back and shoulders.

He wanted her, burned for her, even when in the midst of having her.

Touches, kisses, looks they exchanged.

Not enough.

It'd never be enough.

Emotions rolled over him.

I love her.

After a few dates and a super-hot phone sex session?

Yes.

This wasn't just lust.

Jared loved her.

Completely.

Maybe there'd never been a choice. It'd started that first night at *McAuley's*.

"Mel…" His whisper was sucked into her mouth when she kissed him again. It rocked him as much as his cock moving in and out of her.

She arched into his chest, her breasts going flat as her body stiffened in his arms. Mel panted beneath him and called his name as her sex clenched his, her muscles contracting and releasing in waves.

Pleasure made his head spin and his spine tighten. Jared threw his head back as his cock spasmed and kicked inside her, shooting his release deep. Orgasm stole coherent thought.

Mel nestled her body closer, her arms and legs wrapped around him. Finally her shoulders relaxed into the bed and he collapsed with her, their bodies still joined.

She kissed him, and it melted into something deep and languorous, their tongues dancing in time with the lazy caresses she spread over his shoulders and back. "Stay with me." She pushed the plea into his lips and he shivered.

"You couldn't make me leave. Even at gunpoint."

Mel smiled up at him and his heart fluttered.

Damn, he wanted to tell her he loved her. Jared *couldn't* say it.

I love you would sure as hell blow the *slow* rule out

of the water.

Chapter Twenty-Four

Mel sighed and burrowed deeper into the warmth of her bed. She wasn't overheated—which was odd. She drifted in and out of sleep, having very vivid dreams of big, hot hands touching her all over.

Okay, overheated maybe. But for good reason.

What a nice dream.

A toilet flushing had her shooting up in bed.

Like an alarm clock.

She blinked and tensed.

Jared froze just inside the room from her attached bathroom. "Something wrong?"

The night came flying back. Her *lover* on her doorstep. His touch, his kiss.

Making love.

"No." She shook her head and relaxed, her shoulders bumping the headboard.

He smirked, his eye focused lower than her face.

Mel blushed to her toes. She was naked and popping to a sitting position had caused the comforter to pool at her waist.

He was staring at her breasts. Her detective stalked to the bed and crawled the rest of the way to her as soon as his knees hit the sheets.

She gulped.

"I'm not going to apologize for waking you," Jared growled.

"No?" She gasped when he grabbed her waist and

tugged.

"No, ma'am. I don't like to lie."

She giggled and wrapped her arms around his neck. Met his kiss when he dipped his mouth down. Her heart and stomach fluttered at the same time when he settled his weight on top of her, but she was already burning for him.

Mel felt feminine, vulnerable, but not in a bad way. A moan fell from her lips when he flicked his tongue over a nipple.

As he trailed kisses down her breasts and tummy, she threw her head back into her pillow, biting her bottom lip to keep the whimpers in check.

Jared dragged calloused hands over both of her breasts, kneading and caressing as he went. He brushed her belly then applied just the right pressure as he continued downward. Massaging, soothing. Turning her on even more.

Her blood sang and she squirmed.

Unfortunately, her detective was in no hurry as he explored her body.

She whined when he kissed below her navel.

Wrapping her arms around his neck got her nowhere.

He dislodged her hold, lavishing kisses on her wrists and knuckles then planted her arms to the bed. He gave her a stern mock-glare before releasing her. His eyes dared her to grab him again.

It took willpower, but Mel ordered herself to lie still and let the feel of Jared—his kiss, his touch—roll over her form.

She wiggled when he caressed her hips.

His fingertips rubbed her inner thighs. Then he was there, teasing her sex. His thumbs made lazy circles above, below and *on* her clit.

Applying pressure, taking it away, until she was so hot she could die.

If he didn't get over his unusual patience, she just might.

Ecstasy rolled over her whole form, and it was difficult to split her focus on the multiple sensations.

An orgasm built and receded.

She ached.

Wanted.

Burned.

She needed him.

Now.

"Jared…" His name was a groan.

She lifted her hips and her man finally covered her again. Mel rubbed against him like she was in heat. The friction on her throbbing sex was a relief but it wasn't enough.

Jared chuckled, his lips hovering millimeters above hers. "Baby. Somethin' wrong?"

"You're killing me…"

"Oh?" The inquiry was too thick with desire to have her buy the innocence he'd been going for.

"Kiss me," she ordered.

He flashed a grin before complying.

She eagerly shoved her tongue against his when he slanted for a deeper kiss.

His hands never stopped moving, brushing her

with the same torturous pressure.

Mel was going to climax before he even joined their bodies at this rate. She felt hollow, pulsing for him to push inside her. "Please…I…need…"she begged, as their kiss continued.

Jared got the message. He slipped his hand between them, guiding his erection to her.

She arched when he filled her with one stroke.

He wasted no time, thrusting hard and deep.

It was exactly what she wanted — *needed* — and she wrapped her legs around him. To get as close as she could.

She moved with him, under him, her hands buried in his hair, then on his shoulders, and finally on his ass, urging him even faster.

Mel had never been this bold, but she burned for him. To feel him *more* — completely. She panted as her orgasm roared, her pulse pounding in her ears, and he moved even faster. Her body stiffened and she could feel her core spasming. Pleasure rolled over her in waves. She panted his name, holding Jared even tighter.

He groaned and hid his face in her neck. His arms tightened around her. A shudder racked his powerful frame as his arousal kicked and he came inside her. Then he lifted his head and kissed her.

Their gazes fused.

They didn't talk.

Rough breathing was the only sound that greeted her ears.

They were still joined, and he held himself above

her but hovered.

Her breasts heaved against hard pecs and her head spun as her vision cleared. She was conscious of every inch of her skin touching his.

His heart pounded against hers, but it started slowing from its frantic pace.

"Wow," Jared whispered.

Heat licked her cheeks.

Oh God, I'm probably bright red.

Mel chided herself from the sudden embarrassment. After the intimacy they'd just shared, it was ridiculous. "Good wow?"

"Yes." He kissed her again, twining his tongue around hers and exploring her mouth until heat unfurled low in her belly and her limbs melted even further into her sheets.

When Jared ended their kiss and slipped from her body, she felt a sense of loss that flipped her stomach.

He rolled over and hauled her into his arms.

The contradiction of desire and emptiness warring made her shiver. She snuggled into him, hiding her face.

Mel needed to touch him. Have as much of her skin against his as she could manage. She wanted to clutch him and never let go. She should say something, but nothing would form.

What's wrong with me?

He sighed and started to rub her back in long strokes that made her feel tingly and content.

Warmth licked her whole body and she closed her eyes, resting her arm across his middle.

"Are you okay?" he whispered.

No.

"Yes." She lifted her head, smiling when their gazes met. "More than okay." Emotion barreled into her and rocked her to her soul. Tremors chased each other down her spine and she prayed he didn't notice her trembling.

I'm falling for him.

Mel swallowed.

"Are you sure?" Jared cocked his head to one side, his dark eyes scanning her face.

"Absolutely."

Scenes of lying in bed with David flashed into her mind, a movie on fast-forward that sank her heart to her stomach.

Then stages of their relationship. The innocence of high school, full of chaste kisses and holding hands.

Then college. Their first time, when she was nineteen and he'd been twenty. Supposedly, he'd been a virgin, too.

Endless dates and dinners and holidays.

His proposal, and the modest fourth of a karat ring—since it was all he'd been able to afford. Hadn't mattered, because she'd loved him.

They were supposed to get married.

Mel would've been content with David for the rest of her life.

Right?

Our relationship was a lie.

For. Six. Years.

He'd been with another woman. Got her pregnant.

Never bothered to tell Mel.

What a fool he'd made of her.

Watching her plan their wedding. Helped her, even. Gone as far as booking the church and hall himself.

They'd ordered the cake together. He'd been measured for a tux. Had seen her excitement when she'd finally picked a gown.

David hadn't come to the church.

The coward had left a note—a *note*—when Mel had been at the church full of their family and friends waiting. Waiting.

He hadn't answered any calls.

His father had found the note. David hadn't shared his plans to marry the mother of his child—children now—instead of Mel with *anyone*.

Not even his parents found out until much later, from what she'd heard. The note had just said he couldn't marry her. The ass hadn't even apologized; not really. He'd just said he needed to do what was best for *him*.

He'd moved to Dallas and stayed there. Seeing him at school with his son and pregnant wife had been the first time in almost two years.

Val had wanted to kill him on her should've-been-wedding day.

Mel should've let her. She'd wasted *years* on David.

"Mel? Baby, talk to me." Jared cupped her face, caressing her cheeks with both thumbs.

She blinked. Stared into his beloved dark eyes.

Jared is not David.

They were night and day.

Dark and light.

David's eyes were blue, his hair sandy. He was handsome, sure. But not as gorgeous as the cop holding her in his arms, studying her like he knew what was wrong.

Okay, so he wouldn't know *what*, but he wasn't a detective for nothing.

He was reading her.

God, don't let him see my feelings for him.

She was liable to blurt she loved him.

Especially with him looking at her like that.

"Mel." Her name on his kiss-swollen lips was a mixture of concern and demand.

"I'm good. Promise." She scooted up and kissed him.

Jared buried his hand in the thick locks at the back of neck, holding her to him and slanting his mouth to deepen his exploration of hers.

Their tongues tangled and Mel started to melt all over. Her body prickled, her core throbbing despite the multiple orgasms.

She'd never get enough of Jared Manning.

He broke the kiss on a pant, wrapping his arms around her. "As much as I'd love to have you again, six a.m. is gonna suck."

Mel glanced at the clock on her nightstand and flashed a lopsided grin. 3:02 stared back in bright green. "You're right. Do you care?" She dragged her hand down his chest, paying special attention to the dark strip of hair that led to his sex. She was feeling unusually brave and ignored the fact they both had to wake up in three hours; she was going to go with it.

He watched her and a thrill shot through her that *she* could give him pleasure. Jared's dark eyes were half-lidded and he sucked in a breath when she encircled him. He wasn't hard, but was stiffening by the second, his penis jumping against her fingers.

His skin was so soft. She wanted to caresses every inch. She would.

Mel pumped him and he moaned. When she glanced back at his face, her detective had his eyes closed, his head tilted back, resting against the wooden headboard.

She scooted down his body, still making slow, shallow strokes until he was granite in her palm. Increased her pace a little, watching the thick head disappear and reappear in her grip.

Jared made the most delicious noises, squirming a little. He jolted when she kissed his inner thigh.

She lifted her head and their eyes locked.

"Mel?"

Ignoring the question in his eyes, Mel lowered her head and licked him.

Jared groaned. "You don't have to do that."

"I want to." She *did*. She wanted to make him feel good with her mouth and hands like he did to her.

Mel hadn't admitted she'd never given a blow job in her life, but she had told him she'd only been with one man other than him.

Evidently Jared had correctly gauged her

inexperience.

Darn it.

She dipped down and sucked him into her mouth, running her tongue around his tip before slowly moving up and down.

Her name fell from his lips and she noticed his arms were planted to her bed.

He was making tight fists of her sheets.

"Is it not good?" Heat seared her cheeks.

Stupid, stupid girl, Melody Nash.

She just wanted to make him feel good. Never having done it before, how could she assume he'd like it? Mel went to sit up, but she didn't release her grip on Jared's erection.

"It's awesome. You're driving me crazy," he panted.

"Then why—?"

"You make me want to thrust into your mouth. I don't want to hurt you."

Her cheeks burned even more. "Oh."

Jared smiled. "Mel, you can touch me however, wherever, you want. I love your touch. I love how you make me feel."

His use of the L-word made her heart pound.

"Okay. I want to do this."

"I'll tell you when I'm close."

She figured what he was getting at, even though he hadn't said it. He was worried about her reaction to an orgasm. "I want all of you, Jared Manning."

He paused then caressed her cheek. "All right. Whatever you want. However you want it."

The need to speak faded as Mel pumped him again. She took him back into her mouth, adding kisses and licks up and down his length. She used her hand at the same time, varying her speed, since he seemed to like that the most.

Jared groaned and grunted, and with every sound that greeted her ears, desire rolled over her even more.

She was doing this to him.

She was making him feel good.

He cried out when she cupped and caressed his sac; his hips rose off the bed. When his powerful thighs tensed and his erection jumped against her tongue, she buried him into the heat of her mouth and sucked hard.

"Oh, God, oh, God," fell from his lips as a chant when he climaxed.

She felt the hot rush on her tongue, tasted saltiness but it wasn't unpleasant.

Mel caressed his thighs and abs as pleasure rolled over his handsome features.

His body shook and he hauled her into his arms as soon as she'd released him, plastering her to his chest.

Jared took her mouth without warning, but she kissed him back until need hit in waves and her core bloomed, throbbing in a demand he was already answering. He buried his hand between her legs. He rubbed her clit in circles.

There was no shying away like before when he'd teased her. He touched her, the pressure of his fingertips increasing until she collapsed against his chest in a boneless heap, screaming his name as she came.

They both panted hard.

"Wow."

"Wow," Mel echoed.

"I have no words," he whispered.

She smirked, glancing up at him. "Those are words."

He kissed her forehead in answer and gathered her closer. "What am I gonna do with you, Melody Nash?"

A tender smile curved his full lips and her heart jumped.

'Keep me forever' was on the tip of her tongue, but Mel didn't say it.

She couldn't.

Chapter Twenty-Five

Jared frowned when he reached for his phone, on Mel's dining room table next to him. He looked at the screen, saw Cole's name and number, then set the device face down on the ivory tablecloth.

"Don't you have to get that?" Her brow was furrowed and he wanted to reach across, smooth her forehead and kiss her there.

"No, baby. Tonight is all about me and you."

Besides, something was up with his partner. He'd felt the tension all day, though the guy hadn't called him on whatever was obviously bothering him.

Carrigan had been unusually quiet, too.

Mel covered his hand and smiled. "I'm glad you let me cook for you."

He reclined in the chair and patted his stomach. "Any time. You're awesome in the kitchen, as you are other places."

Her face went crimson, but she didn't avert her gaze.

Jared chuckled and kissed her knuckles. "God, you're adorable."

She rolled her eyes.

He laughed again. "Why do you always argue with me?"

"Me? I didn't say anything." She fought a smile, if her expression was any indication.

He growled and hauled her off her chair, onto his

lap. Right when he was getting lost in her kiss, his phone screamed for the second time.

When he confirmed it was Cole, once again, he ignored the call. He pressed the button on the side, sending it directly to voicemail.

"Jared, you should get that," Mel urged, panting against his chest. She didn't ask who it was, though.

He shook his head. "It's after seven. I'm off the clock, and he knows I had plans with you tonight."

"He?"

"My partner."

"Detective Lucas?"

"The very one." He kissed her nose.

"Does he call you after-hours a lot?"

Jared didn't want to answer. His partner was usually only persistent when it was important, but after the heavy conversation with his brother for the second night in a row, he needed the lightness of Mel's company, her arms, her touch and kiss.

"Did something happen between the two of you?" she prodded.

He frowned. "No, why?"

Cole — and whatever was bothering the guy — would have to hold until the morning.

"You just seem really tense. Is something wrong?"

"No, baby."

She studied him a long moment before nodding.

"Let's go into the living room," he said.

"I need to clean up, and you should call your partner," she admonished, but he ignored it and kissed her again.

She moaned on his lap and his jeans tightened.

Last night he'd had her three times. Held her, slept with her in his arms and it'd been *perfection.*

Jared needed that again. Needed it every night.

The idea should've been jarring, but it wasn't.

He loved her. Just couldn't tell her yet.

Mel pulled away, her cheeks flushed pink and her light brown hair disheveled. The smile she wore was tender and his stomach jumped, despite being full with her phenomenal ranch chicken.

Her breasts heaved as she caught her breath, and he reached to undo the top two buttons on her pink blouse. Needed more than the tease of cleavage peeking out.

She slapped his hand away, but giggled. "Stop. I have to clean up. And *you* need to call your partner."

"I don't do well with repetition." Jared flashed a lopsided grin.

"No? My kids do."

He shook his head, but couldn't stop smiling. He went to kiss her again, but Mel turned her cheek. "I'm not six," he whispered.

"Then don't act like it." She softened her statement with a pat to his chest.

"Oh, all right." He intentionally pouted, and Mel laughed. "I'll keep my hands to myself and help you clean up."

"I can do it myself."

He sighed.

Her crystal blue gaze sharpened and trailed up and down his face. "Are you *sure* everything's okay?"

"Yes." The automatic answer breeched his lips. Jared swallowed another sigh. "I'm with you, what could be wrong?"

She didn't say anything, and her gaze didn't waver.

"Mel, I'm good. Promise." Guilt hit his gut. Pressure and tension stiffened his back. He'd never lied to the woman he loved before.

He was mostly okay, but insisting on it was riding the line.

It's not like I can tell her anything, anyway.

"All right." Her tone said she didn't buy it, but she didn't push him.

He was torn between wanting to tell her the truth and kissing the look off her face. He couldn't talk about the case, or Joe. He didn't *want* to talk about his partner. Not that he knew what was up with Cole, anyway.

Jared helped her gather the dishes and silverware up, and carry them into the kitchen.

Mel wasn't talking much and he hated it.

"Look, I'm sorry," he whispered, setting the platter of leftover chicken on the counter.

"It's fine. I shouldn't push you." Her statement was flat and his chest constricted.

He set down the rubber lid and plastic container he'd reached for from her cupboard. Was at her side in seconds, pulling her into his arms.

"Jared, my hands are wet," she squeaked.

"I don't care." He cupped her face so she'd have to look at him. "You can push me any time. It makes me feel like you care about me."

"I do care about you." Her cheeks went pink.

Jared smiled. "Good. I care about you, too."

God, he wanted to tell her he loved her.

Mel flashed a brilliant smile.

He pressed a soft kiss to her mouth. "Let's forget about all this tension and watch a movie or something."

"Is that code for getting in my pants?"

He laughed. "Oh, I plan to do that, too. Worry not."

"Don't be presumptuous, detective." She patted the side of his face. Her lips quivered as she fought another smile, and his little teacher was trying hard to sound serious.

"I'm not. My conclusion is based on fact and previous experience."

Her eyes twinkled, so he kissed her again. Couldn't help it.

Mel moaned into his mouth, wrapping her arms around him. She buried her hands in his hair at the base of his neck, and he didn't even mind her damp fingers.

She was hot, pliant and supple in his arms, against his chest, and he already ached for her.

His zipper bit into his cock, and he grunted a protest when she pulled away.

"I don't want to leave my kitchen a wreck, but I do very much want to curl up with you on my couch. I want to change, though."

"Okay." Jared forced his breath even. "You change. I'll finish up."

"You'd do that?"

"Oh course, baby. Thank you for cooking for me.

I'm glad we opted to stay in instead of heading to Rizzoli's."

Mel smiled again and stood tiptoe to kiss him. "Me too. I loved cooking for you. Be right back."

Her lips on his did nothing to cool his ardor, and Jared swatted her ass as she headed out of the room.

She threw a mock-glare over her shoulder that had him grinning all over again.

He started the dishwasher and looked around the small kitchen. It was pale yellow and homey.

She had all her utensils in a slim clay cylinder at the center of her small butcher's block that also served as an island. Pots and pans hung from a rack mounted beneath the cupboard next to the stove, and he was impressed at her use of storage in the not-so-large space.

The fridge was new and stainless steel. Very nice, but it sort of stuck out compared to the other older appliances in the room.

Jared suddenly wanted to buy her a matching stove and microwave, and update her porcelain sinks to stainless.

Heh. Who know I could feel domestic?

She brought that out in him.

He could easily come home to this house—and Mel—every night.

Once again there was no fear or uncertainty in that train of thought.

Jared loved her.

His phone rang again, and he groaned, rushing to the table to grab it and put it on silent. Cole. *Again.*

He waited, but there was no voicemail alert.

"Whatever it is, he's not leaving a message."

Must not be important.

He didn't buy that.

At night, Cole belonged solely to Andi and the boys—save work on-call duties and an emergency.

Fellow detective, Kurt Jamison was on-call all this week.

Jared didn't want to fathom *emergency.*

Carrigan hadn't tried to call, so Cole couldn't want something regarding the case, could he?

Nope. Done thinking for the night.

He cursed and stuffed his phone in his jeans. Trotted back to the kitchen and grabbed two beers. "Baby, you want a drink?" he called on his way through the living room.

He grabbed two coasters from Mel's desk in the corner and set both frosty bottles on the end table next to the couch.

"That's fine." She was right behind him. She'd come into the room from her bedroom.

His heart and his cock jumped at the same time when he took her in. She'd donned pale blue boxers and a matching spaghetti-strapped tank top. Wasn't wearing a bra.

"C'mere," Jared ordered.

She crossed the distance between them without hesitation. Rested her palms on his chest, her warmth seeping into his T-shirt.

He dipped his head down and drew her closer.

Mel met his kiss, opening for him and shoving her

tongue into his mouth.

He backed to the couch without releasing her, and they plopped into the plush microfiber together, without breaking the seal of their lips.

She landed on his lap, her thighs split over his, her knees pressing into the cushion on either side of him.

Which was damn fine with him.

Couldn't have planned it better.

He pushed up under her tank, caressing the soft skin of her back. Jared dragged kisses down her neck and shoulders, sliding one of the thin straps down. He layered even more kisses across her collarbone, bringing his hands around to the front and cupped her breasts under the cotton fabric.

Mel moaned when he teased her nipples. She tugged his hair with both hands, but it didn't hurt.

"Take this off," Jared urged. "I need to taste you."

She pulled back and he helped her whip the tank over and off.

He dragged his tongue around one areola before sucking her into his mouth.

She whimpered and squirmed, grinding her barely covered sex over his straining cock.

"Shorts off," he growled against her overheated skin. He traced one hard peak then blew on it.

Mel made a sexy, wanton whine and his dick pulsed.

Jared tugged on her boxers. "Off."

A throaty, deep laugh greeted his ears. When their gazes met, her flushed skin make his heart skip. She caressed his cheek. "You have to let me up before I can do that."

Mel pressed a quick kiss to his lips before backing off the couch. She pushed the blue shorts off one hip, then the other and stepped out of them. She went to climb back on him, Jared stopped her, grabbing her waist.

"Let me look at you," he whispered.

She wiggled in his hold. "You did that last night."

"It wasn't enough."

Their eyes locked and held.

Her cheeks were even more crimson and he had to swallow words of love.

She wasn't ready.

He pulled her forward gently, until she straddled his hips again. Jared dragged his hands down her back, following as much of the curve of her delectable bottom as he could reach. He kneaded her there, until she was rocking in his lap, the heat of her desire burning through the denim of his jeans and the cotton of his tee.

Mel fully naked, him fully clothed.

His blood boiled with the exquisite torture. His zipper bit even deeper and his cock threatened to blow in his boxers at the same time. "I need you," he groaned as she kissed his lips, his chin then nibbled on his earlobe. Electricity zinged up and down his spine, sensation threatening to swallow him whole.

"You have too many clothes on."

His cell started to vibrate in his pocket and she paused, her hands on his shirt.

She'd been about to yank it out of his jeans.

Dammit, she can feel my phone.

Jared went to kiss her, but she reclined back.

"Is that your partner again? Didn't you call him?"

He tried to laugh, but it wasn't genuine. "Mel, we're a little busy."

"No. We're not. Get your phone. If it's Detective Lucas, answer it. If you miss the call, you should call him back."

Irritation boiled up. "Mel—"

"Do it."

"Why is this so important to you?" he snapped.

Her face fell and she looked away.

"I'm sorry." Regret hit him immediately, and Jared sighed.

"Just handle your business."

She didn't move off his lap, but lifted her bottom so he could reach for his stupid cell. Mel wouldn't look at him.

One glance at his call log made him growl.

Six in all.

Of course, it was Cole, and still no voicemail.

His lover sat still while he dialed.

Jared caressed her shoulder, her arm.

She didn't pull away, but she didn't lean into him like before, either. She was stiff under the arm he had around her.

His stomach roiled. He needed things okay between them.

Didn't need blue balls, either.

"Jared," Cole barked before he could even say hello.

"Yeah."

"I need to talk to you."

"Obviously." He kept his answer dry even though alarm washed over him.

His partner's voice was more than simply *urgent.*

Something's wrong.

Mel finally looked his way, and her crystal blue eyes said she agreed.

"Get over to my house."

He stiffened. "I'm busy. It can hold until the morning."

"It can't. I need to you come over here. Now."

The stubborn part of him wanted to bark at his partner for trying to order him around. Jared forced a calming breath that the woman in his arms would no doubt felt.

Mel was paying keen attention to his conversation.

"What's going on?" he managed just short of a shout.

"We'll talk when you get here. Just *get* here."

"I'm with Mel."

"Yeah, tell her I'm sorry, but I have to see you, Jer. Now."

Fuck.

He wasn't going to win.

With either of them, if his lover's expression meant anything. No way would Mel let him stay. She'd push him to go meet up with Cole.

Jared had no choice.

"Fine," he snapped. He ended the call on another curse and tossed his phone to the couch.

Mel's hands on his face should've calmed him, but

his patience was shot to hell along with his ardor.

"That sounded important," she whispered.

"*You're* more important."

Her face softened but she wouldn't let him kiss her when he tried — which prickled all over.

"Just go, Jared. It'll be okay. You can come back afterward — or even tomorrow."

"It's not okay."

I don't have time for this shit.

"It will be. I promise. Just go." She kissed him, hard and fast, but Jared didn't respond.

His head spun. Stress, tension, Carrigan, Joe, and now his fucking partner. It all made mush out of his brain and he couldn't think.

He didn't *want* to think.

Jared wanted pleasure. Wanted to get lost in Mel.

He cursed under his breath, things he'd never said around the woman he loved. "Don't order me around," he barked.

"I'm not trying to. It just seems like Detective Lucas needs you. Something's going on. Something's up with you. You've been really tense all evening, and —"

"Since when do you know me well enough to make that assessment?" The inquiry were out before he could censor them.

Mel blanched, freezing on his lap. Her hands fell away from his face. She averted her gaze, but he didn't miss the hurt in her eyes.

Fuck.

She slipped off his lap and pulled on her shorts

without another word.

He didn't miss the fact that she hid her face a little longer than necessary when she pulled the tank top over her head.

Double fuck.

"I'm sorry, Mel."

"You should just go," she said.

He looked into her eyes, imploring, but his love wasn't having it.

Mel crossed her arms over her breasts as if he hadn't tasted her bare skin moments before. Her face was hard.

God, if she could only read my mind. Or if I could tell her everything.

He'd hurt her on purpose to get her to stop pushing him. He'd never been able to deal with being pressured.

Fucking asshole.

"Mel—"

"Just...not right now, Jared. Go."

"I really *am* sorry."

Mel shook her head, her baby blues shiny and his heart stopped.

She was about to slay him with that look.

He'd made her *cry.*

Jared bounded off the couch, whipped his phone up and snatched his leather bomber off the back of the recliner.

Whatever Cole wants, it'd better be fucking good.

Chapter Twenty-Six

A ndi let him in, but Jared wasn't very gracious. He stalked past her, determined to tell his partner to go to hell, no matter what'd crawled up his ass. Oh, and thank him for the ruined evening.

Ruined relationship?

No way. That's all on you, dude.

He hadn't lost her, anyway. Wouldn't let it go that far.

Jared would let Mel cool off and call her. Apologize. If she wouldn't take his calls—God, wouldn't *that* be ironic—he'd show up on her doorstep and beg her forgiveness.

"You wanna tell me why Carrigan saw you going into a safe house?" Cole sounded casual, mirroring his posture where he sat in the overstuffed recliner, but those steel eyes flashed and his heart sped up.

"What?" His planned verbal attack dissipated and he froze just inside the big living room.

Pete Crane was on the couch, a laptop on the coffee table in front of him, but his eyes were locked onto him and Cole.

Andi had followed Jared back into the room and hovered next to her partner, but her gaze was wary, too.

Great. The spotlight's on me.

Whatcha gonna do now, Jared Manning?

"You tell me *what*," Cole ordered.

"There's nothing to tell." He shrugged and made

himself lean on the wall. Propped one combat boot up behind him.

Casual. Just…act normal.

"Bullshit."

"Bullshit? Nah, man. Seriously." Jared shook his head.

His partner pushed out of the chair and crossed the room. Stopped a few feet from him. Glared then started pacing.

A classic Cole move when his partner was irritated.

"I'm not going to let you do this shit, Jer."

"What shit?" Terror shot down his spine. He chided himself to relax.

"We've known each other a long time."

Jared didn't answer.

"I consider myself pretty damn good at reading you."

Still didn't answer, but he could feel the tension in the room build.

Pete and Andi stared.

He didn't look their way, but in his peripheral vision, he could sense tight shoulders and backs.

Pete's body was pitched forward; could be on his feet in seconds. The guy was biding his time.

Yeah, I've never seen my partner like this, either.

"Something's been up with you lately. I couldn't put my finger on it—still can't. Bought your shit about the teacher."

"I didn't lie to you," Jared said.

About Mel, anyway.

Cole paused, shaking his head. "Carrigan's whispering some heavy shit in my ear, Jer. My gut says it's not true, but you gotta throw me a life preserver, dude. You gotta gimme something."

"There's nothing to give."

His partner froze, giving him the stare-down. "Bull. Shit." He pointed to punctuate the phrase he'd drug out in two words.

Tension spiked and his heart threatened to pop out of his chest as it rebounded against his ribs. His partner's eyes burned him.

"Carrigan thinks you're dirty, man."

"Fuck." Jared closed his own and buried his hand in his hair. He bumped his head into the wall behind him a few times. "What do *you* think?" he managed, but he couldn't meet Cole's gaze.

"What the fuck am I supposed to think?" The question was harsh.

"You're supposed to believe in me." He winced. Was defensive to his own ears, and his partner glared.

"I saw you, too. I went with her. She's been trailing you for a week. Why the hell were you going into a safe house? Keys were never checked out. I asked. Had to play that off too, so thanks for that, dude."

The terror was back, inching in on his vision. Making his sight dance and Jared's limbs shake until tremors started all over his body. Even his teeth shook.

Would his partner save him or condemn him when he came clean?

He had to tell Cole about Joe.

His pulse thundered in his ears and sweat beaded

his forehead. "Did you tell her it's a safe house?"

"No." Cole's scowl could've killed him on the spot. "Come. Clean. Right. Fucking. Now."

"Joe Pompa is my brother."

Rage, pure, thick, like he'd never seen before, darted over his partner's expression. He crossed the room in two steps. "You said you trusted me." The bark came with two fistfuls of Jared's shirt. "You're my fucking *partner*."

Anger roiled his gut, too. Instead of pulling away, he got right in Cole's face. "You're gonna wanna let me go, before you get hurt." Chaos from everything stirred his head—fucking up his thoughts like it had at Mel's.

Mel.

Jared refused to add her as a causality of his situation.

"Whoa, guys." Pete's voice was calm, even as he shot to his feet. He threw his palms out, but they both ignored their fellow detective.

Cole and Jared were almost equal in height and bulk, so if they came to blows, it could go either way.

He clutched the fury with both hands, because it gave him relief from the pain and confusion that'd been swirling around his brain and heart for weeks concerning his brother.

His partner was his brother, too.

It didn't stop him.

Jared shoved Cole. The wall gave him leverage and they ended up in the center of the room. "I did what I had to do," he bit out.

"Fuck you, Jared." His partner pushed him in

return, and Jared stumbled.

He roared, rushing him, then taking a swing.

Cole grunted as Jared's fist connected with his jaw but he absorbed the hit, planting his feet in the carpet of his and Andi's living room.

Blood trickled down his chin.

"Cole!" Andi shouted and ran forward when Jared was making a move to strike again. She slid between them. Her eyes widened and a gasp fell from her lips.

Cole wrapped his arms around his wife and whipped them around, presenting his back to Jared.

"Jesus Christ," Pete spat, shoving the coffee table out of his way.

Jared diverted, but his momentum made him wobble on his feet. He dropped his arm and collapsed in a heap. His ass hit the carpet hard enough to make his muscles smart. His holster bit into his hip.

Anger deflated. His head and shoulders sagged. Regret rolled over him and his pulse pounded in his temples.

What the fuck are you doing?

His partner squatted, planting his face only inches from Jared's. "You almost hit my wife," he growled.

"I'm sorry." He crushed his eyes shut and sucked in a breath, willing his heart to calm.

"Don't fucking tell me. Tell *her*." Cole pointed to the only female detective on their squad.

Jared had always respected and admired Andi. She was a hell of a cop. Now he'd *disrespected* her, her house—her man, in the worst way.

She put a hand on her husband's shoulder and

waved her free hand. "Cole, it's fine—"

"It's *not* fine, Andi."

"She's right." He cleared his throat and met her blue eyes. "I'm sorry, Andi. I'm a shit."

Her partner stood next to her, and Jared winced when the guy muttered agreement.

"It's okay," she repeated.

The hurt in Mel's eyes flashed into his mind and he pushed it away. Couldn't deal with that at the moment, too.

Cole, Andi, Mel, even Pete.

All people he cared about.

Jared had to make things right.

His partner straightened, swiping the back of his hand across his mouth, wiping the blood away. "You want to fucking hit me, fine. You ever get that close to harming her again, and you won't like what I do to you, *partner*."

Jared sighed and let Cole rant. Deserved everything the guy said about him.

Pete watched in silence, appraising as he often did, his arms crossed over his broad chest, eyes narrowed.

Jared felt about five years old. He scrambled to his feet and planted his ass hard on the edge of the dark brown ottoman, dragging his hand down his face. "I'm sorry," he repeated, projecting.

Cole didn't stop pacing.

Andi threw him a sympathetic look and patted his back. At least *she'd* forgiven him.

His partner still raved, but he'd moved on to their case and his secret.

"Fuck." Jared sucked in the hundredth breath of the day and thought about Mel, against his will. He hadn't told her much about his case—hell, he couldn't—but he wished she was here right now. Her presence always calmed him.

"I'll say." Cole paused in front of him, staring him down.

He read mixed emotions in his partner's eyes.

Jared had hurt him, keeping a secret.

Shit.

"I *do* trust you," he said.

Cole flexed his jaw and nodded.

"I pretty much fucked myself here. No reason to drag you down with me. I'll handle this. I'll call Carrigan. My brother's agreed to turn himself in." He needed to call a lawyer. His job was probably gone, too.

Please, God, don't let me get jail time.

Sorrow washed over him when he thought about his parents. Disappointment in their eyes was going to kill him. Jared was torn, because he'd known all along his brother didn't kill anyone.

"Fuck that," his partner spat.

"What?" He squared his shoulders.

"We're not calling Carrigan."

Shock washed over him and he could feel Pete and Andi staring at them again. "Cole—"

"I want to talk to your brother."

Chapter Twenty-Seven

Betrayal hit her in the gut and Taylor's Glock shook in her hands.

Lucas, too?

She'd suspected Jared Manning was a dirty cop. Sharing that info with his partner hadn't been worth shit.

Proof was before her eyes.

The former FBI agent had deceived her as much as his partner.

Her gut had screamed to stay at the house on Montgomery well after Manning had left for the evening, a few minutes after six.

The curtains still prevented her from any clues as to who was inside, but she'd stayed. Watched. Ignored her growling — very empty — stomach.

When Lucas' blue Dodge Challenger had pulled in the driveway about ten minutes before, Taylor's heart had almost exited her chest.

What the hell's going on?

She'd waited in the car. Surely there'd be some logical explanation. She'd see when they came out of the house, right?

The minutes ticked by, and they didn't come out.

When she left her Impala and approached the house, she'd finally gotten a glimpse of what — who — was inside.

Taylor couldn't see his face, but through the

window on the side of the house, a third dark head was visible. There was a black curtain, but it was too short.

A backlit crack allowed a clue to the interior. Appeared to be the kitchen, and three large male bodies were clustered together.

Her pulse thundered in her temples.

Pompa?

She had to confirm. Taylor panted, squeezing her eyes shut and sucking in air.

If the third man was indeed Joe Pompa, what the *hell* was going on?

She'd never imagined in a million years that Cole Lucas would be involved in anything illegal.

Did she now have proof Jared Manning was hiding the man she'd been after for months?

Maybe Lucas' protest about his partner had been too vehement after all.

She'd run up onto the porch, rage fueling her way. She'd had to scream at herself to calm so she could handle this.

Properly. Safely.

Taylor wasn't afraid of Manning and Lucas, but they were armed. If it *was* Pompa with them, he probably was, too.

She gritted her teeth and slunk closer, flexing her fingers on her weapon's thick grip. Her mind screamed caution.

She ignored it.

There was no one to help her — no backup she could call. She needed to act *now*. Against her inner do-gooder, rule-follower, *safely* didn't mean *procedurally* this time.

Taylor sucked in another deep breath, and pushed closer to the house. Siding bit into her shoulder, but she didn't move away. Not just yet. Needed to calm her heartrate.

Three deep voices carried through the door she'd managed to inch open, but she couldn't make out specifics.

"Here goes nothing." Her whisper rang in her ears as she shoved away from the side of the house and kicked the door all the way open.

"Did you hear that?" Lucas was louder; then there was silence.

She could hear them, but she couldn't see them yet.

Taylor glued herself flat to the living room wall and waited, her Glock at-the-ready.

"Hold on a sec." That was Manning, but still no one came into her line of sight.

She heard the crisp sound of a snap being opened and the creak of leather.

Someone must've drawn his gun.

Her eyes darted to the left. She could see a hallway that led to unknown territory. The stairwell on the right curved slightly, but she didn't know how far the kitchen really was.

Taylor rounded the corner. "Federal agent!" fell from her lips, like normal.

The three males were indeed together in the kitchen, right next a marble-topped island.

A round table sat behind them in a breakfast nook,

right up against the bay window that matched the one on the front of the big two-story brick house. Except, this one had revealed the house's secret resident.

Three sets of broad shoulders tensed as she raised her Glock.

Joe Pompa was standing slightly behind Manning.
It is Pompa, after all. After all this time.

Her gaze shot from Pompa to Manning and back. "Shit," Taylor muttered.

Almost the same height as Manning. Same muscular build, but Pompa had a more streamlined torso. Shorn hair, instead of too-long and shaggy like the many pictures in her casefile. Same dark eyes, high cheekbones, strong jaw line.

Side-by-side, they were striking.

Too similar.

Manning and Pompa…Pompa and Manning.
They look alike. Too much for it to be coincidence. Brothers?

"Son of a bitch!" She'd meant it to be a shout, but it came out a agonized whisper.

The cop and the criminal *had* to be brothers.

Both wore expressions that told her they realized what she'd just put together.

Lucas stepped forward, one palm out flat, the other holding his forty caliber Sig. The weapon was pointed down, held by his thigh instead of at-the-ready. "Carrigan, holster up. This isn't what you think."

"Bullshit," Taylor spat. The curse shook.

If it *wasn't* the worst situation possible, they would've had Pompa in cuffs and exited the house minutes after entering, instead of having the conference she'd interrupted.

"Let me explain," Manning said.

Lucas spared his partner a glance before meeting her eyes again. "Let *us* explain."

She glued her gaze to Joe Pompa.

The man she'd been searching for.

The man who'd killed her fiancé.

"No." Taylor raised her Glock.

Ignored the curse that Lucas uttered.

"Fuck that," Pompa barked. He whipped an arm around Manning's neck and yanked the detective against his body.

Audible breath whooshed out of Manning's mouth. His dark eyes widened.

Lucas tensed in her peripheral vision at the same time she straightened her shoulders, but he didn't raise his weapon.

The bastard murderer jerked Manning's gun from the holster in the waist of his jeans. A Sig that matched Lucas'.

Manning didn't struggle in his brother's hold, even as Pompa aimed straight at Taylor.

She aimed her Glock in answer, fighting the threatening shiver. It'd been a long time since she'd been on the wrong side of a gun barrel.

The first kiss of fear inched into her spine, into her arms, but she didn't let them shake.

Pompa's eyes were frantic, his jaw clenched tight. His Adam's apple bobbed and the veins were standing out on both sides of his neck.

"Joe, what're you doing? Let me go, give me my gun, and take a breath. This doesn't have to go down like this." The detective was calm, betraying no fear that his brother would actually harm him.

Taylor didn't let her stare — or her forty — falter.

This guy's unpredictable.

A murderer.

Pompa waved the gun around. The sheen of sweat beaded his brow. "Fuck that. You know she won't listen. She doesn't want justice. She wants me fucking dead."

"Put the gun down, or I'll shoot," Taylor shouted.

"No you fucking won't," Lucas said. The order was hard, deadly. The former FBI agent's eyes narrowed as he slid forward, like he was going to move between her and the brothers. He hesitated, but finally took one step.

"See? She's got death on her mind. Doesn't give a fuck about me. Or what really happened."

Taylor tensed even more, until her shoulders ached. She swallowed. Twice.

"Joe, please." The plea from Manning was still calm, steady.

Pompa's arm around his neck flexed, but he didn't release his hostage. If anything, he tightened his grip.

Manning's hands flew to his brother's forearm, but if he tugged, it was to no avail. The detective winced, the first sign of any discomfort.

"Joe. Listen to your brother," Lucas urged.

Taylor didn't have any satisfaction that she'd surmised correctly. Just more fury that Manning had hidden the man after knowing what he'd done.

"This is gonna work out like we talked about." The former FBI agent's gaze shot daggers at her. "Put the fucking gun down, Carrigan."

"No." She narrowed her eyes.

"Taylor." Lucas's voice dropped. "You don't know what's going on. Put it down. Do it. Now."

"Fuck this, fuck her," Pompa hollered, raising the Sig again.

He aimed at Taylor.

"No!" Manning and Lucas shouted at the same time.

Pompa's shot went wide, up above her head.

Glass shattered from somewhere behind her and made her jump.

The miss was intentional, but it didn't change her mind.

Despite the continued shouting of the two detectives, Taylor pulled the trigger.

"You fucking shot him!" Jared's shout had a frantic edge but he didn't give a shit. "He fired a warning shot. You fucking *know* he missed on purpose. He just wanted to get away! You fucking killed my brother!" He wanted to shake her or choke the shit out of her, but Carrigan watched him rail on with an unreadable expression in her eyes.

"I called 9-1-1. See if he's alive, partner." Cole was calm.

It was what he needed.

His gut clenched when he lowered himself to the linoleum floor.

Next to his brother's crumpled form.

Blood was everywhere, including all over Joe's clothing and face.

Jared's too.

"Joe." His brother's name fell out, a whisper instead of a shout.

His brother didn't move.

Jared's chest constricted. Anguish rose from up from his gut and breathing became even more difficult. His hand shook when he felt for a pulse. "He's alive!"

Barely.

The slight press-back on his index and middle fingers was thready at best.

"Fucking bitch!" he barked, glaring up at the FBI agent. "He didn't kill your fucking fiancé. Carter Bennett did."

Cole had told him what her game really was with this case.

John Murray hadn't been her partner.

He'd been her lover.

"Jer." His partner's use of his nickname was an admonition, but Jared didn't look away from Carrigan. "Concentrate on your brother, partner."

Jared looked down at his brother's face.

Too-pale skin underneath the five-o'clock shadow made the blood spatter stand out even more. The right side of his face was covered in blood and a pool had already started beneath his head and shoulders.

"Head wounds bleed a lot," Cole said. "It might

not be as bad as it looks, dude."

He ignored the words, as well as his partner's encouraging squeeze on his shoulder. "Where the fuck are they?"

They should've heard sirens by now.

The closest fire station—his dad's station—was only the next block over.

Unless the medics were already on a call. There were only two squads.

No...Joe needs them. Now.

"They're coming. Don't worry."

Jared shook his head, disregarding Cole's attempt to make him feel better.

How could he *not* worry?

"I just found you again, big brother." He blinked, but his vision didn't clear. "Don't leave me now."

His partner's grip on his shoulder tightened, but he couldn't look up. He'd never meant to say what he had aloud. The guy was going to think he was a pussy.

Crying at a scene.

The word made him still.

Scene.

Like *crime* scene.

Murder scene.

Death scene.

He searched his brother's pallid face. Jared was afraid to feel for a bullet hole—entrance or exit wound—but the thready pulse still pushed against his seeking fingertips.

Carrigan stood too close for comfort, but he couldn't look at *her*, either. He saw shiny wet spots on her black loafers.

Joe's blood.

He crushed his eyes shut as soon as sirens finally —
fucking finally — greeted his ears.

It was forever until the paramedics and cops
poured into the kitchen of the big house.

How long's it been?

Jared had to force his legs upright and lock his
knees in order to hold himself on his feet as he watched
them work on Joe.

His stomach jumped when his brother's arm
flopped off the side of the gurney, but one of the medics
just placed it beside him.

They wasted no time getting him up into the
ambulance.

The slam of one door then the other, resounded in
his ears…his heart.

Rocked him.

Please. God. Let him live.

Over the years, he'd never asked whether they
thought someone would live or die. Good thing he
didn't have the balls to start today.

He looked at the FBI agent hovering near the door
as Sgt. Crowley and his guys set up a perimeter. Fury,
and crippling agony boiled up from his gut and Jared
stomped over to her, ignoring Cole when he shouted
his name.

Maybe his partner thought he was going to hit her.
Good.

"He was going to turn himself in," he barked at the
bitch. "You just rushed in here and shot him. You didn't

know what the fuck was going on. He could've helped your case."

Carrigan said nothing, but she didn't back down, either. Squared her shoulders and stood taller. Glared up at him.

If he didn't hate her ever-loving guts Jared would've admired her. Just a little.

"I did what I needed to do," she said finally.

He clenched his jaw until pain shot into his teeth. He planted tight fists at his sides so he *wouldn't* hit her. Had never wanted to hit a female in his life.

First time for everything.

"Jer." Cole's voice. Close. His partner had a hand on his right biceps. The grip was tight, but not painful. "Let's head to the hospital. Crowley's going to take over the scene. Neil and his team are on the way. Chloe is too."

Shit.

Chief would be next. As soon as he heard what happened, he'd make scene. Then, most likely, head to the hospital. And Jared would be fucked.

He didn't budge for a moment. Couldn't.

Carrigan's hazel gaze was unwavering on his face and he wanted to scream. There was no apology in those eyes.

Doesn't she know how wrong she is?

"Jared. Let's. Go." Cole's order was reinforced as the pressure on his upper arm increased.

He nodded and his partner released him. Instead of turning to follow, he intentionally towered over the FBI agent. Stuck his index finger in her face.

Carrigan didn't even flinch.

"If he dies, I'm going to fucking kill you."

Chapter Twenty-Eight

Mel wiped her face. "You're being ridiculous. Stop it."

'Since when do you know me well enough to make that assessment?'

His demand played on a loop in her head. Like a recording stuck on play.

Jared was right.

She didn't know him well.

It didn't matter.

She still loved him.

But don't we know each other?

No, it hadn't been very long. However, the time they'd spent together, laughed together, ate and talked together, made love.

Counted for something, didn't it?

She'd known him enough to recognize something was wrong tonight. Her gut had seen it. Her heart had, too.

When a new tear rolled down her cheek, Mel growled.

"What's your problem? What he said wasn't even that bad!"

David had told her worse. Much worse.

Things about her body she hadn't even admitted to Val. Her best friend would've killed him.

Jared had been stressed and rightly so, if that phone call was any indication.

God, I hope he's okay.

Her heart took a dive to her stomach.

Antioch wasn't the big city. It was affluent and mostly safe, but bad stuff happened everywhere, right?

She gulped and said a few prayers.

He'd hurt her for the first time, but she didn't want anything bad to happen to him. Couldn't fathom it. Wouldn't get over it.

"But I'm not gonna sit here crying, either."

Jared had been a jerk. What he'd said had been a slap in the face. Her doubts about relationships, love and trust had whizzed back into her head. David's betrayal had stung like it was new.

Which is totally stupid.

"This is why I don't date."

Oh, but she wasn't *just* dating Jared, was she?

Mel had fallen head over heels for him in a week. She winced.

A friggin' week.

She'd taken longer than a week to pick out a television at the big electronics store when she'd bought her house. Where was her sense and careful planning?

Gone.

She sighed.

The first time, she'd pushed him, and it'd shut him down. She'd failed the girlfriend test, big time. He'd lashed out. It hadn't *really* been his fault—even if she'd been right.

"Wait. Knock it off." She was inching dangerously close to the self-blame crap she used to do with David.

Mel had made herself suffer from the things her ex

had said too many times to count.

Jared was still different. Still *wasn't* David.

On the other hand, this isn't my fault.

Yeah, sure, she'd pushed him, but he'd been the one to throw hurtful words. Had it been on purpose?

Had Jared been *trying* to hurt her?

She blew out a breath and reclined into her overstuffed couch. Crushed her eyes shut and willed the pain away.

Knowing it and *feeling* it were two different things. Her heart was heavy and her chest burned, because she loved him.

Mel was torn between relief and sadness that she hadn't told Jared how she felt about him. He'd been so fantastic about taking things slow with her — well, until he'd showed up on her doorstep the other night. Although, that'd been okay; she'd been ready to be with him again.

It'd been perfect. Hot and passionate, but tender and sweet, too. The look in his dark eyes, the way he touched and kissed her. With reverence. Caring.

He'd *made love* to her that night, and every time they were together after that. Perhaps he had from day one, the night he'd brought her home from the bar.

The night she'd met Jared at *McAuley's* hadn't started a new chapter in her life, after all.

She'd gone and fallen for her one-night-stand the first chance she'd gotten.

Mel pulled the quilt she kept on the back of the couch around her and reached for the remote, shaking her head. She flipped through channels on the big TV and turned the volume up a little. Wasn't really watching it.

Still couldn't stop replaying the evening like some stupid movie. Horrific, but she couldn't look away. Like watching a car accident or something.

"You're sick. Seriously ill in the head. A glutton for punishment." Her voice just made her even more disgusted with herself.

She scowled when she caught her reflection in the glass-top coffee table her dad had given her when she'd been trying to furnish her living room on the cheap.

It was from a garage sale and was probably older than her, but it worked. However, at the moment, she'd rather throw it out. Or smash that clear clean mirror into a thousand pieces.

Her eyes were puffy and red. Her hair mussed — and she didn't want to remember Jared's hands in her long wavy locks.

He always went on and on about how he loved her hair.

The waves were natural, and had always been her nemesis. As a kid, it'd always been a mess. The kinks never lying flat or even in a semblance of order until her dad had finally allowed her to have a straightener when she was a teen.

Somehow, her hair being disheveled from Jared's hands didn't bother her so much.

"Ugh!"

Stop thinking about him. Stop saying his name.

She couldn't.

Maybe she should just go to bed.

Mel groaned and glanced at the clock on the cable box. It was only ten after nine. If she tried to sleep now, she'd only have trouble later, in the middle of the night.

I could call Val.

No.

She wasn't ready to tell her best friend about her argument with Jared.

It was just a little thing anyway. It'd blow over, wouldn't it?

Her breath caught and her heart skipped.

What if it didn't?

He'd said he cared about her, but what if he couldn't handle a clingy—pushy—girlfriend?

Her detective had admitted he'd not had a relationship in a long time.

What if Mel had shown him he didn't *want* one?

A lump formed in her throat and she swallowed as her vision blurred.

Her cell rang and Mel jumped.

Jared.

She grabbed the phone off the coffee table, her stomach fluttering.

Not Jared.

The number flashing wasn't in her contacts.

"Hello?" The greeting came out shaky, so she cleared her throat and sniffled.

"Miss Nash?" The voice was familiar but she couldn't place it.

"This is she."

"This is Cole Lucas, Ethan's dad."

"Jared's partner," she breathed.

He paused. "Yes, that, too."

"Is he okay?" she blurted, gripping her phone tighter.

"Yes. Well, mostly. That's why I called."

Mel's heart plummeted to her stomach. "What happened?"

"Can you come down to the hospital?"

"Hospital?" she squeaked.

"Not for him, he's not hurt. I'm sorry, Miss Nash, I didn't mean to scare you. Jared's fine. But his brother got shot, and he's in bad shape. I think if you were here, my partner would be a lot calmer. When can you get here?"

His brother?

Jared had told her about his younger sister, Jenna, but had never mentioned a brother.

"Now. I'll come now."

"Lucas!"

Mel heard a feminine shout in the background then muffled voices as if the detective had put his hand over the speaker.

"I've gotta go," Detective Lucas said a few seconds later.

"Tell Jared I'm on my way."

He crushed his eyes shut and let his head fall into his cupped hands. Jared didn't know where Carrigan or Cole was, and he didn't give a shit.

His legs had given up holding his weight as soon as he'd hit the waiting room. A room he'd been in a dozen times.

Just never in this capacity.

"Fuck me." The curse greeted his ears, fragmented and really a half-sob. He was only two seconds from losing it.

"Jared?"

When he heard her, Jared kept his eyes closed and froze in his seat. He'd never told Mel about his brother. Had no idea how or why she was here, but he couldn't look at her. He swallowed when she slipped onto the chair next to his.

She slid her arms around him and he sucked back an honest-to-God sob. No way he was going to cry like a little bitch in front of the woman he loved.

"Jared," Mel whispered.

It was just like her to comfort without asking questions. After he'd been such an asshole tonight, why did she even care?

He didn't know whether to be grateful and yank her to him or shake her arms off and flee the room.

"Why can't this be some sort of sick nightmare?" The question cracked on its way passed his dry lips.

He felt her warm fingertips above his left ear as she ran a caress through his hair.

"I don't know, but I'm here for you. Anything you need."

Jared choked as his throat started to close around a lump. "Cole call you?"

"Yes." She paused, but he knew what she was going to add before she spoke. "I didn't know you had a brother."

He closed his eyes again. "God, hope it's not *had*."

Mel's grip around his torso tightened. "I'm sorry. I didn't mean—"

"No worries, baby. I guess I shouldn't be morbid." He finally raised his eyes to her beautiful face. Jared read compassion and concern in that crystal gaze and his heart skipped. He threw his arms around her and plastered her to his body as best he could in their side-by-side chairs, burying his face against her. He inhaled deeply and squeezed his eyes shut.

Mel's scent was comforting. Familiar and normal, and all *his*.

"Thank you for coming," he croaked. "I'm so sorry about tonight. I was a complete asshole."

"It's okay. I pushed you and I shouldn't have. I'm sorry, too."

"You should've. You were right."

She hugged him tighter. "We can worry about that later."

God, she's too good for me.

He nodded into her neck.

A companionable silence fell, and they sat in the small waiting area, just holding each other.

It wasn't the right time to finally admit how he felt about her, but Jared wanted to.

He wasn't through apologizing for what he'd said. Needed to see that she *believed* he was sorry; only then could he bare his heart.

"I couldn't tell you about Joe." He cleared his throat. "He was—is. Fucking *is*—involved in my case."

"I know." Mel met his eyes when he lifted his face

and caressed his cheeks with her thumbs, a small smile on her luscious mouth. "It's okay. Now I know why you've been so tense."

Jared nodded.

What the hell else could he say?

I love you hovered on his tongue.

"Detective Lucas said you needed someone to calm you. He told me your brother was shot. What happened? That he didn't say."

He stared into her pale eyes.

Where to start with *that*?

"Manning."

The person he wanted to see *least* in the whole world had his head swinging around to the waiting room door.

Cole was on Carrigan's heels.

"Carrigan," his partner warned, but the FBI agent ignored the guy, continuing her stride forward.

Jared shot to his feet.

His love's arms fell away from his body and he was cold.

He gripped the feeling with both hands and embraced the rage washing over him. "Get the fuck away from me."

Mel gasped.

"Manning, I'm sorry."

He ignored Carrigan and made eye contact with his partner. "Get this bitch away from me."

"Jared!" Mel admonished, but he ignored the love of his life.

"Jared." Carrigan's use of his first name for the

first time—*ever*—made him wince. "Lucas explained things. I'm so sorry."

He narrowed his eyes. "It's too fucking late for that, isn't it?"

"Will you let me explain?"

"What's to *explain*? You rushed in, ignored our commands and fucking *shot* my brother." Jared took a step toward her, intentionally towering over her like he had at the house.

"Jared!" Mel's hands enclosed his forearm, and he glanced into her crystal blue eyes. "Take a breath. It's going to be okay."

Agony warred with the fury that surrounded him like an aura.

He looked at the FBI agent and back at the woman he loved. He just wanted the hurt to stop. Wanted Joe to be okay, and he wanted Carrigan to pay. "My brother didn't kill anyone," he whispered.

"I know." Her hazel eyes were clouded with regret—and perhaps a little pain of her own.

Jared laughed, but it sounded bitter to his ears.

His partner winced from where he hovered over Carrigan's shoulder.

Mel tightened her grip on him.

"Lucas told me just how wrong I was, and I'm *sorry*, Manning."

Jared sat hard, the plastic chair creaked a protest.

His love sat next to him and threw her arms around him again.

He didn't pull her to him, but he didn't yank away, either.

"*Sorry* doesn't fucking cut it. My brother has a bullet in his head." His voice broke. He was two seconds from sobbing, and he wasn't about to do it in front of Carrigan. He averted his gaze, even though he could still feel her eyes burning his face.

"What the *hell* is going on here?" Chief Martin barked from the waiting room door. His wide shoulders filled the frame and he wore a scowl the size of Texas.

Jared sucked in air. Couldn't talk to his boss right now. Just *couldn't*.

If the man was still his boss, anyway.

Fuck.

"Boss, good to see you." Cole was on it, meeting the chief of police before he could come into the room. "Let's step out and I'll brief you."

Chief grunted, but threw a nod, then they were gone.

Thank you, partner.

"Manning, I'm genuinely sorry." Carrigan's apology was thick and laced with regret.

Jared didn't give a shit.

"Get out. Just get the fuck out of here. You better pray my brother lives, or I'm coming after you."

Mel gasped, but he didn't give a shit about that, either.

Chapter Twenty-Nine

"That went fucking brilliantly, didn't it." Taylor crushed her eyes shut and sucked in the side of her cheek. She bit down to stave off threatening tears. The sting made her face throb but she didn't care. Pain was good.

Tears?

"You've got to be kidding me."

And you're still talking to yourself.

She needed something to focus on.

Now.

How had doing the right thing ended up so skewed?

Joe Pompa wasn't a murderer?

Manning had no clue how hard it was to admit she'd been wrong about him—about *them*. Yet he'd rejected her apology like it was nothing.

She'd been chasing Joe Pompa since the morning John's body had been found.

Taylor would never forget that awful day for the rest of her life. Had insisted on identifying him herself. Seeing his olive complexion so white had rocked her to her core.

Lying on the cold metal table with a paper sheet covering him up to his chest, he hadn't looked like the man she'd loved.

She'd seen his hand first.

Then his bare—bruised—arms and shoulders.

She'd had to force herself to look at his face.

His dark hair had been swept off his forehead and John's eyes had been swollen shut. He'd been beaten badly.

Her fiancé had looked like he was asleep, as if he was resting, pain free from his wounds.

The repose was false.

He'd never wake up again.

Taylor bit her fist as the first tear spilled. She couldn't cry. She'd been done with that.

Emotion is weak.

She turned toward the wall outside the waiting room, swiping at her face, but her vision just blurred all over.

"No."

She wasn't going to let Pompa—and Manning— do this to her. She'd done what she'd had to do.

How was she supposed to know he wouldn't actually shoot her?

That he actually *wouldn't* harm the detective who happened to be his brother?

Taylor had been protecting Manning *and* herself. Lucas, too.

Pompa could've easily turned and taken a shot at the former FBI agent.

Doubts started to eat at her as she replayed the scene in her head.

Lucas and Manning both shouting.

Pompa screaming and waving that gun.

When he'd aimed, she recognized it was high and to the right, but she'd still feared he *would* shoot her.

She'd pulled the trigger. As she'd been trained.

It hadn't been textbook, but what real world situations were?

Their jobs were hard. Dangerous. They had *split-seconds* to make decisions that effected people for *years*. In most cases, for the rest of their lives. Even worse, if people died.

"Great. Now you're justifying yourself," Taylor whispered. She sucked in a breath and squared her shoulders. Her gut clenched.

I screwed up. Shot the wrong man.

Suddenly, she wanted—no, *needed*—Pompa to live.

"Stop this." She needed to stop tearing herself apart.

Carter Bennett had killed John. She needed to pick herself up, wrap things up in Antioch and go after him. Her case wasn't over.

Far from it.

Taylor *would* get the bastard.

"Special Agent."

She jumped, then cursed. Whirled around to meet a pair of amber eyes. Taylor fought a shiver but trembled anyway, until her teeth rattled. Tried to tell herself it was because of her current mood. *Wishy-washy* was unfamiliar and she hated it. "Sergeant."

Shannon Crowley threw her a nod. "Do you have a backup weapon?"

"Yes, why?"

"I need yours."

Her heart plummeted to her stomach.

Of course.

She'd shot someone.

APD was going to run the investigation, unless her boss was planning to send in another agent to be a liaison since she'd been involved.

Taylor didn't know. Hadn't had the guts to call in.

Matthias Baker trusted her judgment. Knew her well, and they'd worked together for a few years. He'd know she wouldn't shoot unless it was necessary, so perhaps he'd let the small department handle things.

Did her boss guess she'd been *wrong* this time?

Her heart skipped.

Words deserted her as she looked up at the handsome uniform cop. She tried not to stare, and ordered a wave of emotion to go to hell. Refused to cry in front of anyone, let alone a cop.

What's wrong with me?

She *never* cried. Well, she hadn't until John had been taken from her. She'd always bought what her father had sold about emotions—life wasn't as messy without them. Had she had a personality transplant or was weakness just a part of who she'd become?

Hell no.

Taylor cleared her throat.

"Special Agent, are you all right?"

The concern in those oddly hued eyes made her frown.

She stood taller and yanked her blazer straight, even though it was already lying flat. "I'm fine. You wanna do this right here?" She gestured to their public location.

"We don't have to. Just giving you a heads up. Your office called my chief. We're handling things. I'm supposed to get your statement. I'm running point for Sully — Detective Sullivan — until he gets here. He's in charge of the investigation, with your boss's blessing. You're supposed to check in with Special Agent Baker when things settle down."

Taylor nodded and bit back a sigh. Baker was patient; he wouldn't contact her. So she needed to woman-up and make the call.

She hadn't met Detective Sullivan, and perhaps that was for the best, as far as the investigation was concerned. Personally, she would've rather had Andi or her partner, Pete Crane, run things. Familiar felt better.

Sergeant Crowley studied her and she straightened her spine. Didn't like the appraisal.

"Are you sure you're all right, ma'am?"

"This isn't my first rodeo," she snapped.

When he frowned, regret washed over her. The guy was just showing he gave a shit about how she was feeling on some level. Crowley didn't deserve her angst.

"Doesn't matter. When you shoot someone, it's hard to process. You need to decompress." The statements were even. If he'd been bothered by her attitude, he hid it well.

She respected that he hadn't minced words, either. Taylor bit her bottom lip. A lump formed in her throat and her nose tingled. She swallowed hard — twice.

Do not cry. Do not cry. She chanted over and over,

praying it would work.

"I'm FBI," she blurted.

Crowley took a step toward her. "You're still human. This shit is hard. Every damn time." Something flashed in those whiskey-colored eyes. He reached for her hand and squeezed.

Since John, she sure as hell didn't feel human most of the time. For some reason, Taylor couldn't pull away. Or look away.

"C'mon, let's go back to the PD. You can turn your weapon in and we'll talk until Sully finds us." The sergeant put his arm around her shoulders.

She froze in his grip but only for a second. Her should-have-been protest died before it was born. The scent of cologne or aftershave tickled her nose. Clean and fresh. Very masculine, and somehow fitting, although she didn't really know the man. But Taylor remembered the scent from the night he'd opened the door for her at the bar.

When Shannon Crowley started to walk, she went with him. The warmth of his body seeped into her shoulders and back.

Somehow, despite everything, she felt better than she had in a long time.

"He's stable, for now."

Jared sagged in her grip, but Mel just held him tighter.

"For now?" His inquiry cracked and he stared the doctor down.

The surgeon's brown eyes were somber, when he nodded. He removed his surgical cap and ran his hand through his thinning gray hair. "We won't really know anything until he comes around from the anesthesia, but surgery went well. We're hopeful."

"Can I see him?"

"He's in recovery, and he's unconscious."

"I don't care." His jaw was a hard line, and she wanted to kiss him there, soften his expression, but the best she could do was *be* there for him.

Hold him like he was holding her.

Love him.

"Very well. Ten minutes, tops, and only because you're a detective."

The doctor left, and Mel squeezed her arms around Jared's torso. "Do you want me to stay here?" Her heart clenched when their eyes met, and his were misty.

"Will you go with me?"

"Of course."

"I love you," Jared blurted.

Her heart flip-flopped, but she didn't hesitate. "I love you, too."

He paused, staring hard. As if she'd grown a second head. His Adam's apple bobbed and his lips parted, but he didn't speak right away.

Like he *couldn't*.

"W-what?"

Mel blinked. "What d'you mean, '*what*?' Did I not answer appropriately?" She fought the amusement rising up, because now was *so* not the time. Elation warred with the seriousness of his brother's injury. Her heart and soul soared.

Jared loves me!

"Did you mean it?" The question was heavy and low.

She gave into the smile hovering below the surface. "Yes. Did you?"

He nodded and her breath caught.

When one tear rolled down his cheek, she regretted the teasing challenge and wiped it away, taking a moment to caress the stubble on his cheeks.

"Something in my eye," Jared muttered.

Mel grinned, couldn't help it. "What a guy thing to say."

A smile played at his lips. "I don't deserve you."

"Yes you do. And I deserve you, too. Now kiss me."

He flashed the first smile she'd seen since she'd arrived at the hospital. Given the weighty circumstances, it was a good thing to see.

She met his lips halfway, snaking her arms around his neck. Tried not to lose her head to desire, but it was impossible, as always when he kissed her. She moved as close as she could get, flattening her breasts against his chest.

When he slanted his mouth for a second, even deeper kiss, she gathered all her strength and pulled away.

They were in the hospital waiting room, and they needed to check on Joe.

Jared rested his forehead against hers, and they

both panted. "Thank you for being here for me. Thank you for forgiving me for being an ass, too. Thank you for loving me." He smiled. It was tender and serious, all wrapped into one.

"You're not going to yell at me for bossing you around?" Mel teased.

His expression turned sheepish. "I'll admit it. I'm a control freak."

She laughed and entwined their fingers. "So am I."

"So you tell me how we avoid another collision," he said.

She leaned into his side when he wrapped his arm around her shoulders. "I don't think we will. It's a part of a normal relationship. It's all about willingness to compromise. You know; give and take. And of course, love. A lot of it."

"I'm willing, if you are."

"I love you," she whispered.

"I love you, too."

After another bone-melting kiss, Mel hugged him and took his hand again. "Let's go see your brother."

Epilogue

"**M**aybe Christmas Day *isn't* the best day to meet your parents for the very *first* time." Mel shuffled on her feet, her cheeks adorably pink.

Jared fought a smile. Lost the battle. His parents were going to love her. Just like he did. "Why not?"

She hedged, swaying back and forth. Her knuckles were white around her purse strap.

"Hey."

His love wouldn't look at him.

He gripped her upper arms and squeezed. "Hey." He firmed up his voice and those pretty eyes finally focused on his face. "I love you."

Mel smiled.

"I *love* you. Do ya hear me?" Jared tried to hold onto a stern expression, but when her smile slid into a grin, he couldn't help but return it.

"I hear ya."

"Good." He dipped his head down and claimed her mouth.

She moved closer, slipping her arms around his waist and squeezing.

He could feel her body heat through her puffy winter coat. Craved more. Didn't care that they were standing on his parents' front porch.

She opened for him like always, and their tongues melded.

Place and time faded as Jared got lost in her kiss.

He hauled her even closer, kissing her deeper, swallowing her little whimper. Fusing their bodies from chest to breasts, hips to hips. His cock stirred.

The diamond ring was going to burn a hole in his pocket, but he'd held back all morning. He wanted to see her eyes light up when he asked her. Wanted Mel to throw her arms around his neck. Wanted one thing to lead to another so he could have her in his bed again.

He'd forced himself to wait.

Be patient.

Planned on a proposal in front of his family.

Should he ask her in his parents' living room?

She *was* meeting them for the first time, after all. She'd be embarrassed.

God, what if she says no?

He scolded himself. She wouldn't say no.

She loved him.

He loved her.

Jared's heart soared and he ripped his lips off hers before the temptation to shove her up against the brick or lay her on his parents' porch swing became too much to cope with. Sex in public, on a holiday nonetheless, was probably *not* the best thing.

"Hmmm," Mel murmured, resting her forehead against his chest.

He chuckled and cupped her face so she'd look at him. "I should've done that before we left, so I could call Mom and Dad and tell them we'd be late."

Her blush deepened, and he stole a tiny kiss.

"They're gonna wonder why we've been languishing on the porch. I'll probably just blurt the truth. I'm a huge wimp. I'm no good at meeting people older than five."

Jared laughed again. "God, I love you."

She beamed. "I love you, too."

His pulse thundered in his temples and he had to swallow hard. His heart demanded he ask her to be his wife *now*.

While she still had that look on her face.

Cheeks crimson, lips swollen from their kiss. Her smile chased away the vulnerability in her crystal blue eyes, but she was so endearing.

So *his*.

"I have a good reason."

"What?" Mel asked.

"For languishing on the porch."

"Oh yeah?" Amusement flickered across her beautiful face.

He released her and took a step back.

Now she looked confused, head cocked to one side, but he flashed a smile and buried a hand in his pocket.

Jared put his index finger up. "One sec."

"What're you doing?"

"Just wait." He pulled out a small bundle of artificial mistletoe and held it out.

She arched an eyebrow. "Umm…aren't you a bit late? You just kissed me. I think you're supposed to hold that up first or something."

He shrugged. "Oh well."

"Besides, it's not like you need mistletoe to kiss me."

He laughed and grabbed Mel's hand. Jared turned her palm up and set the fake leaves and berries in it.

Her engagement ring was attached to the tiny bottom branch.

He didn't care that his long-thought-out plan was now a moot point.

The diamond caught the light at the same time the love of his life gasped.

His heart slid into overdrive and heat crept up his neck. "The wires were poking me. Can't keep it in my pocket anymore." Nonsense slipped out, but she wasn't looking at him.

She studied the plastic greenery and white gold in her hand. "Jared…" Mel gripped the ring reverently, as if it would fall apart. Her eyes were shiny when their gazes collided.

"Merry Christmas, baby," he whispered.

"This…this—"

"Will you marry me?" Jared blurted.

She nodded. One tear rolled down her cheek and he thumbed it away. Swallowed and he wanted to kiss her throat.

He took the bundle from her and detached the ring from the fake mistletoe.

Her hand shook when he slid the diamond onto her left ring finger.

They both stared at it in silence.

It fit like a glove and looked awesome on her.

Joy washed over him. "Are you okay? You're so quiet."

Mel nodded again.

"You're kinda freakin' me out. Say something. Please."

"Yes," she croaked, but she grinned through the tears on her cheeks.

The smartass remark died on his tongue when their eyes met again. Jared's stomach somersaulted and he crushed her to him.

She met his lips when he dipped down, and he kissed her until he couldn't breathe. Until they were clutching at each other and winter coats were too much for the heat they'd worked up, despite the outside temperature.

His jeans were tight. A groan was torn from his lips when Mel wiggled against him.

The porch swing was looking good —

"Oh, my God. Get a room." Jenna burst through the fog of passion clouding his head, and Jared pulled away from his fiancée.

Fiancée!

"Mom! Dad! They *are* here. Necking on the front porch. In *broad* daylight!"

Necking?

Mel snorted beside him and he scowled, but at least she wasn't embarrassed.

He glanced at her, ignoring his bratty little sister. His hard-on already started to deflate, although it throbbed a protest on the way down.

His love's cheeks were still pink, the light brown waves of her hair mussed from his hands. She glowed. More gorgeous than he'd ever seen her.

Which didn't help his ardor, but his sister standing

at the front door sure as hell did.

"You must be Jenna." Mel's voice was steady and she took a step forward, thrusting her hand out to his sister.

Jenna beamed and nodded as they shook. "I'm the smart one."

Jared rolled his eyes as they stepped into the house, and his fiancée laughed.

"I don't doubt that. You're in medical school?"

"Yes, ma'am."

"I'm impressed."

"God, don't encourage her."

Mel patted his chest after he slipped out of his leather jacket. "Be nice to your sister."

"Oh, I like her," Jenna said.

He helped his fiancée out of her coat and hung both in the closet. "Well, you were right about one thing, baby."

"What's that?"

Jared winked. "You have no problem meeting five-year-olds."

"Hey!" Jenna propped her hands on her hips and mock-glared.

There was no way his sister had heard Mel's insecurities, but she was a quick study when she was being insulted.

He laughed.

Their parents interrupted them, preventing her from one of her famous retorts.

"Who is this lovely creature?" Dad said.

Mel's face went even more crimson.

Jared set his hand at the small of her back and urged her forward. "Dad, Mom, this is my fiancée, Mel Nash."

"Fiancée?" Jenna waggled her eyebrows.

Mom hushed her and politely met his love, but she refused a handshake and pulled her in for a hug.

His mom had always been a hugger.

At least Mel's shoulders loosened at his side afterward.

Pleasantries came and went; his fiancée relaxing more as conversation flowed. They moved into the living room and took seats to chat.

Mom offered drinks, and refused help. She disappeared into the kitchen, Jenna on her heels anyway.

"How's Joe?" his dad asked, somber, his mouth a line.

Jared had had to call his parents and explain what'd happened — including the three-week suspension without pay from APD. The write-ups at work had made him wince, but at least he still *had* a job, and there were no legal charges pending.

Even Carrigan had fought to help save his ass.

They hadn't really settled things between them, but he respected her a little bit. She hadn't had to put in a good word for him. He'd been the one in the wrong — *illegal* wrong.

He was damn lucky things were going to work out.

The mar on his permanent record was nothing less than he deserved.

The disappointment in Chief Martin's eyes had about slayed him. The same had reflected in his father's eyes when they'd seen each other for the first time after a full confession.

That look from both men was way worse than the reality of a low bank account. Also no less than Jared deserved.

Cole was going to have to babysit him when he finally was allowed to come back to work. His partner had had to make promises to their boss. *His* ass was on the line, too. But Jared wasn't going to screw up—like that anyway—ever again.

However, he was going to have to work to earn Chief *and* Cole's trust again. A position he'd never fathomed ever being in.

He and his partner had promised Carrigan they'd help in any way they could with her case. She still had to catch Bennett.

Both his parents had come to the hospital the morning after that horrible night. He'd called at Mel's urging—after he'd made her go home to get some sleep.

It'd been the right thing to do.

They were a family, and he'd needed their support.

Joe did, too.

Jared surveyed the room before he could meet his dad's hazel gaze, the question still bouncing around in his head.

Mel squeezed their already entwined fingers, as if she could read his mind, and he took strength from her grip—and her love.

He took in the giant fake Christmas tree, smiling when he saw a homemade ornament with Jenna's face plastered on it. Her toothless grin told him she'd been about six.

The one he'd made that year was probably on the tree somewhere, too. His mom would hold onto those childhood items until they fell apart—and probably even longer.

"That bad, huh, kid?" He shook his head when their eyes met.

"He'll be okay. Eventually. The doctors don't know if there'll be permanent damage or to what extent. One side of his body is stiff—but not paralyzed. He'll have to do physical therapy when he's on his feet. His mouth still works." Jared smirked.

"Oh yeah," Mel said. "Joe expresses himself quite well. Extensive vocabulary."

Dad chuckled. "Ah, so he's a patient like his little brother, then."

"I plead the fifth on that one." He smiled, despite the serious conversation.

His love grinned.

"Just ask his mother if you want some stories."

"I think I will."

"Thanks, Dad."

His father winked, even though there was no mistaking Jared's sarcasm.

Ranger trotted over from his bed by the fireplace as if he was just noticing them, his Bassett Hound bay making them laugh.

"There you are, old man," Jared said.

The dog made a beeline for Mel, wagging his tail hard.

"Oh, he's precious," she breathed, reaching down to pet him.

Ranger groaned in pleasure, leaning into her leg.

Jared and his dad both chuckled again.

"Well, he has good taste in women," Jared said.

She beamed, her cheeks going pink all over again.

"So what's next?" Dad asked.

"With Joe?" He sighed when his father nodded. "Healing. Trial. Prison. Prosecutor says they'll offer a plea since he's cooperating, but he's looking at five to ten. What's worse is he's got charges in multiple states, so it's a *'we'll see'* more than anything else. It's killin' me, but it's how it has to be."

The older man nodded and Mel sat up, slipping her arm around Jared.

He slid his arm around her shoulders and pulled her closer.

"He'll be okay. He was always a strong kid," his dad said.

Emotion clogged Jared's throat. He forced a nod.

Dad reached to pat his forearm. "All right. Enough of this on Christmas. I wanted to ask before your mom comes back. She's pretty torn up over the whole thing. Be warned, after dinner we're making a family trip to the hospital. Joe deserves family on Christmas, too. Jenna's on board. Don't give your mom a hard time about it, okay?"

Mel's eyes misted over. "Joe would like that," she whispered.

Again, he could only nod at both of them. His voice had packed bags and moved out.

His mom's tears over Joe when everything had come out—car theft then him getting shot—had just about killed him.

Jared's work suspension drama had just made it worse.

His parents were embracing his brother as if he'd never left—pretty much what he'd expected—but his throat was clogged, his tongue thick in his mouth.

Mel had accepted Joe, too. Had spent time speaking with him, getting to know him. It just made him love her more.

Family for Joe. Finally.

"Christmas is a time for family. Fun. Laughs. Love," Mel said.

Tension melted out of Jared's shoulders, his back, when he looked into the eyes of the woman he loved.

His dad, Ranger, and the room faded until there was only *her*.

Her expression was soft, glowing with love.

For him.

I'm the luckiest guy in the world.

"Damn straight." Mel grinned.

His dad laughed and heat rose at the back of Jared's neck, scorching his cheeks.

He'd spoken out loud?

Don't care.

Not when she was looking at him like *that*.

He couldn't even form a tease for her swearing. He cupped her face and kissed her.

The End

About The Author

USA TODAY Bestselling, award winning author of historical and epic fantasy romance, as well as romantic suspense, C.A. loves to dabble in different genres. If it's a good story, she'll write it, no matter where it seems to fit!

She's a hopeless romantic and always will be.

Risking it all for Happily Ever After is what she lives by!

C.A. is originally from Ohio, but got to Texas as soon as she could. She's happily married and has a bachelor's degree in Criminal Justice.

She works with kids when she's not writing.

WEBSITE: http://www.caszarek.com
BLOG: http://www.caszarekwriter.blogspot.com/
TWITTER: https://twitter.com/caszarek
FACEBOOK: http://www.facebook.com/caszarek
INSTAGRAM: https://www.instagram.com/caszarek/
GOODREADS:https://www.goodreads.com/author/show/58 15085.C_A_Szarek
NEWSLETTER SIGNUP: http://blogspot.us7.list-manage.com/subscribe?u=296abc5983ebc51c1d4d0972b&id=fb 22ce93be
EMAIL: ca@caszarek.com

www.ingramcontent.com/pod-product-compliance
Lightning Source LLC
Chambersburg PA
CBHW051629180726
48284CB00006B/1664